ACCLAIM FOR VICTORIA DENAULT'S BOOKS

SCORE

"Denault launches a new series, featuring the bad boys of the San Francisco Thunder, with gusto, passion and heaps of tension and sensual detail....Several genre-defying complications make the story feel unexpectedly fresh."

—*RT Book Reviews*

"Sexy, sassy, and a perfect new adult read for fans who love hockey and romance, not necessarily in that order. An excellent new sports series launch."

—*Library Journal*

ON THE LINE

"Once again Victoria Denault has written a sexy, sweet story with characters who draw you in and get you invested in their lives as though you're living in this fantastic world of hockey with them."

—Fiction Fangirls

"*On the Line* was a complicated friends-to-lovers romance that was fun and sexy, yet intense and poignant."

—Guilty Pleasures

WINNING IT ALL

"Victoria Denault delivered a fantastic story that kept me glued to the pages. Between the sizzling chemistry and creative dialogue, I loved Shayne and Sebastian's relationship."

—Smut Book Junkie

THE FINAL MOVE

"Victoria Denault's writing is awesome, her character development is some of the best I've encountered and her dialogue is on point. This whole series is a must read!"

—Fiction Fangirls

"The perfect amount of heat, angst, romance, and humor."

—Shameless Book Club

ONE MORE SHOT

"This book is sexy, funny and has a lot of heart…I can't wait until the next book comes out!"

—Hashtag Avenue

MAKING A PLAY

"Victoria Denault's Hometown Players is sports romance perfection."

—Biblio Junkies Blog

"[*Making a Play*] was a breath of fresh air in a genre saturated with games and contrived misunderstandings…I loved the way the author was able to pull everything together in a plausible way."

—Badass Book Reviews

"I think this series might be turning me into a puck bunny because I cannot get enough of these hockey studs!"

—Fiction Fangirls

ALSO BY VICTORIA DENAULT

SLAMMED

A SAN FRANCISCO THUNDER NOVEL

VICTORIA DENAULT

FOREVER

New York   Boston

Cover design by Elizabeth Turner. Cover photography by Claudio Marinesco.
Cover copyright © 2017 by Hachette Book Group, Inc.

Forever
Hachette Book Group
1290 Avenue of the Americas, New York, NY 10104
forever-romance.com
twitter.com/foreverromance

First Edition: December 2017

Forever is an imprint of Grand Central Publishing. The Forever name and logo are trademarks of Hachette Book Group, Inc.

The publisher is not responsible for websites (or their content) that are not owned by the publisher.

The Hachette Speakers Bureau provides a wide range of authors for speaking events. To find out more, go to www.hachettespeakersbureau.com or call (866) 376-6591.

Library of Congress Cataloging-in-Publication Data

Names: Denault, Victoria, author.
Title: Slammed/Victoria Denault.
Description: First edition. | New York: Forever, 2017. | Series: San Francisco Thunder; 2
Identifiers: LCCN 2017029727 | ISBN 9781455597680 (softcover) |
ISBN 9781478916277 (audio download) | ISBN 9781455597703 (ebook)
Subjects: LCSH: Hockey teams—Fiction. | Hockey players—Fiction. | Sports stories. |
BISAC: FICTION / Romance / Contemporary. | GSAFD: Romantic suspense fiction. |
Love stories.
Classification: LCC PS3604.E525 S58 2017 | DDC 813/.6—dc23
LC record available at https://lccn.loc.gov/2017029727

ISBNs: 978-1-4555-9768-0 (trade pbk.), 978-1-4555-9770-3 (ebook)

Printed in the United States of America

LSC-C

10 9 8 7 6 5 4 3 2 1

For my cousin Lisa. For always being there with advice, support and wine.

ACKNOWLEDGMENTS

To my husband for everything, and I mean *everything*. I couldn't do this without your support and encouragement. You never let me give up, and I am so grateful for you, even when you're making me run Runyon.

To my agent, Kimberly Brower, thank you for being my compass on this journey. I'd be lost without your guidance. I can't express how much I appreciate all you do.

To Leah Hultenschmidt, my editor, thank you for your enthusiasm, your positivity and your skills. Dixie and Eli are smarter and sassier thanks to your input. To Lexi, Michelle, Estelle, Monisha and the rest of the crew at Forever who have helped with this series, you make it look easy and I know it's not. Thank you for all you do!

Thank you Jenn Watson and Social Butterfly for your magical marketing skills and being my advertising gurus. Also my freelance graphic artist extraordinaire, Michele Catalano, your beautiful graphics, banners and teasers are much appreciated.

To my fiesta siblings, because you're more like blood than just plain old friends, thank you for your support and love. Ray, Mel, Peter, Ari, Sue Stalker, Ruthe, Devon, Joe D, Carlos and the rest of you amazing humans. I never write in July because I'm recharging my batteries with you all, and I wouldn't have it any other way. YFM.

DeAnna Zankich, my soul sister and fellow author, thank you for getting me like no one else does.

To my fellow authors who have been so kind and generous—Melissa Marino, Parker Swift, Amy Reichert—I'm an anxiety-filled ball of awkward at signings and conferences and you ladies keep me from imploding (although next time, someone stop me from throwing chili at people, okay?). Helena Hunting, Lex Martin and the rest of "Kimberly's Kids," thank you for always being so generous with advice and support and promotion. Stephanie Kay, Kat Mizera, Kate Willoughby and all the other talented ladies in our little hockey author support group (you know who you are), I'm so grateful I'm a part of such a supportive, informative group. Also loved meeting a bunch of you in Atlanta!

Bloggers and readers who gave this book, or any of my books, a spot on your e-reader or bookshelf, thank you so much.

SLAMMED

PROLOGUE

DIXIE

Come on…where is the damn elevator?

I glance at my phone to check the time and then shove it into my blazer pocket. Tonight is not going as planned. I was almost late getting to the arena because of an accident on the freeway, and as soon as I arrived I realized I forgot my employee pass. So I had to skip the PR briefing and run to security to get a temporary pass. I managed to print out the press list, but now I'm late for a meeting with the owner of the team, Ryanne Bateman. She's the reason I wanted to work for the San Francisco Thunder hockey franchise to begin with, and I'm about to mess up my first impression. The thought has me so panicked my skin is itching.

I jam my thumb into the elevator button again. And again.

"Punching it repeatedly doesn't make it come any quicker, you know." The voice rumbles through me like an earthquake. My first thought as soon as my eyes land on him is *Ooh…he's pretty*. If a scientist mixed the DNA of a Disney prince and an action hero, this guy would be the result. Tall, dark, rugged, muscled and exuding calm confidence. Who the hell is he?

I glance at his chest, which is expansive, to say the least, looking for the pass that should be around his neck if he's a guest or staff, but there's nothing there. My eyes move up from his chest to his face, and on the way they land on a scar. It's hard to miss because it's pink and puffy and takes up a lot of real estate on his strong neck, moving from below his ear to an inch or two from his Adam's apple. There's only one person with a scar like that who would be in this arena.

"You're Levi's brother," I announce, like he doesn't know his older brother is captain of the Thunder.

"Just Eli is fine," he corrects and his voice is even deeper than before, which is both unbelievable and unbelievably attractive.

He's in a suit that fits him like a glove, and the charcoal gray color compliments his shock of thick, dark hair. His eyes are…green? I'd have to step closer to find out, and I almost do but catch myself. Then he smiles, something that his constantly brooding brother rarely does, and it's sexy as all hell.

"Are you lost? Are you looking for the friends and family lounge or something?" I ask and glance at the elevator, which still isn't here. "I'm heading down that way. You can come with me."

Eli's sexy smile grows bigger. "There's nothing I'd rather do."

He winks at me. Wow. Talk about cheesy. So why am I smiling? I bite the inside of my cheek to stop it from spreading as he takes a step closer so he's standing right beside me now. He's looking down at me with those definitely green, like dewy moss or freshly cut grass, eyes. Wow. He's hot. Am I breathing? I don't think I'm breathing. I take a deep, deliberate breath. "You're going to need to get a pass from security." I hold up mine as an example. "All non-players walking around the VIP areas need a pass on game days."

"I don't need a pass," he replies casually and then dips his head a little to read the name on my pass. "Dixie Wynn, PR intern."

I glance down. "Crap. They printed my old title. I'm PR staff now. Since June," I mutter, annoyed. "Also, I know you're the captain's brother, but you still need a pass."

He smirks at that. "I don't."

Wow. He's entitled. I decide not to argue with him. He'll find out quick enough when the security guard at the players level won't let him off the elevator.

The elevator dings and the doors open. No one is there. That's weird. Why was it taking so long if no one was in it? I step inside and he follows, once again standing right next to me even though we have the whole elevator to ourselves. It's disconcerting and yet somehow flattering at the same time. I keep my eyes focused on the elevator panel after I punch the bottom floor.

"There might be something wrong with my eyes," he murmurs and his rough, deep voice seems to reverberate off the walls of the elevator. I look up at him and he smiles. "Because I can't seem to take them off of you."

Oh God. Is he serious? Who uses lines like that? Our eyes meet and he grins, and it makes me grin. Damn it. I'm enabling him.

"That was cheese-tastic. You need to work on your pickup lines," I say. "On someone else."

He chuckles lightly. This guy must think because he's the captain's brother he can do whatever he wants.

"You clearly don't know why I'm here, so how did you know who I was?" Eli asks, and it makes me look up at him again.

"You're here to visit Levi, obviously, and I recognized you because…" My eyes linger on the scar instead of his face, and when I do make eye contact I can see a scowl cross his face, but he quickly smiles.

He raises his hand to his neck. "I got it saving orphans from a knife fight."

I bite back a laugh. "Do you actually tell women that?"

He nods. "Sometimes. Other times I say I was saving puppies from a hostage situation. Women love heroes, Ms. Wynn."

"Are you for real?" I ask, and I can no longer hold back my laugh. "Do cheesy pickup lines and ridiculous lies honestly work for you?"

He laughs too. "Yeah. Because it gets women to laugh and it starts a conversation. And it takes the stick out of even the tightest little asses, like yours."

"You really can't talk to me like that!" I warn him, but I can't sell it because I'm not all that angry—mostly just stunned. "Are you sure you share DNA with Levi? He's way more…refined than you."

He chuffs at that. "Refined? You mean boring."

Before I can answer there's a noise—a horrendous grinding sound that makes the hair on the back of my neck rise—and then the elevator shimmies and stops abruptly. I reach out and grab for the small railing along the walls, and he reaches out and grabs me. His hand around my waist is tight and firm and it causes a tingle that has nothing to do with the fear from the faulty elevator. I can't remember the last time I was this close to a guy this hot, which seems pathetic, but I've been busy with work, and since I found out about my dad being sick, I haven't exactly been in the mood to go out and meet people.

When I'm convinced it's not going to move again I step forward, out of his protective embrace, and look up at the lights telling us what floor we're on. No floor is lit up. I punch the bottom-floor button again. Nothing happens.

"No," I say out loud. "Just no."

Eli steps forward. I can feel his whole body like a warm, muscled wall behind me. "It's stuck."

"No."

"Yes."

"Fucking hell. Fuck my life!" I blurt out and instantly hate myself for it. I couldn't be more unprofessional right now. Embarrassed by my outburst, I step away from him, closer to the panel of buttons, and hit the one marked Call. A ringing sound fills the elevator.

"It's okay. We'll get out of here," he says in a soothing tone. "It's not going to turn into a survival movie where one of us has to eat the other. Although I'm open to that…"

I snap my head up to stare at him. He's grinning again. Jesus, does this guy take anything seriously? Why is everything sexual? And why is it suddenly warm in here?

Before I can chastise him the ringing stops and a voice comes out of the little speaker above the floor numbers. "Security."

"Hey! We're trapped in an elevator!" I yell, panicked.

"Okay, ma'am…" the security guard says. I bristle at that term and see Eli chuckle. "We have fourteen elevators in the building, so can you read me the number at the top of the panel? It's engraved in the metal. That will tell me which one you're in. I don't see an alert on our system."

Oh fuck. That can't be good. "S4," I say.

"Okay…" His pause fills me with dread. "We'll figure this out. I will send someone over there to see if they can manually reset it and call the elevator company immediately. It will take a little bit of time though, so hold tight."

"How long?" I ask and the anguish in my voice is more than a little apparent. It's so strong Eli drops a hand on my shoulder and squeezes. "I have somewhere to be."

"We'll work as fast as we can, ma'am."

"We'll be fine. Thank you," Eli says. "We'll buzz you again if we need an ETA."

He hits the button again and the little light that was lit up fades. I look up at Eli. "What did you do?"

"Ended the call so he can get to work getting us out of here," Eli explains casually. I want to argue with him, but I don't know why. He didn't do anything wrong. I'm just raging inside that yet another thing today has totally backfired and I want someone to blame. Being late makes me crazy. I'm always early to everything—meetings, parties, doctor's appointments, funerals.

I pull out my phone and pull up the PR director's number. I text Mr. Carling that I'm stuck in an elevator. I'm about to make a bad first impression on a woman I've studied and admired since college.

"Who are you texting? Your boyfriend?"

I roll my eyes. "My boss. He was going to introduce me to the team owner, but now I've screwed that up."

"It's not your fault the elevator crapped out," he reminds me.

"Yeah, she's not going to care. She's just going to see me as a screw-up," I tell him, my voice filled with disappointment. "In her memoir Ryanne says all mistakes must be owned, and nothing is out of your control. If something goes wrong, there's a reason, a choice you made, that should have been different. Like I could have taken the stairs."

"Wow, you've read her memoir?" he says, his green eyes wide.

I nod. "She made her first million by twenty-eight. She's a marketing genius and the only woman to own a professional hockey team. And the Thunder are the most popular California hockey team in the league, thanks to her marketing savvy."

Eli's expression seems to cloud a little, dimming the flirtatious twinkle in his eyes. "I'm sure she has flaws. Maybe even a dark side."

I roll my eyes. "Yeah, men often say that about successful women."

He chuckles. "I'm just saying. We all have a little fault in our stars."

I glance at my phone screen to see that Mr. Carling replied.

She's done meeting staff, gone to meet with the team. Maybe I can introduce you after the game. Hope you get unstuck soon.

I slump against the wall and cover my face with my hands for a moment, fighting to rein in all these hideous emotions. "Dixie? Tell me what I can do to help."

He's suddenly serious and it radiates through his tone. It's low and rough and I *feel* it inside me like the bass in a song coming out of a kick-ass sound system. I drop my hands and look up into his eyes. "Your voice is so deep it's kind of insane. It sounds like sandpaper but feels like velvet."

He stares at me. His expression is intense, but his face is passive and calm in an unnerving way. "You *feel* my voice?"

Somehow he said that with even more sandpaper and velvet. I feel it *everywhere*. I try to swallow and nod my response. The elevator suddenly feels claustrophobic and hot. I move away from the wall, and him, and shrug out of my blazer. The air swirls around my bare arms, and I pinch the front of my sleeveless silk shirt and move it, creating a breeze.

"If it makes you feel any better I have somewhere important to be too," Eli tells me quietly, still serious. "And I could use a little luck right now also."

I have no idea what he's talking about and I open my mouth to ask at the very moment the elevator lurches up but stops just as abruptly as it did before. It makes me squeak in shock at the sudden movement and stumble, but he grabs me again, this time with both hands on my waist, and I face-plant into his chest. It's rock hard and warm, and he smells unbelievable. I look up at him. "I guess we both need something good to happen."

"So let's make something good happen." Before I realize what he's doing he's got his hands against my cheeks and he's tipping my head back.

His mouth hovers so close to mine as he tilts his head slowly. His lips part just a little bit as his mouth gets even closer. I feel like the whole world has stopped just like this elevator. We're frozen in this almost kiss. And then his lips are against mine. It isn't sudden. It isn't rushed. I'm not taken by surprise. I knew exactly what he was going to do and I let him do it. Still, somehow I'm surprised. My pulse races and my breath catches, but I kiss him back. With everything in me, I kiss him back.

It's long, it's deep and hot and perfect, and I find myself suddenly begging the universe to leave us here in this elevator forever. But the universe isn't taking my calls right now, obviously, because the elevator shudders and starts moving down. This time it doesn't stop.

He steps away from me abruptly and my hand flies up to cover my mouth. He just stares at me, a victorious smile on his lips. "That was something good," he says in that deep velvety voice.

Oh my God. Suddenly he's way more than just a pretty face. And just like that I am totally, fully and completely crushing on Elijah Casco.

The elevator stops, smoothly this time, and the doors slide open. I rush out. He follows. We're on the player level, my original destination. I turn to him and I start to open my mouth because I need to say something—but what? Do I ask for his phone number? Do I ask him out for drinks? Do I act like that kiss didn't just curl my toes and set my insides on fire?

"Dixie!" Mr. Carling's voice shatters the euphoric post-kiss haze that had engulfed me. "You're out!"

I spin to face him as he approaches. "Hi, Mr. Carling. Yes. We're out."

He glances past me at Eli and his entire face lights up. "Elijah! You were trapped in the elevator too? We've been looking for you everywhere! The rest of the team is already dressing, and Ryanne wanted to meet you before the game."

Rest of the…*what?* I blink. My eyes fly up to Eli. He's giving Mr. Carling an easy smile. "Sorry. I would have called but my phone is in the locker room."

"You still play?" I blurt out, stunned and horrified. Eli nods. His back is to Mr. Carling because he's about to walk away, so Mr. Carling doesn't see the smug smirk and the wink. That's just for my viewing pleasure.

Mr. Carling looks at me with confusion and a little judgment, which makes me feel like I just let him down somehow. "You didn't know?"

"I mean, I knew he played in college…" I mumble like an idiot. "I saw the news reports on the accident a couple years ago, but I assumed he quit hockey after that."

Eli frowns, hard, but I ignore him and concentrate on Mr. Carling, who's still looking at me like I've just failed some test. "He's been with our farm team for almost a year now. We called him up for the game tonight. I guess you haven't see the team roster yet."

"No. Sorry," I mumble, stunned and confused. It's like the world just stopped and then started spinning in the wrong direction.

"I figured you wouldn't even need the roster since Levi is best friends with your brother. I'm surprised Jude didn't ever mention Eli was playing in the organization." Mr. Carling glances down the hall and smiles. "Oh! There's Ryanne. Let me go get her."

He starts to march down the long, curved corridor. I try not to fall headfirst into a panic attack because holy shit, the hottest kiss of my life just turned into a giant mistake. There's a strict policy against fraternization between employees and players, and I'm fairly certain having Eli's tongue in my mouth in the elevator counts as fraternization. I don't break rules. Ever. Especially ones that can cost me my fledgling career.

"Why didn't you tell me you're a Thunder player?" I whisper harshly when Mr. Carling is out of earshot.

"Why didn't you tell me you were Jude Braddock's sister?" he counters, looking just as stunned as I feel.

"Because I don't tell anyone. That's why I use my middle name as a last name," I reply sternly. "I don't want the team to think he got me the job, so you can't tell anyone. Just like you can't tell anyone about that kiss. *Please.* Because this is the only good thing I have in my life, and I'm not losing it over a kiss."

"For the record, I didn't tell you I play for the Thunder because I don't. I play for the Storm," he tells me calmly. "And I won't tell anyone your real last name, but who cares who knows about the kiss?"

"I care! They have a strict policy about that stuff here," I explain. My eyes keep darting down the hall. Mr. Carling is coming our way now with Ryanne. "That kiss could cost me my job."

"Okay. Okay. If you want me to pretend that incredible kiss didn't happen, then I will. But I don't think either of us will forget it," he manages to whisper before Mr. Carling and Ryanne are standing in front of us. She looks equal parts power and beauty in a pair of tailored black pants, with her long dark hair pulled back in a low ponytail that looks as silky as her red blouse. I open my mouth to introduce myself, but her eyes are on Eli, not me. She extends her hand to him. "Mr. Casco. I'm looking forward to seeing what you can do out there tonight."

He shakes her hand and flashes a confident grin. "I'm looking forward to impressing you."

Ryanne glances at Mr. Carling. "This one is much bolder than his brother. Let's hope he can back it up."

"I should get into my gear," Eli says and then puts a hand on my back, which makes me bristle. "I'll leave you to talk to your best and brightest communications team addition. Nice meeting you."

Eli walks away and I'm left frazzled again, but I try not to show it as I look up at Ryanne and give her what I hope is a poised smile. "Dixie Wynn. I'm very happy to meet you, Ms. Bateman. You're the reason I wanted to work here."

She smiles and shakes my hand. "I'm flattered. Your whole department—hell, the whole organization—has nothing but positive remarks about you."

I smile brighter, my nerves starting to dissipate. She leans in and winks at me. "And I admire the fact that you haven't told them who you are. You earned your fantastic reputation on your own."

She stands straighter and turns to Mr. Carling again. "I'm heading to my box. Looking forward to seeing you all at the party later tonight."

And just like that she's off down the hall, her four-inch heels clicking loudly against the concrete floor. That went way better than I thought it would after all the drama leading up to it. I turn to Mr. Carling. "I'm going to go brief the team on the media info for after the game."

His phone buzzes and as his eyes slide to the screen, I leave him to head into the locker room. I march right in, even though some of the guys are in various states of undress. I learned early on that being timid or shy with these boys caused them to give me more grief than if I just walked in on them when they were half naked.

"Boys! Listen up!" I bellow and ninety percent of the heads in the room snap to attention. Only one of them is glaring at me in horror—my brother, Jude Braddock.

"Hey, Ms. Wynn," he says, accentuating the Wynn part. "Maybe knock before entering or something!"

I give him a quick *I don't give a fuck* smirk. He knows the look well, and I know it annoys the hell out of him, which is why I do it. The only thing I love more than Jude is irking the hell out of Jude.

"I'm not the Virgin Mary, Braddock." I let my eyes sweep the room, but they somehow get stuck on Eli. He smiles and casually reaches up, touching his lips with his fingertips, subtly reminding me…teasing me…I blink and wrench my eyes away. "Nothing I haven't seen before."

I shoot out my directions about press after the game like a drill sergeant, explaining it's a light schedule tonight because the media only want to talk to the Casco brothers after the game. The irony is I was holding this list the entire time. If I'd just read it in the elevator I would have known Eli was playing for us. I leave, forcing myself not to look back at Eli even though every fiber of my being wants to. I have to let it go—forget the kiss and how attractive I find his bold, goofy personality.

Fifteen minutes later the players are filtering out to take the ice. Eli is the last one out of the locker room and as his eyes connect with mine, he grins and gives me a wink. Everyone continues down the hall chattering away, excited for the game. Eli pauses for just a second right in front of me and in a rough whisper says, "Admit it. That was one hell of a kiss."

"Go!" I command sharply and he struts off down the tunnel with the rest of the team.

Alone in the hall, my fingertips brush my lips absently, my breath hitches. He's not here to see my response, but I can't help nodding my head in agreement.

1

ELIJAH

One Year Later

I walk into the dark apartment and drop my keys on the coffee table as I toe off my shoes. I don't bother turning on the lights as I make my way to the kitchen. I swing open the door of the fridge and blindly reach for a bottle of water. My hand hits a can of beer instead. Even better. I usually prefer mixed drinks, but tonight I don't care. I grab the Coors Light and crack it open, taking a sip as I make my way to the back of the apartment.

It's only nine at night. The whole team has gone out to drown their sorrows—at least that's the excuse, but the fact is they go out, win or lose, after every game. I rarely do because I rarely have something to celebrate, and when the team loses I don't want to commiserate, I want to stew. Especially when I was in goal, like tonight.

I make it to my bedroom and decide that turning on a light, as much as I don't want to, is the best option because my room is a mess, and I'm likely to trip on something if I don't. I turn on the small lamp on my desk and put my beer beside it while I shrug out of my suit jacket and start unbuttoning my shirt. My laptop is open on the desk with the screensaver looping silently. It's made up of images from my cloud. I set it to one specific folder filled with images from my hockey career. The good times—championship wins, MVP trophies, medals, press photos of amazing saves. I thought reliving those moments would help. Positive reinforcement. But it hasn't. I'm still playing like shit.

I let in three goals tonight, and only one of them was forgivable. The other two should have been easy saves. But I tensed and froze for the slightest second at just the wrong time on both. My heart was pounding the entire game. I could feel my knees wobble. I couldn't get a decent grip on my stick. It sucked.

I let my shirt fall to the ground and kick it out of the way so I can pull out the desk chair. I drop into it and run my hand over the mouse pad so the screensaver goes away, then take a long, slow sip of beer. If positive reinforcement doesn't work, maybe negative will.

I pull up a browser and search for the video. It's not hard to find. I've only watched it once. Right after I got out of the hospital and went back to the dorms, my roommate pulled it up to show me. I didn't ask to see it, and I didn't realize how much I didn't want to see it until I was watching it.

I don't want to see it now, but maybe I have to. Avoiding the memory hasn't helped me, so maybe I need to watch it repeatedly and desensitize myself. I'm surprised by how much of it I do remember.

It was a good game. We were winning, and I was five minutes away from a shutout. I was in control. I was relaxed. I was confident. I was me.

I stopped a shot, but the puck bounced free. There was a scramble for it by players on both teams inches from my face. The video shows a big blur of body parts and jerseys. I used to love those dustups and fed off the frantic energy. I almost always dove into the mix and ended up with the puck. I'd done it a million times. I watch myself drop closer to the ice and lunge forward, reaching for the puck everyone is battling for.

I think that's where my neck guard tears free. We tie them on with skate laces—which is ridiculous but works. It's pretty rare that the guards break or get torn away. Then the puck pops free and skitters half a foot to the left of the group of players. I see it at the exact same time two other players do. We all lunge for it. It's impossible to see whose skate gets me in the video. I found out afterward it was one of the defensemen on my own team. He got pushed down in the pile of people, and his skate came up as he fell and connected with my neck, slicing right through it.

The video doesn't show the impact clearly, but the result is plain as day. The player goes down and I pop up to my feet, bright red blood suddenly spraying the ice in front of me. I drop my gloves and grab my neck and skate. I skate as fast as I've ever skated in my life, both hands wrapped around my throat, blood still gushing from between my fingers and staining the ice as I rush to the bench.

The announcers' voices have changed. They're talking over each other now in frantic, horrified tones. "He's cut." "It's his neck." "Oh my God." "Never seen anything like this."

The trainer and medical team rush the ice and meet me just before I make it to the bench. I won't move my hands, so one of them just covers them in a towel, pressing his own hand on top of it, and the other is pulling me toward the tunnel. The video ends, but my memories right now don't.

I remember making it off the ice and into the tunnel, and that was the point when I started to have to fight for consciousness. I remember stumbling against the wall and someone yelling, "Get a stretcher!" and then the team doctor was in front of me and wrenching my hands away. I remember he had brown eyes—wider than I've ever seen anyone's eyes. He knew it got my artery. He knew I was bleeding out. His fingers went right into my neck. Into it. I remember the feel of that. He pushed past the torn skin and pinched the artery closed.

"Get the ambulance *now*!" he screamed. I've never heard a doctor scream like that. "Catch him!"

That's the last thing I remember.

I blink. The video is over and the next one in the queue is halfway through. It's another one of the accident, filmed from the stands, and you can hear the fans screaming and freaking out. Even with the grainy quality of the cell phone footage and the distance, you can still see the spray of red with every pump of my heart.

My phone rings, and it's like an alarm waking me from a nightmare. I jump and realize my right hand was rubbing the scar on my neck. I pull it away, slam the laptop shut and dig my phone out of my suit jacket pocket on the floor. I should have read the display. "Hello?"

"Elijah?" My mother's voice fills my ear, and I bite back a groan. "Is that you? You sound funny."

I clear my throat and try not to let my sigh be audible. "Yeah, Mom. It's me."

"Oh. Are you sure you're okay?"

"Yes. I'm just tired. I had a long day," I explain tersely. I don't know why she's calling me, but I know it's probably going to end in a fight.

"Your father and I wanted to officially confirm your dad is running for Senate again," my mother announces.

"Okay. Thanks for letting me know," I reply and try not to sound as disinterested as I am. My dad is a California senator and I assumed he would run for a second term, just like the media assumed he would. "Tell him good luck and everything."

"We thought you should know because the press might ask you questions," she goes on in her typical clipped, brisk tone. "He's making the official announcement tomorrow, and we didn't want it to seem like we hadn't told you boys first. So can you let your brother know, please?"

"Levi or Todd?" I ask just to be a brat, because I know the answer. It's Levi.

"Todd knows. He talks to us almost weekly, and he comes home for visits," my mother responds pointedly.

"Yeah, well, you're not giving Todd the cold shoulder for following his dreams and doing what he's good at," I counter, even though I know it's just going to make this conversation a nightmare. But I'm in the mood for a fight, and she's volunteering as tribute.

"Because Todd is a realist," she shoots back. "Not all dreams are meant to be pursued. You boys had the world at your feet and could have done anything, but you both chose something reckless and pointless."

"Great talk, Mom. I have to go now."

"I know you're not doing well, Elijah," she blurts before I can hang up. "Your father is keeping track. He said you should have been playing with Levi by now."

My jaw is locked shut, and I grind my teeth. I'm so furious and humiliated that I can't speak. She pauses and I hear her exhale, and then her tone is soft, which is rare. "Elijah, sweetheart, it's okay to walk away from something that isn't working out. There is no shame in it. I know you don't believe it, but we just want what's best for you, and it feels like you're doing this now to spite us, not because you're good at it. If that's the case, please just stop and move on from this and go back to school."

"No," I manage to reply through my clenched jaw.

"But you only have a semester left to finish your degree," she reminds me. "We can get you back into Harvard. And you can always join a recreational league if you insist on still playing hockey."

"I'll let Levi know about Dad. Good night, Mom." I hang up before she can say another word.

I haven't heard from her in four months, and now I hope it's another four before she calls again. I down the rest of my beer. I used to have a little sympathy for my mother's stance about professional sports because her brother was permanently injured playing football. But at some point she needs to let that go and let my brother and me follow our dreams. Even her brother supported us.

I crush the beer can as my phone rings again. Goddamn it, if she's calling back, I swear I will block her number. But it's not my mom. Just a number with a San Francisco area code. I hesitate before answering because I really don't want to talk to anyone, but I'm worried it might be someone from the Thunder.

"Hello?"

"Hey, Eli?" I don't recognize the female voice. "This is Dixie Wynn."

Holy shit. My memories of the tiny blond bombshell fill my brain. And so does that kiss from a year ago.

"I work for the San Francisco Thunder in their PR department, and I—"

"Are you really introducing yourself like I have no idea who you are?" I interrupt.

"Yes."

"Dixie, we've played tonsil hockey, the only kind of hockey I like better than ice hockey," I remind her not so gently. "You think I'd forget you?"

"This needs to be a professional conversation," she responds flatly. "I'm calling about work."

I have a brief but powerful surge of hope that she's calling to tell me that the Thunder are bringing me up to play with them. I've been on their farm team here in Sacramento for two years now, which is one and a half years longer than I hoped to be here. But my mother wasn't wrong in her assessment. I haven't been playing great, definitely not great enough that they'd put me on the Thunder unless they had no other option. And besides, they don't have their PR department call with that news.

"The Thunder is hosting their annual silent auction and cocktail party, and management would like for a couple of Storm players to be there as well," she explains, her tone all detached and businesslike, which I take as a challenge. "It'll give our fans a chance to see our up-and-coming—"

"I'm sorry, can you Skype me instead?" I ask interrupting her again.

"What?"

"Skype," I repeat. "Can you Skype me with this invitation?"

"Why would I do that?" she demands, annoyed.

"Because I'd prefer it," I reply and then I start to lie to help my case. "My phone network is horrendous in Sacramento. I drop calls all the time, and the connections are bad, like right now. I'm not sure I'm hearing everything you're saying. Thunder charity? Fans? You should Skype me."

"Are you serious?" she asks, still annoyed.

"I absorb information much better when I can look into the pretty blue eyes of the person delivering it," I add. I know she can hear the cocky smile through the tone in my voice, but I want her to see it too. "I'll be ready and waiting."

I hang up and open my laptop again. It takes less than a minute before the Skype icon starts flashing. I click it and her face fills my screen. She's gorgeous, just like I remember.

Her hair is longer than the last time I saw her, dusting her shoulders now instead of just grazing her chin, but it's still glossy, straight and that perfect yellow-blond. She's dressed, from what I can tell, in one of those hot power suits she wears daily to work, even though it's after nine on a Friday night. She's wearing a teal blouse with simple gold hoops, and her makeup is subtle. I wish I could ask her to stand up so I could see the full hot look, but she'd hang up on me.

Her eyes grow wide. "Are you naked?"

I look down. Right. I took my shirt off. "No. Do you want me to be?"

Again, she ignores me. This girl is way too good at that.

"As I was saying," she starts again. "The Thunder wants you and one of your teammates to represent the Storm at an upcoming charity event we're doing here."

"Will you be at the charity event?"

She ignores that, her eyes leaving mine and glancing down at something in front of her. "I've already informed your teammate Jasper, and since he returned my voicemail I know he's coming and can make his travel arrangements. I assume you're in too?"

"Yeah. If you're going to be there, I will be too," I reply and wink when she finally looks back up at me through the screen. I glance back down at my phone on the desk beside me and realize I do have a voicemail. Oops.

Again she ignores that. "We've already cleared the time away with your coach, and the event is scheduled in between your games."

They picked Jasper. That's cool. He's become my closest friend on the team, and he's also my roommate here at the apartment. "You'll arrive next Friday. The event is that night, and then we'll send you back to Sacramento Saturday afternoon."

I check my calendar. "I don't have another game until Tuesday. Can you book me on a flight home Sunday instead? I'll stay with someone in the city Saturday night, so no need for a hotel."

"You mean Levi and Tessa?" she asks.

"Yeah. Or I could stay with you."

She looks absolutely appalled by the idea, and I have to work hard not to be too insulted by that. "Are you propositioning me?"

"I'm just warning you." I shrug. "I've gotten better-looking, and when you see me again you're going to want a sequel to that kiss—and a whole lot more. And I'm willing to let that happen."

"Why are you so ridiculous?"

"Because it's fun," I reply. "And I like acting a little crazy. It's charming."

"Or it's just crazy," she counters and lets out a breath so deep and long it borders on a sigh. "Eli, I never would have let that kiss happen if I realized you'd been drafted by the team I work for."

"Yeah, but you did let it happen, and we had a connection. Admit it."

She presses those gorgeous lips together. She's physically trying to stop herself from answering, which is totally an answer unto itself. I grin. She blushes. I can even see it through the screen, and it makes me grin bigger.

Her defenses seem to be crumbling. "You're growing a beard?"

I reach up and scrub my jaw. "I was going to try it out. What do you think?"

She smiles but then forces her lips into a straight line. "It's…it doesn't matter what I think."

I lean closer to the screen and decide to really push her limits by hitting her with one of those pickup lines she loves to hate. "My beard wants to know if you would like a comfortable place to sit down?"

She laughs—a loud, high burst of a sound that causes her to clamp her hand over her mouth to try to contain it. I laugh with her.

"It's good to talk to you." I say it with a softness and sincerity that shocks even me, and it quells both our laughter.

She's smiling now though, not looking horrified, which is a victory. "How have you been?"

"Okay," I reply vaguely. "I'd ask you how you are, but you can tell me in person when we spend the night together after the charity event."

"Elijah, you can't stay with me," she replies sternly. "You have to forget that kiss ever happened. Truly. And you can't ever tell anyone about it. Please say you haven't told anyone."

"I haven't and I won't," I promise. "But it was fun. I don't have enough fun in my life, and you definitely don't seem like you do."

She looks confused, like she can't decide if that was an insult or not. It wasn't. I was just stating a fact. The last time I saw her she was way too stressed for a single, sexy woman under thirty. She bites her bottom lip, and for some reason watching her do that turns me on and solidifies my decision. "I'm spending an extra night in San Fran, so book it that way or I'll just stay anyway."

"You can't stay with me or see me. Not outside of the event."

"We can talk about it more later," I say and I give her another cocky smile. "After all, I have your phone number now and a week to convince you otherwise." I stand up, knowing the camera is now directly focused on my bare waist. I reach for my belt and start to undo it. "Would you like to see what you'll miss if you don't change your mind?"

"Eli. Don't you dare." Her eyes grow wide and her mouth starts to fall open.

I get the belt undone and reach for the button.

"Good night, Eli!"

The screen goes black as she ends the call.

I laugh, close my laptop and continue to take off the rest of my suit, smiling the entire time. Somehow, talking to Dixie completely one-eightied my mood.

I've thought about Dixie more than a few times since that night we kissed. I hadn't had a chance to see her since that preseason game last year because the Thunder didn't call me up again. They tested me out, and I failed miserably. There was a party after the game at the team owner's house, and I was feeling like shit and sulked by the bar. Dixie found me and we spent a big chunk of that night bantering—hell, flirting—and even though it didn't go further than that, it saved me from the darkness of my own thoughts. And this call a year later, out of the blue, just did the same thing.

I walk back out to the kitchen naked and grab another beer, bring it back to the bedroom and crawl into bed. All the bullshit of the night seems less important now. The frustration of losing the game, the anguish of watching that video, the annoyance of talking to my mother—it's all forgotten by the unexpected pleasure of seeing and talking to Dixie again.

I don't know how, but Dixie keeps popping back up in my life right when I need something good. And since the bad is far outweighing the good these days, I'm not about to let her disappear again, whether she likes it or not.

2

DIXIE

Morning, Dixie!"

"Holy crow! You popped!" I exclaim and grab Zoey in a hug as I walk over the threshold and into the house she shares with my brother. My arms barely make it around her now. "I'm going to have to side hug you from now on. Nugget is taking up too much space."

"Don't call him nugget!" I hear Jude bellow from the kitchen at the back of the house. "And why on earth can't you eat a meal at your own place?"

Zoey rolls her eyes and ushers me into the house. I kiss her cheek excitedly and can't help but pat her ever-growing belly. I start the never-ending battle against tears because every time I see this woman and my brother—and the bump they created—I get mushy. He had a horrible track record when it came to relationships, and even though I knew he had the potential to be the best boyfriend on the planet, he didn't know it. Zoey, thankfully, made him see his own potential, and they've been madly in love with each other for a year now. The baby was unexpected and sudden, but I've never seen Jude so happy or grounded in my life.

I bounce into the kitchen. He's leaning against the counter in nothing but a pair of sweats, holding what I'm guessing is a piping-hot cup of coffee. I sort of hug him, trying not to bobble his coffee. "Have you had a sip yet?"

"No."

I wrap my hand around the mug and take it from him. He rolls his eyes but doesn't fight me. Instead he walks over to the fancy coffee machine on the hutch next to the kitchen table and starts to make another. I smile victoriously as Zoey walks back into the kitchen and sits beside me. She leans forward and pushes the pink box of donuts toward me. "I knew you'd swing by this morning, so I had Jude make sure there were two maple bacon cream ones."

I flip the box open and groan like I'm having an orgasm. It makes Zoey laugh and Jude shudder. I reach for the sugary, salty goodness. "You are the best."

"You know bacon and maple on a donut is disgusting," Jude laments as he lifts a new coffee to his lips. "Zoey is pregnant, so what's your excuse for eating that?"

"Hush now" is the only answer I can come up with because it's short, sweet and to the point and I just want to shovel more donut in my mouth. I groan again as I take a bite. Jude looks horrified. "And give me a lift to the arena."

"Okay." Jude sighs and pushes himself off the counter. "I'm going to go get dressed."

He walks toward the hall, stopping to kiss the top of Zoey's auburn head. She smiles serenely. I take another giant bite of donut. As we wait for Jude to get ready, we talk about the baby. She tells me she's starting to have trouble sleeping and that she feels like she looks like a baby Beluga whale.

"You haven't gained weight, you've gained baby. There's a difference," I remind her and grab her wrist to lift her arm. "Look at those chicken limbs. It's all tummy and it's all nugget. Did you find out the sex yet, or is Jude just using 'he' for the hell of it?"

Zoey smiles and reaches for her fancy green teapot and pours some more herbal tea into her cup on the table. "He still doesn't want the doctor to confirm it. He's just convinced it's a boy because there are too many women in this family. Apparently he *deserves* a boy."

I roll my eyes at that, but I'm smiling. My brother has always acted like having three younger sisters was a hardship, but deep down I know he adores us and wouldn't trade us for all the brothers in the world, even though we live to tease him.

"So…how about you?" Zoey asks casually as she sips her tea. "How are things?"

I shrug. "Work is great."

Zoey puts down her teacup. "So how is everything else? Besides work?"

I almost snort at that because there's no "besides work," and she knows that. She looks sad when she sees the expression on my face. I pat her hand. "I'm not looking for love right now, Z. I've got an empire to build. Between my career and the family stuff, it's not a good time at all."

She laughs. "There is no right time."

"There's a right and wrong time for everything," I counter and stand up as I hear Jude's feet stomping down the stairs.

"Sometimes what seems like the wrong time is actually the right time," Zoey tells me, rubbing her belly. "Like getting pregnant by your teenage crush less than a year into your relationship."

"Nothing about us is wrong," Jude declares as he walks in and right over to Zoey, pulling her into his arms.

"You two are sweeter than this donut," I reply.

Jude ignores me and turns to Zoey. "You have a full day?"

"Meeting a new client in the morning, paperwork at the office, then an open house later this afternoon," Zoey replies and he kisses her forehead before using his thumb to tilt her face up so he can look in her eyes.

"Take it easy, okay?" Jude advises. "Text me the location of your open house, and I'll meet you there afterward."

Zoey nods and Jude gives her one more small kiss and then turns to me. "Let's go, kid."

I grab one more donut from the box and he glares at me. "Road donut."

He rolls his eyes and takes a napkin from the holder in the center of the table and shoves it at me. "Do not spill those sprinkles in my car."

"You are such a neat freak," I declare as I follow him out the front door. "Hopefully your little girl is more relaxed. Like me."

"It's a boy," Jude replies firmly as he slides into the driver's seat of his Tesla. I open the door and jump into the passenger seat. Sprinkles leap from the donut and cascade around the car, mostly between my seat and the console.

Jude glares at me. I smile. "Sorry. You know kids are messy. You should get used to it."

"You're not a kid anymore. Stop eating my food, messing up my car and demanding I chauffeur you everywhere," Jude grumbles and starts the engine. He pulls out into San Francisco traffic and I take another big bite of donut. I'm begrudgingly careful with the sprinkles this time.

"How are things going for the charity event Friday?" Jude wants to know. "Please say it's not going to be some big, long thing."

"Short and sweet," I promise. "Cocktails and bidding. A little mingling. Should be over by ten."

He looks relieved. I bite back a smile because thinking of the charity event makes me think of Eli. My phone buzzes in my purse, so I dig it out. I have ringtones for just about everyone, so the minute the first strands of Justin Bieber's "Baby" start, it makes my smile grow.

"Who do you hate enough to give them that ringtone?" Jude asks.

"Never you mind," I mutter, still smiling as I silence it and glance at the text.

Good Morning. It's so cold out. Can I use your thighs as earmuffs?

Before I can respond, Eli sends a photo of his very naked, very sculpted torso lying in bed and the sheet clinging precariously low on his hips. Sweet God. He's been texting me every day since I called him about the silent auction, every text more suggestive and flirty than the last, but this picture takes it to a new level.

"Donut!" Jude barks and I look at my hand, which is accidentally tilting the donut. Some sprinkles have landed on his gearshift. Oops. I quickly turn my phone screen down in my lap and pick up the sprinkles with my fingertips. I smear them onto my napkin and grab my phone again, making sure to angle it away from Jude, who has a habit of glancing over at stop signs or red lights, and quickly text him back.

> If I said you had a nice body, would you hold it against me?
> How did last night's game go?

I shouldn't be asking him about his games, but for some reason I can't help myself this morning. He answers just as I swallow down the last of my donut.

> Fine. I didn't go down in history but I will go down on you.

This boy. Oh boy…

"Who the hell are you texting with?" Jude voice is almost menacing. I glance up and find him wearing his best overprotective brother face.

"Nobody you need to know about," I reply flatly, because I know if I say it's work or one of our sisters he won't believe it.

"Are you dating someone?" He says it like the idea is as likely as a UFO landing, which is mildly offensive.

"No." I glare at him.

He turns to stare at me, arching an eyebrow and glaring at the same time. Damn it. Why can't he be a dumb jock? "I'm just going to get it out of Sadie or Winnie. And if I can't, Zoey will."

"My sisters don't know about any imaginary boyfriend, because he's imaginary," I explain. "As in he lives in *your* imagination."

"You're smiling like a cat on catnip, and your face is like glowing or something," Jude says.

"Cats don't smile. Even when they're on catnip," I reply, but his description is kind of on point. This ongoing, escalating text flirtation with Elijah Casco makes me feel pretty high. "Also, if I wanted to date someone, I don't have to clear it with you. I don't even have to tell you."

"Who are you dating?" he demands, completely horrified and not even trying to hide it. "And yes, you do have to clear it with me. You're the baby, and Mom and Dad would want me to look out for you since I'm the only one living here with you."

I roll my eyes, huff and tip my head back. "Well, you won't be the only one shortly. Soon the whole family will be here."

He doesn't answer that, but a cloud of darkness seems to fall over the car, as it always does when we talk about our family…at least since Dad was diagnosed with ALS almost two years ago. He's been steadily declining in recent months.

Dad, Mom and my sisters are all still living in Toronto, where we grew up, but with Zoey pregnant, and Dad needing more help and a place to live that doesn't involve stairs, like our family home, he decided he wanted to move here. My mom already quit her job and my sisters did too, because they want to be where my dad is. I am of two minds about the move. On one hand, it's going to be great to have my whole family so close. I've missed them desperately and haven't lived near my sisters since before college. On the other hand, I'm sad that it's happening because it means my dad is getting sicker.

"You know there's room for you in the new place," Jude tells me for probably the tenth time since he bought our parents a condo in the city. "You can get rid of your apartment, save some cash and spend time with Mom and Dad."

"Do you remember the last time Winnie, Sadie and I were under the same roof?" I ask him and give him a pointed stare. He's fighting a smile, which means he remembers that we tend to fight like cats and dogs when we're confined together for too long. "Besides, I'm a grown woman and I need my space."

"You're twenty-five and you spend more time monopolizing my Netflix and raiding my fridge than you do in your dorm-sized apartment," Jude says as he turns into the parking lot attached to the Thunder Arena and waves his pass out his window in front of the automated gate. "That's not being a grown woman, Dix. Just accept defeat and move back in with the 'rents. You can save money for a while, spend time with Dad and eat Mom's cooking. And you'll be within walking distance of your new nephew."

"I'll be twenty-six in a couple months. And shut up, jerk."

It would be kind of cool to be just down the block from Zoey and Jude's place, especially after the baby comes. Jude's going to be an amazing dad—not that I'll ever let him know. I'll tease him relentlessly about everything he does, from diaper changes to burping, but I can't wait to see him in action. If he loves this kid half as much as he loves Zoey, it's the luckiest kid alive. And to be able to see my dad with his grandkid, who I know will be over at my parents' new place every day, would be incredible.

Jude knows he's getting to me—I can tell by the smug little smirk dancing across his annoying mouth as we get out of the car. I ignore him completely. "Remember, if anyone sees us, we carpool because I'm friends with Zoey."

He nods dismissively. He doesn't hate that I refuse to admit we're related, but it's definitely not his favorite thing. He thinks that people won't judge me if they find out my brother is one of the star players on the team I work for, that it won't look like nepotism. But I think it will.

Being a woman working for a pro hockey team isn't the easiest job in the world to begin with—it's filled with biases and people looking at you like either you don't belong or you're there for the wrong reasons. That's why I love Ryanne so much. She not only owns a very successful company she built from the ground up, but she did what no woman has ever done—she bought a hockey team. She has constantly given talks about breaking down stereotypes and shattering glass ceilings. I knew from the moment I learned about her, when I was researching women CEOs for a paper in college, that I wanted to work for her somehow.

There weren't a lot of women majoring in sports media at Ithaca and even fewer with a minor in sports management. I got a lot of misogynistic bullshit while I was there—stuff like how I was only doing it to date athletes. It didn't help, I'm sure, that Jude was already making a name for himself in the NHL, and I happened to date a hockey player in college. Well, two actually. But two in four years hardly makes me a puck bunny. Still, I'd experienced enough double standard bullshit to know that when I applied to internships with the NHL, I should use my middle name, which also happened to be my mom's maiden name, as a last name.

I've been working here for almost two years, and still the only people who know I'm Jude's sister are the HR director and PR management. Oh, and Levi Casco. I still work extra hard just in case someone does find out.

"So you going to move in with the fam?"

"No." I shake my head. "Maybe in the new year. Maybe. For now I need space."

Justin Bieber blares from my cell again as if in agreement. Because the guy assigned to that ringtone is the reason I still need a place of my own right now. I can't risk anyone finding out that we're…doing whatever the hell it is we're doing.

I pull my phone out of my pocket again and check the text message.

Say you'll hang out with me this weekend after the event?

Jude walks closer, craning his neck to see my screen. In a flash I have both hands around the phone and the screen pressed into my chest. I glare at him. "I will gut you."

He looks startled. "Okay! Jesus, Dixie, you're wound tighter than a whore in church. What is up with you?"

"I need to get laid." The words tumble from my lips before I realize who I am talking to. Best I can do now is try to blow this off as another attempt to annoy him and not the truth. But it is the truth. Jude gives me the typical look of disgust. "What?" I say. "Isn't that what you'd tell one of the guys if they were bitchy? Go get laid? So I guess I need to get laid."

"Why do you insist on breaking the boundaries that have existed for centuries between brothers and—" He stops midsentence and clears his throat. "Anyway, thanks for the baby shower ideas. I really appreciate it."

I look up. My co-worker Trish Shaw is walking toward us. Jude noticed her in time, thankfully, and I'm sure she didn't hear anything she shouldn't have. I smile casually at my brother.

"Glad to help. Let me know if you want any more advice. We love Zoey!"

Trish is beside us now, smiling. "Oh! You're planning her baby shower?"

Jude nods casually. "Just asking Dix for some ideas. She knows Zoey well, and I've never planned something like this before."

"We'd love to help, when you're ready to throw it," Trish volunteers. "Of course the Thunder girls will do something for her too. We're so happy for you both, Jude."

"Thanks, Trish," Jude replies. "I've gotta go. Can't be late for practice this early in the season."

I watch him disappear through the players' entrance. Trish and I veer right to the doors that lead to the staff side of the building. Trish started in July. I was on vacation, and when I got back she had "borrowed" my stapler, my pens and the extra phone charger I keep in my desk drawer. She apologized profusely and I acted like it was no big deal, but it made me instantly not like her, even though we have the same position and have to work pretty closely together.

She's been nothing but a perfect co-worker ever since, and that's why I still don't like her. Perfect people are creepy. She reaches the door first and opens it for me, smiling brightly. I walk in and thank her, and she's beside me again a second later. "So how well do you know Zoey Quinlin that Jude is asking for baby shower advice?"

"I've gotten to know her really well since they started dating," I mutter. "I'd call her a friend."

"We're allowed to be friends with the wives and girlfriends?" she asks. She's got an innocent tone, but it feels fake.

I push open one of the double doors and hold it for her as

we enter the lobby where the elevators will take us up to our offices. "We work closely with them on charity events, so it's not uncommon that we become close to them. It can actually make the job easier if they like us."

"So we can be buddies with the wives and girlfriends but not the players?"

"We can be friends with the players. Just friends," I remind her as we step into the elevators and she presses the button for four. The arena is state of the art and only five years old. Our offices are on the top floor of the building attached to the arena.

"It's a good thing all the hot ones are taken." Trish sighs and winks at me conspiratorially like we're besties. God, it's awkward. "If Levi Casco and Jude Braddock and Duncan Darby were single when I started working here, this job would've been much harder."

Gross. That's always my first reaction when someone finds my brother attractive. I can be a little more objective about Levi. I get that the tall, dark and brooding thing is an instant panty-remover for a lot of women, but considering he lived in my basement for three months when he was a teenager, I don't see him as anything more than a pseudo-brother.

Trish yawns. It's a huge yawn—her mouth is open so wide her hand can barely cover it—and she makes a weird noise while she's doing it. She giggles when she's done and puts a hand to her chest like Scarlett O'Hara or some such nonsense. "So sorry! I was here until almost eleven last night working out the last auction items for the event. Did you figure out all the travel details for the Storm players coming?"

"Yep!"

My skin starts to tingle at the mention of the Storm players.

"They played last night, right?" She nods and struggles to cover another yawn. "How'd they do?"

"I'm sure Nadine will have the report ready for you when we get off this elevator." Trish seems overly amused for a second and then she seems overly impressed. "I swear, Dixie, I have never met a person on the business end that's as interested in the sports end as you are. I mean, you probably know more about the prospects on the farm team than the coaches."

"I've always been a hockey fan," I explain as the elevator doors open and we both step off. "Some of these guys may make it up to the team, and I like to keep an eye on them now so I've got a handle on their performance and personalities before I have to sell them to the press."

Nadine is at her desk when we walk by. She's the intern for our department, the job I started here with. She's basically our slave, but if she works hard enough and well enough she'll get a position like I did. She smiles and hands me the sheet she's gotten in the habit of preparing for me. It's clips from media articles and posts from the last twenty-four hours. Anything that mentions the Thunder or the Storm. I take the papers and smile. "Thanks, Nadine. How are you?"

"Right as rain," she responds cheerily. "I'm almost finished with the programs for the auction."

"Great! Send them my way as soon as you're done," Trish tells her and breezes by to her desk. It's always a relief when she's gone. I feel like an ass for thinking that, but then I catch someone else—like Nadine right now—with the same look of relief flickering across her face and I realize I'm not a judgy bitch. Or at least, I'm not alone in my bitchy judgment.

I move to my own desk, which is about two feet from Trish's and separated by an opaque glass partition. Before my butt is even firmly in my seat, I'm flipping through the pages Nadine gave me and reading everything about the Storm game last night.

Elijah wasn't the starting goalie, but they put him in halfway through the second period. Eli did okay. Not great, because he let in two goals in quick succession, but he blocked eight others. Well, that's better than he's been doing. Damn. I wish I could ask Levi what he thinks is going on with his brother, but he'd want to know why I'm so concerned, and I can't explain that to him. He's already keeping my identity a secret. He doesn't need to keep my crush a secret too.

I met Levi when I was fourteen at Jude's boarding school graduation. He had been Jude's roommate and they'd quickly become best friends. Levi's parents weren't at graduation, just his older brother, Todd, who seemed like a bit of a doofus. When Jude explained Levi's parents had disowned him because he was going to enter the NHL draft that summer instead of going to college, my parents offered to let him spend the summer with us. He was a quiet, reserved kid and rarely talked about his situation. I did hear him mention a younger brother, but he didn't give details and I didn't ask.

The attraction to Eli when I met him in that elevator was intense and out of nowhere. It was easy to dismiss him, and the feelings, as some weird chemical reaction. But now that we're in contact again and he's texting me all the time, I realize it's not just chemical. I like him, which is even weirder because he's brash and wild. I'm usually attracted to guys with a serious side, something Eli seems to have been born without. But we seem to just really click with each other.

I remember that he texted me about this weekend and I never responded. I grab my phone and pull up his message again. There's a new one that's just a bunch of question marks. I sent his itinerary this morning, so he knows I gave in on his request for an extra day, and that's why he's pushing me.

I quickly type him back: We can't.

Then I put my phone down and turn on my computer. I bury my brain in work to avoid thinking about this man who has become the biggest temptation of my life.

3

ELIJAH

asco! See me when you're done with your weights," the coach barks as he pops his head into the weight room. I feel my heart sink. This can't be good. We have three days off. There's no reason he should need to talk to me right now…unless it's about the charity auction. Maybe they changed their mind and are sending a different player. My heart sinks at the thought.

I finish my set of leg presses and stand up. My teammate Jasper walks over. He wipes his face with his towel and gives me a sympathetic grin. "What's that about?"

I shrug. "Doesn't feel like it's good news."

"Yeah," Jasper agrees and runs a hand through his hair. "But you did a decent job last night. And we eked out a win."

I nod and take a sip from my water bottle as Jasper sits on the weight machine I just vacated. He looks up at me as he positions his feet in the machine. "Well, good luck. At least we have a weekend in San Francisco to look forward to."

"If I'm still going," I reply and try not to frown. "Maybe that's what this is about."

Jasper doesn't look the least bit concerned. "Nah. You're a media dream and the captain's brother. Everybody loves hockey siblings. I'm sure you're still going."

I give him a fleeting smile and leave, heading down the hall to the coach's office. Rationally, I know Jasper is probably right. Still, I've gotten really used to things not being predictable in my life lately, so as I walk into the office I totally expect him to tell me that I'm not going to San Francisco.

I haven't looked forward to anything in a long time, but I'm really looking forward to seeing Dixie Wynn Braddock. It's all I've thought about since she called me to tell me about it. Something about our crazy flirtation makes me feel something I haven't felt since before the accident—normal. Probably because she never asks about the injury—or even talks much about hockey—so I can almost forget it happened.

I rap my knuckles on Coach's open office door. He looks up from his desk, spinning his chair away from his computer to face me, and motions for me to take a seat across from him. He levels me with a stern stare. "You're starting on Tuesday."

"Oh. Okay," I reply and it sounds as emotionless as I feel.

He stares at me wordless for another minute, and then his expression turns into a scowl. "Fuck, Casco. That's it?"

He's pissed off. What did I do? I lean forward. "I don't know what else to say."

He sighs and swears under his breath. "What happened to the kid I watched in college? You were so fucking pumped back then. You were so hungry for ice time, and you fucking owned the goal."

I feel the two things I always feel when someone questions my game since the accident—anger and humiliation. I clench my jaw and fight to remain cool. "I'm happy I'm starting. I'll do my best."

He's still looking at me with frustration. "The Casco I saw at Harvard would have answered that with something more along the lines of 'I'll kick everyone's asses, Coach.'"

My jaw gets tighter and I'm scared to unclench it for fear I'll tell him to shove a hockey stick up his ass. He sighs again and puts his elbows on his desk, giving his face a rub with the palm of his hand. "Look, I get that injury you had was a big one. But it was a fluke. A one-in-a-million chance of happening, so the chance of it happening again is even less. I need you to start thinking like that."

"Lightning doesn't strike twice," I mutter, because I've heard that before, and it brings me zero comfort.

He doesn't hear the skepticism in my tone, so he smacks his palm on the desk. "Exactly! You're not going to get sliced open again, so turn back into that fearless maniac that we need. That we signed. Okay?"

Yeah. Sure. It's that easy. Thanks for the pep talk. I'm going to forget all about having my neck sliced open now. You're a fucking genius. You missed your calling. You should have been a fucking psychologist.

I smile, large and fake but hopefully not detectable. "I'll kick ass, Coach. I promise."

He doesn't seem completely convinced, but he's convinced enough that he's done with this conversation. "Great. Now have a good weekend with the big boys, but remember, if you still want to join your brother permanently you have to get your mojo back. It's now or never, Elijah."

"Yep!" I smile again and stand. He nods and I get the fuck out of there without picking up the chair I was sitting in and smashing it over his desk and possibly his head. So that's a win in my book.

I storm out of the building, skipping the locker room because I can shower at home. I need to pack and I need some time to myself. Jasper texts me as I drive to our apartment.

Where are you? Did you forget we drove in together? Again?

Right. Shit. I pull over and pick up my phone and text him back that I did forget—again. And tell him I'll turn around. Before I can do that, though, he texts back that he'll grab a ride with someone else and see me at home.

How he puts up with me I'll never know. He's been in my corner since I dropped out of college and joined the team. He is younger than me. He was born and raised in Sweden and drafted last year after playing a year in the Swedish hockey league. Most of the team knows my history and knows who my brother is and expects me to be better than I am. Half are annoyed by the fact I'm not, and the other half seems to enjoy my struggles. Jasper is in neither category. He's just been a good friend. He's probably going to be moved up to the Thunder any day now, and he'll never be sent back down to this league. He's that good.

I used to be that good. Hell, I used to be better than that.

I park my Jeep and walk across the parking lot of our apartment complex to our unit. I open our front door, drop my keys on the coffee table next to the tangle of Xbox controllers, and head into my room. We're on the top floor of the two-story building, with a balcony overlooking the pool. It's not fancy, because we're on entry-level contracts, but it's decent and it's clean. My parents are wealthy and I grew up with a lot more luxury than I have in this place, but I'm happier here, and that's what counts.

I have to remind myself of that fact—that I'm still happier here, on the farm team for the San Francisco Thunder, than I would have been giving up on hockey and finishing a business degree in college. I'd wanted to head straight into the NHL like Levi, but I knew my parents would be devastated. So I went to an Ivy League school just as Christopher and Catherine Casco had wanted, but I purposely picked Harvard because it had the best hockey program.

I can see my scar in the mirror across the room. I see it everywhere. I feel it too. I don't know how to explain it, but when I laugh or turn my head I feel it like a rope tightening around my neck. I've been to specialists and plastic surgeons and everyone says it's psychological. The skin healed well, and the scar fades more as time ticks by. So how come I notice it every second of the day? Even the permanent almost-beard I've started keeping on my face doesn't mask it. It glares at me—mocks me.

I take a deep breath and force my eyes off my reflection. I pull my suitcase out from under my bed and toss it on top, flipping it open. I start to walk around the room grabbing what I need for the weekend in San Francisco. A suit, jeans, underwear, socks, tie, dress shoes…I stop at my night table and pull open the drawer. Inside is a box of condoms I bought a couple months ago when we moved in. It's unopened.

I've been too miserable to pick up chicks the way Jasper and the others have been doing—the way I'd planned to, and quite frankly dreamed of, when I thought about playing pro hockey.

But I don't need Dixie to know that. If I'm lucky, I'll convince her I'm a loophole in the no-fraternization clause. Because I did a little research last night and I am. The clause talks about Thunder players and staff, and I'm a Storm player right now. Total loophole. Hopefully I can convince her to take a shot because, man, I want her. I want her like I haven't wanted anyone or anything in a very long time.

I open the box, pull out a strip and leave it in my drawer. I put the remaining condoms—eight—into my suitcase and then head into the bathroom. I shower, and as I'm wrapping a towel around my waist I hear Jasper come home. I grab my toothbrush, hair product and clippers, to keep my almost-beard from becoming an actual beard. While I'm heading back across the hall to my room, I see Jasper standing by the front door kicking off his shoes.

"Sorry about the lift thing," I tell him sincerely.

"You suck, but it's fine." Jasper smiles. "You're still going to San Fran with me, right?"

"Yep. Coach wanted to see me to tell me I'm starting on Tuesday," I explain and turn into my room as Jasper's face lights up. I don't want to look at his excitement. It's going to give me nerves. I never used to be nervous about playing. Fuck.

He leans on my doorframe. "Dude, that's great news!"

I nod and shove my toiletries in my travel bag and drop it on top of the clothes in the suitcase. My phone rings and vibrates on my desk, causing it to bounce around the wood surface. Before I can reach it, Jasper picks it up and glances at the screen. He smiles. "It's your new girl. How have I not met her again?"

I smile, not really at him, but at the idea that Dixie is calling—or "Julie," as he knows her, because that's the fake name I have her number stored under. "She lives in San Fran. We're reconnecting on this trip."

Not a lie... I hope.

He tosses me the phone. I catch it and wait until he leaves the room to answer. "I can't remember exactly what you look like. Can you send me a naked selfie so I can find you at the event tomorrow night?"

She laughs. It's this loud, quirky sound I can't quite describe, but it's adorable. "Sure, right after you send me a dick pic so I can make sure the team orders you the right sized jock."

"I'm not playing for the Thunder yet."

"We like to be prepared." If comebacks were an actual art form she'd be a master. It's like a gift. "I'm just making sure you and Jasper have all your flight details."

"Yep. And I can't wait to no longer need a selfie or my imagination to know what you look like naked."

"Elijah." She says my name with a little lilt, even though she's trying to be cautious. "You know the rules."

"I know that you, as an employee of the Thunder hockey organization, cannot fraternize in a romantic way with members of the current roster of the San Francisco Thunder." I'm almost whispering, even though I can hear the distant sounds of the *Walking Dead* video game coming from the living room. Jasper can't hear this conversation. I gently kick the door closed before walking toward my bed. "I am not on the current roster of the Thunder."

"You're in the organization," she replies.

"So is the dude who plays the mascot, but I bet no one would care if you gave him an orgasm," I counter and sit on the edge of my bed.

"He's fifty with a beer gut and smells like fake polyester bear fur," Dixie retorts, and I chuckle. "But even if he were Chris Hemsworth, he's not worth risking my career for."

"Chris Hemsworth, huh?" I smirk. "That's who does it for you?"

"He's on the list, yeah," she replies. "So are you."

"Good to know." I keep my tone light, but inside I'm feeling like a peacock with my feathers out. I like the idea that I'm on her list—a lot.

"The list is titled 'People I Can Never Touch,'" she adds. Damn it.

"Lucky for you I don't mind doing all the work," I quip and flop back on my bed. "You can just lie there. I'll do the touching."

"You're the worst."

"I'm the best," I argue and let my hand wander to the front of my towel. I'm already half hard and she's not even talking dirty or anything. "I'm so good that I also read the fine print in my Storm contract and the no-fraternization policy expressly states with other Storm employees. You, sweet Dixie, are not a Storm employee."

She doesn't respond at first, and I know that means she's thinking it over. I may actually get to do more than kiss her. And I honestly can't wait. My hand moves from the growing bulge to the left side of my neck. I run my fingertips over the slightly raised, lightly puckered line that runs almost to the middle of my throat.

"I have to go. I have a meeting," she says finally, which isn't exactly the *You're totally right, Elijah, let's fuck* I was hoping for, but it's better than *I still won't let you in my tight little power suit.*

"You know, if this PR thing doesn't work for you, you can always buy one of those little carts and sell hot dogs. You'd be great at it." I smile up at the ceiling. "Because you already know how to make a wiener stand."

She rewards my ridiculous pickup line with her adorable laugh again. "That one is groan-worthy."

"But you're not groaning," I reply. "I can make you groan…or moan. Moaning is better actually."

"Good-bye, Elijah."

"See you tomorrow, sweet Dixie."

The line disconnects, and I drop my phone beside me on the bed. My hand goes directly to my half-hard cock. I palm it and press down, giving it a firm rub through the rough towel. It feels good. I would love to make it feel even better, while fantasizing about Dixie, but I can't. I have to finish packing, and Jasper will want to go out to eat soon, which means he'll come barging in here.

I reluctantly let go of my dick after a few more rubs and pick up my phone again. Pulling the thin towel as taut as I can, I snap a picture. The outline of my now fully erect cock is perfectly visible. I text it to Dixie with the words See? You make wieners stand.

I don't get a response and I don't expect one. She's working and I've got to give her some space to think about what I said. I don't want her to lose her job, but the idea that I'll be near her again and not be able to pick up where we left off is painful.

She just came back into my life at the right time. She is turning into the perfect distraction from the trouble I'm having on the ice. I don't think this can go anywhere because our career trajectories make it impossible, which is probably fine. I just think we should work it out of our systems as soon as possible. A little harmless naked fun before it's completely off-limits. She's like this prize now. Something I have to conquer. And if I can win Dixie I'll feel like I can do anything, maybe even get my damn hockey mojo back.

I spend the next several hours hanging out with Jasper—going out for food and coming home and playing video games—but the whole time I'm hoping I can convince her to feel the same way when I see her this weekend. Then, around eleven thirty when I crawl into bed, she texts me again. It's a photo—a selfie taken in a mirror with her head cropped out. She's wearing only a lacy black bra and undies with red piping. My jaw hits the ground and my cock grows rock-hard in seconds.

Before I can get my hand into my underwear and around my cock, she texts again.

I'm thinking of getting a job with UPS so I can handle your package.

I'm smiling so big it aches. This fucking girl…I text her back.

You can handle my package no matter who you work for.

Then I put the phone down to take care of the riot she's causing in my boxer briefs. Man, she better reread her HR paperwork and see my point. I have to have this girl.

4

DIXIE

So?" I ask and give a long, slow spin in front of my computer so Winnie and Sadie can see the back of the white cocktail dress with black lace panels that I'm thinking of wearing to the charity auction tonight.

"Don't you have something…sluttier?" Sadie asks casually.

I glare at her pixelated face through my computer screen. I'm not sure she's absorbing the depth of the look, so I add, "It's a work event, Sadie."

"It's a gorgeous dress, but it is a little…" Winnie, the only one in our family with the slightest amount of tact, searches for the right word. "Safe. Pretty but tame, you know?"

"It's the white. It's virginal," Sadie adds helpfully. "You're twenty-five. No one wants a twenty-five-year-old virgin. Wear a color."

I frown because I really like it. It makes me feel confident. But so does making Elijah's eyes bug out of his head, and that's the ego boost I'm going for tonight. I hold up a finger to the camera and scurry over to my closet.

"How's the packing coming along?" I call out from inside the walk-in closet. I live in a studio. It's small and basic but it's afford-able, which trumps everything else in San Francisco.

"The big stuff like furniture is already in San Fran. We're just go-ing through some boxes in the basement now. What to keep and what to toss. Mom doesn't want to leave too much junk here while we're gone. But Dad's doing a better job with it than her," Winnie informs me. "He's great at purging stuff. Mom keeps finding things and getting weepy."

"Yesterday she found Jude's first pair of skates and cried for like an hour," Sadie explains and I can hear the exasperation in her voice.

I grab the teal cocktail dress with lace across the top and the hem. It's clingier than I've worn to a work event and a much bolder color. I tend to stick to basic black or white at work functions, and much looser. But the Elijah factor is changing everything.

"Give Mom a break, guys," I tell my sisters as I shimmy into the dress. "This is brutal on her even more than us, and probably more than Dad. She's never lived anywhere but Toronto, and she's mov-ing and watching the only man she's ever loved fight a losing battle at the same time."

I walk out of the closet and over to my desk, where my laptop is perched. I can see the instant look of approval on both their faces through the screen. "Yes!" Sadie says emphatically.

"So much yes!" Winnie agrees.

I glance over at the full-length mirror on the wall next to my dresser. The dress is sexy but not racy, so, although it's not some-thing I would normally think of for work, I'm going to go with it.

"Wear Gran's pearl necklace and earrings with it, Dix," Sadie advises.

"Pearls are old-fashioned, aren't they?" Winnie says.

"No way," she argues back, shaking her head so quickly her dirty blond hair flies and hits Winnie in the face. "Any man worth your time will equate a pearl necklace with a pearl necklace."

She grins and gives me an exaggerated wink. Winnie wrinkles her nose. "Gross."

I laugh at both of them. "I'm not trying to get him to think of that. I'm just flirting. We're just flirty friends."

"You have never called us for fashion advice because someone is just a flirty friend," Winnie reminds me.

"Well, there's a first time for everything," I retort. "I have to go! Have to be at the event in half an hour to make sure the setup is going well."

"Have them set up a mattress behind the stage so you don't have to waste time bringing him back to your place," Winnie quips with a grin.

"Besides, your place is too small for really rowdy sex," Sadie advises. "And this guy's a goalie, so it's going to be hella rowdy. Trust me."

Winnie rolls her eyes. "You banged one goalie in your senior year of high school and now you're like an expert?"

"It's one more than you've banged," Sadie counters. "When she starts lusting after librarians and accountants you can give out the advice."

"Later, sisters. I love you."

They wave and blow kisses and I hit End on our Skype session and shut my laptop. I love my sisters more than anyone else in the world. They've been my best friends my entire life, but I'm still not ready to admit to them that this thing with Elijah is anything more than innocent flirtation. Still, as I rush to the bathroom to give my makeup and hair a final primp, I grab the pearl necklace and teardrop earrings Sadie mentioned earlier. In case she's right and it does make Eli think inappropriate thoughts. Then I head to the hotel where the event is happening.

If flirting with Eli is playing with fire, then I'm a goddamn pyromaniac. I can't stop doing it. It's too much fun, and I feel like ninety percent of the fun was sucked out of my life in the last two years. Eli brings it back.

It's not anyone's fault—not even mine—that life got so serious. Finding out your dad's clock is ticking down way faster than it should makes life refocus and forces you to grow up fast. I know that I don't do the things most twenty-somethings do. I spend most of my free time with my family because I'll be damned if I'm going to miss a moment with my dad on purpose. And my mom and my sisters—and Jude, even though he'll never admit it—need me as much as I need them to get through this. The idea of throwing a boyfriend into that just doesn't feel right. Sadie stopped dating when we found out about Dad too, and Winnie's relationship with her long-term boyfriend is a disaster. Because we're barely holding it together. If…*when* Dad finally dies, I am going to be a mess. An inconsolable, devastated, broken mess. No outsider needs to deal with that. So I haven't bothered with guys and dating. I'd rather just focus on what's important—my family.

Flirting with Elijah is the exception to that rule. I get to be wild and inappropriate and horny and all the other things young career girls should be in their spare time. But hooking up with him would be careless…if the no-fraternization clause applies to the Storm players. I just assumed it did, but I didn't read the paperwork all that carefully when I signed it as an intern. I was just thrilled to be a part of the organization and start my career working for Ryanne Bateman. I didn't think the policy would ever matter.

As I walk into the hotel, I head straight to where the event is happening. I smile at a few employees as I pass by. They smile briefly and scurry past. Everyone is in hustle mode already. Good.

Nadine is standing at the entrance to the tiki-themed lounge we've rented for this event. It's a great intimate location with mood lighting designed like tiki torches and funky bamboo tables. The Thunder do three major charity events during the year—this is actually the smallest. Nadine looks stressed as she surveys the employees. "Are you okay with the silver napkins? They gave me a choice of silver or black because you know, team colors. But Trish wasn't here and I didn't want to call you because I thought I could handle it, but now I'm worried I made the wrong call."

"Silver is perfect. The black ones always seem morbid rather than classy." I pat her shoulder reassuringly. She looks so relieved I almost laugh. I remember being that eager and panicked all at once. "You're doing great, Nadine."

"Thank you." She smiles proudly. "Oh, and I brought the HR handbook you asked for. It's in my purse."

She walks over to a nearby table and grabs her purse off the seat. It's honestly the size of a suitcase, which was one of the first things I noticed about her. It's her quirk. Everyone has a quirk, and ever since I was a kid, I've loved finding them in people. I haven't been able to find one in Trish yet, and that's one of the reasons I find her off-putting. Nadine pulls out the thick, neatly bound Code of Conduct for Thunder employees.

"Thank you!" I immediately open it and start flipping pages.

"Hey, ladies! It looks great in here!"

We both turn and see Trish walking toward us with a purposeful stride. She's wearing a simple black cocktail dress with a flared skirt that lands below her knee and strappy silver heels. Her eyes widen a little as they land on me, and I can't decide if she's shocked or offended by my dress choice, but either way it makes me uncomfortable.

"What's that?" Trish asks, pointing to the HR manual in my hand.

"Nothing." I shrug casually. "Just some HR stuff."

"Are you going to read the fraternization clause out loud before the guests get here?" Trish asks, grinning.

My heart stops. Oh my God, she knows? How does she know?

Trish keeps talking. "Out loud to the players? I mean, we should if you think it'll get them to finally stop hitting on the cute female fans at these events."

Oh. She doesn't actually know why I have the book. She's making a joke. I almost sigh audibly in relief. Trish giggles lightly and turns to Nadine. "I heard Jude Braddock rents hotel rooms where we have events so he can sleep with guests."

"Not anymore," I reply quickly. "He's settled down now and has a kid on the way."

Trish nods. "Oh, I know. I wish some guy would look at me the way Jude looks at his girlfriend."

She sighs longingly. Nadine smiles. "It's amazing that a guy who once had a dick pic on the internet could now be in a relationship goals meme."

"Oh God!" I groan like I always do when Jude's famous dick pic comes up. "Please tell me the guests are about to arrive so we can stop having this conversation."

Trish glances at the pretty rose gold watch on her arm. "Actually they are. Nadine, do a last-minute sweep of the room to make sure everything is in place. Dixie, double-check that the bartenders have everything they need. I'm heading to the kitchen to make sure the appetizers are hot and ready to circulate."

Nadine scurries off and I force myself to nod and walk toward the main bar, even though the fact that she's throwing around orders makes me bristle. She's not my boss. In fact, I have seniority over her, but right now that doesn't matter. We just need to make sure everything is ready.

The bartenders are good to go, so I decide to sneak off to the bathroom to freshen up my lipstick and then read every single word of the nonfraternization clause. I leave the tiki bar and head down the long hallway toward the restrooms. I swing open the door and glance around. It's empty, so I walk over to the sink, barely glance at my reflection and start flipping through the booklet again.

I find the clause I'm looking for on page nineteen. I hold my breath and read the section so fast the words get blurry for a second and then I let the air out of my lungs and read it again much more slowly. It doesn't say "and their affiliates." It doesn't include Sacramento Storm in any wording. It says that although connections on a friendly level are encouraged between staff and rostered players of the San Francisco Thunder, romantic involvement of any kind is not condoned and can result in termination.

"What's so exciting?"

My eyes fly up and as I close the handbook and put it behind my back, I see Ann, our assistant manager of communications, standing at the end of the line of stalls. She's smiling. "You didn't even hear me come in, but whatever has you distracted also has you smiling."

My free hand flies up to my mouth. She's right. I am smiling. Oops. Her brown eyes move to the mirror and down. Then she points. "What are you reading?"

"Oh…I…" Oh my God, how do I get out of this? I have fifteen seconds before it's awkward if I don't answer, but I can't think of a single thing to say that will make it perfectly normal to get caught smiling while reading the HR handbook in a public restroom.

The universe must like me today, because her phone rings and her attention is completely refocused. "Ann speaking."

I quickly turn away from her, partly to give her the aura of privacy but also so I can shove the book in my purse. It's kind of too big, so I can't close my purse, but at least it's hidden. I try not to eavesdrop as I apply my lipstick in the mirror but I can't help but notice Ann's voice is getting more excited.

"Yes…Yes…Why thank you…"

I grab my purse and start toward the door because I think she needs privacy and I don't have any more reasons to be in here. The guests are probably already in the bar, and I should get to work. The players should be here any minute too, which means Elijah will be here. I give Ann a little wave as I start to pass by her, but she reaches out and gently grabs my wrist. She keeps talking into her phone, though, so I wait, worried she'll want to talk about the HR book again.

"Great. I look forward to reviewing it. Thank you so much and have a good weekend." She says good-bye, presses End on her cell phone and then lets out an excited squeak and pulls me into a hug.

"What in the world is happening?" I ask, laughing at her enthusiasm.

"I got it!" Ann pulls back and grins wildly at me. "I applied for a director position with Finley Coyne Global in New York and they just offered me the position."

"Oh my God!" To say I'm shocked would be an epic understatement. I didn't even know Ann was looking for another job, let alone one on the other side of the country. Finley Coyne is the biggest sports communications firm in the country. A director position with them, at their head office, is an incredible accomplishment. I hug her again. "Ann, that's amazing. You deserve it, and they're lucky to have you. But on a personal level, I'm devastated you're leaving."

She pulls back from the hug and smiles. "I'm going to miss you and the team, but I'm originally from New York, and I've wanted to move home for a while. And this position…it's a dream come true! They're emailing me the offer tonight, so please don't tell anyone yet."

"Sure." I can't believe she's leaving. She's been my boss since I was an intern, and she's been such a great mentor.

Ann reaches out and squeezes my shoulder. "I want you to apply for my job."

"Really?" I'm stunned.

She nods emphatically. "Yes. You want it, right?"

"Of course I do," I reply automatically. "I really feel like I'm ready for it too, but I don't know if management will see it that way."

"I see it that way," Ann says. "And I'm going to tell them that before I go."

"Thank you. I really appreciate that." If I'm promoted to Ann's position now I'll be exceeding my own goals. I've had a five-year plan mapped out since I started interning here. If I take over for Ann this year, I'll be two years ahead of my goals.

"Remember…" She lifts her finger to her lips. I make a cross over my heart. "See you out there! I'm just going to call my mom and tell her!"

I leave her to it and slip out of the restroom. I can see the guests pouring out of the elevators at the end of the hall, and I make my way toward them. I'm still reeling with the news that Ann is going to leave. A million questions are flying through my head. Will she really recommend me to replace her? Will Mr. Carling go for it? Have I done enough to prove myself?

I'm lost in those thoughts when I pass the elevator banks, so I don't notice the doors are opening on not one but two elevators. I end up almost walking into a large group of people, and my heel catches abruptly on the carpet. I stumble and my body lurches forward. For a swift, panic-filled moment I think I might fall face first, but then a strong hand grabs my arm. It stops me from falling but causes my purse to fly off my other arm.

And of course, because it's not closed, most of the contents fly out across the hotel hallway. Ugh. The person who grabbed my arm to stop me from face-planting is my brother, and of course he was getting off the elevator with a bunch of other hockey players, including Levi Casco, Duncan Darby, Eddie Rollins and Elijah "Fucking Hot as Hell in a Suit" Casco.

"Jesus, Dixie, be careful!" Jude says in his overprotective brotherly voice.

I want to level him with a withering warning stare, but I can't make my eyes leave Elijah. So instead I gently tug my arm out of his grip and coolly say, "Thank you."

I think he clues in that he's on the verge of blowing our cover because he doesn't do what he'd usually do in brother mode, which is lecture me to wear more sensible shoes or something stupid like that. I still can't take my eyes off Elijah, though, so I can't see Jude's face.

Elijah's blue suit is wrapped perfectly around his broad shoulders and tapers neatly down his taut torso. His white shirt is perfectly pressed with French cuffs. He's got the fullest five-o'clock shadow possible without actually being able to classify it as a beard. It's neat but somehow still gives him a rough, wild look—the smirk he's wearing and the way his green eyes glimmer as he looks at me also help with that—and it's in direct contrast with the immaculate outfit. It's hot as hell.

I clear my throat and drop to my knees—not to blow him, which is actually what I'd like to do, but to retrieve my purse and its contents. Levi and Elijah also bend to help me. "I've got it guys, it's fine," I mutter and reach for my lipstick and phone.

Levi grabs the purse itself and hands it to me. Elijah grabs my wallet. Eddie bends and retrieves the last item that happened to land at his feet—the HR handbook. He flips it over and reads the title out loud. "Do you carry this with you at all times? What are you going for? Employee of the year?"

Eddie chuckles at his own lame joke and hands me the book. Elijah is staring at me. I can feel it, and when I look up and meet his eyes, he grins. It's victorious. He knows why I'm carrying that book in my purse. I keep my face passive so he doesn't get any glimmer of satisfaction that he was right and he is not currently off-limits. I tuck the book under my arm. "I have to get this to our intern, Nadine. It's hers. You guys can follow me. The party is this way."

I start walking and I can hear them shuffling along behind me, but I don't turn around. I wiggle my ass enough to be noticeable but not ridiculous, hoping it's Elijah who notices and not Eddie, the team manwhore.

The lounge is nearly full when we get there. I turn and look at the guys. Eli's eyes are slowly making their way up my body to my face. He's still smirking and it's still hot. I force myself to look at someone else—and land on Jude. His face is all scrunched up and his eyes keep sweeping over my dress. Brother mode is still on. If we weren't in public he'd tell me my dress is too tight or something. And I'd tell him to stick it up his ass.

"You know the drill, boys," I say, all business. "Mingle, make polite small talk, pose for photos, stay relatively sober. Absolutely no exchanging of bodily fluids with guests."

My eyes move to Eddie and he tries to look innocent, which actually just makes him look even pervier than normal. I focused on him because he is now the only guy in this group who is single. Well, other than Elijah, and, as the handbook indicated, he's not subject to the rules just yet.

"Have a nice night." I turn and walk away because, yeah, I might let him come home with me, but I'll be damned if I'm going to make it easy.

5

ELIJAH

Even though Dixie is clear across the room, it's impossible to stop looking at her. Damn, she's hot. I've never seen her in anything but business wear. That dress is not business wear. I keep wanting to walk up to her and trace the lace hem with my fingertips.

"Eli!" Levi barks in a harsh whisper at me.

I blink and refocus on the people in front of me, two puffy businessmen who are also season ticket holders. I can tell by the expectant look on their faces they asked me a question, but I have no idea what it was.

"Eli likes playing with the Storm, right, Eli? They're a good group of guys," Levi tells the businessmen with an easy smile.

Oh. We're talking about my career. Great. I press my lips into a smile like I'm perfectly okay with these guys who have probably never laced up skates weighing in on my life's dream. But I give them an easy grin and say, "It's a fun team filled with really talented guys."

"Seems like you're struggling a little, though. No offense, but I saw that you got pulled last game," says the man in the blue suit.

My smile grows brighter as my thoughts grow darker. "Everyone has an off night." *You raging pile of pompous douchery,* I add silently. "I'm just getting it out of my system now so I don't have off days when they call me up."

The businessmen chuckle and Levi smiles. Then they both ask for selfies, which we provide, and they tell us they're going to check on the Mexican vacation package they bid on. They shake our hands, and the one in the blue suit leans in and says, "How's the neck?"

"Like nothing ever happened." I give my automatic standard answer to this question, trying not to let my tone sound clipped.

He grins and winks. "Good to hear it. And I bet that scar gets you a lot of tail."

They saunter off, which is great because I don't know how much longer I can hold this happy-go-lucky look on my face without physical pain. All I want to do is scowl. I fucking hate that everyone and their brother thinks they get to weigh in on the most horrible moment of my life. Seriously. It happens all the time, and it's making my blood boil more and more every time. Levi steps closer and squeezes my shoulder. "Sorry, bro. They can be invasive."

"It's fine. And he's right. Chicks dig scars," I say and run a hand through my hair. "And speaking of chicks, I'm going to grab another drink and take a look at the eye candy in this place."

There's only one girl I intend to ogle, but he doesn't need to know that.

Levi's expression grows stern. "Thunder players can't pick up women at team events."

I grin. "You know, you should really consider acting after hockey. You could play the angry old curmudgeon in just about any movie without even trying." I laugh, but he doesn't. "Relax, I'll behave. And besides, I'm not technically a Thunder player, Thor."

Using the "God of Thunder" nickname he's earned since joining this team gets the reaction I hoped for—he scowls. Triumphant, I wink at him and walk away.

I have no idea where I'm going. I just know I don't want to talk to him anymore—or anyone. I'm really fucking done with everyone's opinions and advice. I need to get in a better headspace if I'm going to stay at this event and convince everyone I'm in a great mood. I find myself by the large bar on the far end of the room so I order a Stella. Normally in this mood I'd want something with hard liquor, but Dixie warned us to take it easy on booze.

"Forget the beer. Make that two Piña Coladas," I hear her say to the bartender before I see her. "And put extra umbrellas in his, please. Extra maraschino cherries in mine."

I smile and turn to find her about half a foot down the bar. My mood instantly lifts and for the first time all night I'm not faking the smile that forms on my face. The pretty teal color of the dress stands out in the dim light, accentuating the way her hip curves as she leans on the bar. Her golden hair shimmers in the light from the tiki torches. It's always so perfectly straight and sleek, and, man, I can't wait to try to mess it up.

"Ms. Wynn, we are not supposed to be getting inebriated at team functions," I tell her sternly and sidestep closer to her. "I believe you have a handbook on your person that will confirm that."

"I gave the handbook back to our intern, Nadine," she explains with a smile playing on her red lips. I want to smear the lipstick off them.

"Why did you have it in the first place?"

"Double-checking one of the clauses," Dixie replies innocently. "I like to make sure I'm not a rule breaker."

The bartender slides two icy Piña Coladas at us. Mine has two frilly paper umbrellas and hers has three cherries as requested. I chuckle. Dixie grins and clinks her glass against mine before putting those perfect lips to the straw. I take a big sip and then put my drink down on the bar.

"Do you mind if I follow you home tonight?" I ask her with a serious stare. "Because my mother always told me to follow my dreams."

She laughs so loudly an older couple a few feet away looks over. Dixie slaps a hand over her mouth to try to stifle the sound. When she regains composure she whispers, "That was the best one yet."

"Thank you." Getting a compliment from her is quickly turning my mood around. I take another sip of the Colada and smile, more at the fact that she ordered for me—with extra umbrellas—than at the drink itself. I'm a huge fan of fruity, slushy drinks. Piña Colada, Margarita, you name it, I love it. And ordering them in bars, with all their fruit and umbrella garnishes, gets attention from women, so I embrace my fruity drink fetish. She knows this. I told her when she caught me drinking a Margarita at Ryanne's party last year after our elevator encounter, and it's cute that she remembered.

"You shouldn't though," she says, bringing me back to reality. "Follow me home."

"But you read the HR book, and you know, like I said, Storm players are not included in the nonfraternization clause." I'm leaning as close to her as I can while still looking casual to anyone who glances over.

She looks up at me from under her lashes, and she looks so damn coy I want to pick her up, throw her on the bar and climb on top of her. I subtly reach down and readjust myself because my pants are getting tight.

"I read it and you're right." My victory smile is cut off as she shakes her head. "But tonight you're here to be part of the team, so you're off-limits. Technically."

"Lucky for you I'm not a technical person," I counter. "I'm about feeling and instinct. You should forget rules and technicalities and just let yourself have a little fun. With me."

She focuses her pretty blue eyes on me, and I can see she's considering it. "We agree though, if this happens, it's one and done. We get naked, get each other out of our systems and move on. That's the plan, okay?"

"You're kind of obsessed with rules and plans, huh?" I watch her take a long sip of her drink and use the tip of her little pink tongue to swipe a dollop from her lips.

"Plans are good. Rules keep chaos at bay," she replies.

"Chaos can be fun." I grip my Piña Colada glass tighter so I don't reach out and wipe away that little drip that landed on the corner of her lip. "I'm going to make you love losing control, sweet Dixie."

Her eyes darken and her cheeks slowly fill with color. But she fights it like a champ, clearing her throat, throwing back the rest of her Piña Colada and taking a step away from me. "You should mingle, Elijah. That's what you're here for."

"I didn't come for the fans. I came for you." I lower my voice and put my now empty glass down on the bar. "Let me come for you."

"Holy shit…" She whispers it softly, and I see the words form more than I actually hear them. "Play by the rules, Elijah."

"For now," I relent and wink as I reluctantly walk away.

I make my way over to Jasper, who is standing by the auction items table taking a picture with an attractive blonde who has wrapped herself around him. I stay a safe distance back until they stop talking and she leaves, because I'm kind of maxed out on the casual banter and I'm still sporting half a hard-on, and the last thing I want is some fan wrapped around me.

Once she's walked away, I join Jasper. He looks like a kid in a candy store. "I see you're enjoying yourself."

"This is insane," he confesses excitedly. "The Thunder have a lot of hot fans. Man, I can't wait till they call me up now. I could get used to this kind of attention very easily."

I laugh. "The problem with fans is they're off-limits."

Jasper gives me a sly smirk. "There's no such thing as off-limits in my world. Just have to be stealthy. Like a ninja."

"You're a fucking nut, you know that?" I shake my head, but honestly I love the guy. At least I think I do until he takes another sip of his drink and then points subtly across the bar to my girl.

"Who is the hot little blond package you were talking with at the bar?"

"She works for the team," I reply, my voice stiff. "Sorry, my ninja buddy."

The glint of mischief in Jasper's eye gets even more glinty and mischievous. "What's her name? What does she do?"

"Dixie Wynn. Publicist, player relations." I sound like my dad suddenly. He always sounds like someone just scratched his Benz. "You touch her and you'll likely be in the minors forever."

The grin on his face falters for a second. "Why? You claiming her?"

"I can't. She's off-limits," I mutter back and suddenly wish I had another drink. "Once I make it up, full-time, I'm not doing anything that will get me shipped back down. The rules are pretty clear. Even Braddock didn't screw around with employees."

Jasper seems to really consider that, furrowing his blond brow. And then he shrugs and takes a sip of his drink. "Well then, fans it is!"

He wanders off to a gaggle of twenty-something women who've been ogling us from the bar. I don't join him. Instead I walk the other way in search of Levi. I find him with Jude and a defenseman they call Marchie. I come to a stop beside Levi just as someone from Thunder staff takes the stage and thanks everyone for coming.

"Good. It's over and I can get home to Zoey." Jude sighs in relief and I try not to look shocked that he's excited to leave a party.

"How's she doing?" Levi asks Jude quietly as they start to announce the winners of the various auction items.

"She's great," Jude whispers, smiling. "The baby dropped, so it looks like she swallowed a basketball now. I think it's adorable, but it makes it uncomfortable for her to sleep. I was Googling it and I guess sometimes a body pillow helps, so I ordered her one."

I chuckle. They both look over at me. "I'm sorry. I just…I'd love to see the difference in your browser history now compared to like a year ago. I'm betting it's hysterical. From porn sites to Babies 'R' Us."

My brother laughs and so does Marchie. Jude kind of glares at me. "Unlike you, Baby Casco, I didn't have to use Google to see naked women. I could just open my front door and invite one in."

Marchie lets out a juvenile "Burn!"

"Ha. Ha." I roll my eyes. "I did great in college."

"Sure ya did, kid." He pats my shoulder.

"I fucked my English professor's wife." It flies from my mouth in a hushed whisper before I can stop it. I mean, it's true, but why do I feel the need to share it right now? Why am I trying to prove myself to these guys?

They're all staring at me now with the surprise and awe I was hoping for, but somehow it doesn't make me feel better. I've never sought approval before. I've never given a shit what anyone thought of me. This is just a further reminder that I'm not the person I used to be, and I hate it.

"How come you never mentioned this professor's wife before?" Levi wants to know.

I shrug. "I did, actually. Remember Lilah? The one I went skiing with one spring break?"

"Whoa!" Marchie looks impressed.

My brother's stubbled jaw drops. "You went skiing with the professor's wife?"

"They have a ski cabin in Vermont. He stayed in Boston to grade papers," I explain quickly because I don't want to talk about this anymore, even though I'm the one who brought it up. "And there wasn't actually much skiing involved."

"Little brother has impressive game," Jude says with a smile. "Which means you're going to know how to take advantage of the opportunities you'll get when you join us. Levi never did learn to enjoy the puck-bunny perks."

"You did it enough for the rest of us," Levi snarks at his best friend.

Jude grins and nods in agreement, and then he looks over at me. "I sowed a lot of oats, but I couldn't be happier that chapter is closed. You'll want it to end one day too, Baby Casco, so enjoy it now while you can."

I nod. I don't add that I want to sow my oats with his sister, but man do I ever. We stop talking as the Thunder employee announces the winner of the biggest auction item—that trip to Mexico the businessmen were yammering about. The winner is an old guy wearing an expensive suit. A woman who looks to be in her twenties takes the stage to claim the voucher with him. She looks thrilled. I can't decide if she's a trophy wife or a daughter.

"Okay, the night is over and I can go, right, Captain?" Jude asks Levi.

Levi nods. "Yeah, let's go."

I follow the guys out, my eyes scanning the room for one last sight of Dixie. All I want to do is stay, find her and flirt with her until I break down her defenses—every last one of them. I'm close. I fucking *know* it.

Jasper joins us by the door, and as we make our way down the hall to the elevators he immediately starts kissing my brother's ass, like it's a job interview. I roll my eyes as I walk behind them. *Jesus, Jasper, he's not the one making the hiring calls.*

There's a large group of guests waiting at the elevator bank, and I can tell, even from a few feet away as we approach, that they're from the event. If we get in the elevator with them it'll be like a continuation of the invasive conversations from the event, only this time with no personal space. Yeah, no. I lean in and say to Levi, "I'm going to hit the restroom. I'll see you in the lobby."

He nods but he's got this look in his eye I've only started seeing recently, and I don't like it. It's concern. Levi is a serious dude. He was born that way, it's how he's wired. He's quiet to a disturbing level. He's calculated and risk-averse and loathes extreme anything, be it sports, music or emotions. But this look…the way his eyes soften but his brow pinches and his jaw stays hard, it's new and I really hate it. It's sympathy or guilt or concern or a mix of all those things I never want anyone to feel over me.

I turn away from it, and him, and decide to find a bathroom not near the elevators or the bar so I don't run into anyone and start an accidental conversation. I pass the ones Dixie came out of earlier and turn left, down an even longer hallway. I see the brass signs the hotel uses to indicate restrooms hanging way at the end of the hall near the doors that lead to the hotel gym. I keep my eyes glued to it to avoid eye contact with anyone and, more than anything, to avoid seeing someone staring at my scar again. That's happened enough tonight.

I swing open the door and am happy to find the space empty. It's a small restroom with only two urinals and two stalls with bamboo doors. I use the urinal and then wash my hands slowly at the sink, my own eyes staring at the scar just above my shirt collar. I honestly can't decide if the sort-of beard I've been keeping actually helps to hide it or just makes it stand out more. Most days it seems to hide it, but next to the crisp white of my dress shirt and in the shitastic fluorescent lighting in this restroom it feels like it's more apparent than ever. I have this fleeting but intense moment of wanting to punch the mirror and shatter my reflection into a million jagged pieces. The urge has me gripping the sink until my knuckles are white as I take a deep breath to gain control.

The door swings open and two sharp clicks rebound through the tiny space as high heels make contact with the tile floor. I turn at the sight of her wheat-colored hair in the mirror and face her, trying to pull a smile over my face to cover the shock I'm feeling. Sweet Dixie just followed me into the bathroom? Plot twist.

"Oh, I'm so sorry! Is this the men's room?" The look of horror on her face is adorable because it's in complete contrast with the flat, calm tone of her voice that says she knows exactly where she is.

"It is, but you know, I don't mind sharing," I reply, grabbing a paper towel and slowly wiping my hands with it.

She doesn't respond, just stands there and sinks her teeth into that full bottom lip. It's cute because she seems a little nervous. Either that or her bottom lip just tastes delicious. I hope to find out soon. I take a step away from the sink, toward her. "Dixie?"

The sweetest little hint of a smile tugs on the corners of her lips. She lets go of the door and reaches for something in her purse, moving toward me swiftly, her heels making purposeful clicks with every step. And then she's so close I can smell her—the vanilla shampoo and the rich but faint flowery scent of her perfume. It warms my blood. She presses one palm flat to the lapel of my jacket and I feel the other one snake into my pocket, my eye catching a glimpse of paper between her fingers as they move.

"You remind me of my big toe," she whispers, her head tilted up to face me. I tilt mine down so I can look into her eyes, and now our lips are just inches apart and perfectly lined up.

"Why is that?" My voice is low and deeper than normal. The urge to kiss her is more overpowering than the urge I had earlier to punch the mirror, so I start to lean forward, but she immediately uses her hand on my lapel to push me back gently.

Our eyes lock and she replies, "Because I'll probably bang you on my coffee table later."

And with that she's gone—just spins around, flings open the

door and disappears so swiftly that I swear there's a whooshing sound. I reach into my pocket, pull out the paper she placed there and carefully unfold it. It's a page from the Thunder HR handbook, the page about employee fraternization, and at the top of the page, in her beautiful cursive, is the word "midnight" and her address.

6

DIXIE

Holy shit, I did it. I am going to do it. I am going to do *him*. I really am. What the hell is wrong with me? It's not my fault. It's that kiss. I've been kissed before. I'd actually say I'd been kissed a lot. But his kiss was different. It was the beginning of something I've been longing to finish ever since.

I climb the crappy staircase to my apartment, taking the steps two at a time. As soon as I unlock the three dead bolts Jude insisted on installing when I moved in, I close the door behind me and start sniffing. Good, the usual smell of soy sauce and fish that wafts up from the sushi place below me isn't as strong as normal. Still, I decide to light most of the Anthropologie candles I have peppered around the place. Then I gather as much mess as I can—shoes, piles of clean and dirty laundry, papers brought home from work, purses, coats—and shove it all into my walk-in closet. That baby is why I rented this place.

I spend another ten minutes darting around to tidy up, then run to the bathroom and dab a little more perfume on my wrists, smooth my hair and reapply my lipstick. I glance at the clock. I told him to come by at midnight. That way he could hang with the guys for a little bit, if they asked, and I had time to come back here and get ready.

But I still have twenty minutes and the waiting is going to make me doubt my decision. I head into the kitchen and decide to busy myself doing the few dishes in the sink—a mug, a bowl and a spoon.

I have to do this now. I realized that as the night went on. Not tomorrow, not next week, now. Elijah will be on the team one day in the not so distant future, and then it'll be against the rules. And I am so impossibly attracted to him that I just need to get it out of my system. If I don't work him out of my system before he's a player for the Thunder, my job is going to suffer because I won't be able to do anything but drool over him, and chances are I'll slip up and somehow end up with my lips on some part of him and then I'll lose my job. I know it's just a physical attraction. He's hot and charming in a completely off-the-wall way that I've never experienced. But he's too wild and doesn't have a serious bone in his body. So not my type. Still, I've never had a stronger chemistry with someone, and it's time to indulge that, so I can get back to my life and my goals.

There's a soft knock on my door. The mug clatters from my hand and shatters in the sink. Shit! The second knock is much harder. "Dixie!"

"Come in!" I call absently and reach for the faucet to turn off the water.

"Well, this is unexpected." His voice fills my apartment, not because he's yelling but just because he's got that kind of voice.

I turn and realize instantly why he's got an amused look on his sexy face. My hands are encased in rubber gloves, one with a dish brush in it and the other with a large chunk of mug. All the while I'm still wearing my sexy dress and high heels. He looks completely turned on right now.

"You have a maid fetish?" I question.

"No. And this isn't maid…This is…" His green eyes sweep up and down my body. "I don't know what this is but yeah, it's a fetish."

I laugh and drop the chunk of mug in the trash, drop the dish brush on the counter and start to pull off the rubber gloves. I toss the gloves on the counter. "Sorry. Show's over. And so is my mug."

"Debutante does dishes?" He's still trying to define my look. "No…maybe heiress does dishes? Or…sexy businesswoman does…"

"Goalie?"

A slow smile spreads over his face. "Now that's a fetish I'll confess to having."

He's just standing there staring at me and smiling. I could honestly look at that smile all damn day long. I can't explain what it does to me. It's honestly the most charismatic, charming and sexy smile I have ever seen. It draws me to him like a cat to a laser pointer.

"Can I get you something? Beer? Water? Wine?"

"Just you," he replies casually, still smiling.

Oh God, we are really going to do this. Suddenly I feel nervous. Still, I find myself walking slowly toward him. He reaches toward me, palm up, and I drop my hand into his and then suddenly, with a whoosh, I'm over his shoulder. My head is dangling over his back and my ass is on his shoulder, my feet hanging at his waist.

"Sweet Dixie," he says as I squirm. "This is going to be fun."

I feel his mouth, more specifically his teeth, as he turns his head and bites my butt cheek. Not hard enough to hurt, just hard enough to notice. So I haul off and smack his ass, since it's the only thing within swatting distance. And then his hands grip my waist and I'm flying through the air then land on my back in the middle of my bed, which is covered with throw pillows since I use it as a couch too.

I prop myself up on my elbows and look up at him. He's shrugging out of his suit jacket. "Tell me you've been thinking about this as much as I have since we met?" he says.

"I wasn't…" He raises an eyebrow at that. Just one—his left one. I bite my bottom lip. "At first."

"I know you love to say that, but I felt the vibe coming off you the moment our eyes locked," Eli replies, confident as he starts to undo his cuff links. Jesus, I feel like I should be filming this and selling it to a suit manufacturer for their next campaign. It's hot as hell.

"There was no vibe, rookie," I reply.

"I'm not a rookie yet. You're going to have to come up with a new annoying nickname." He starts to unbutton his dress shirt. "How about Sex God?"

I snort.

He grins, eyes wide. "Did you just snort?"

"Hell yes. That was a snort-worthy level of machismo."

"Machismo?" He laughs loudly. "I know you're older than me, but no need for vocabulary from the forties."

"I'm only one year older than you."

His shirt is completely unbuttoned now and hanging from his shoulders. My eyes take a long, slow journey from his collarbone down his perfectly toned chest and abdomen.

"A year and two months," Elijah corrects. "You're a certifiable cougar, Dixie Wynn Braddock."

I regretfully pull my eyes off his gorgeously ridged abs and up to his face. But he's not looking at mine. His eyes are on my legs. I glance down. My dress hiked up quite a bit after I was tossed on the bed and he likes what he sees. I want to show him more so I move a little bit and the dress slides to the top of my thigh. He takes a step closer.

"Take off your shirt," I whisper and our eyes finally connect.

Without a word he removes his shirt and lets it land at his feet, then he bends and once again he's deliciously close, his face inches from mine.

"Now," he says, reaching up with one of his hands and gently wrapping it around the back of my neck. "Where were we?"

"I think we were right about here." I tip my head ever so slightly so our lips connect.

Yup. He's as good at kissing as I remember. I don't know what it is about his lips or his tongue or how he moves them, but it's blowing my mind like it did the first time. I'm the definition of hot and bothered. His fingers press gently into my neck, and he tilts my head back farther and leans into me, pushing me back onto the mattress. My hands roam over his bare chest and graze a small but perfect amount of chest hair. I let out a little grunt of satisfaction at the feel of it. Jesus.

"You like the chest hair?" he asks, his lips still against mine, his words basically spoken against my mouth.

"Mmm...it's awesome," I whisper and let my fingernails scrape through it and over his nipples, which makes his pecs clench. "Helps me forget what a baby you actually are."

"Stop," he says, laughing.

"Make me."

His mouth covers mine again and his tongue sweeps over mine, and seriously, why is this so damn hot? Just kissing him makes me ache between my legs. I move my hands down his stomach and then I move them back up so I can slide my fingers down it again. Because seriously, it's so hard and rippled with glorious muscle it deserves double the feels. I deserve double the feels.

I'm suddenly, fleetingly, self-conscious. I'm in no way out of shape, but I am also in no way in shape. Definitely not the kind of shape he's in. His body looks like he's auditioning for Jason Momoa's naked stunt double. He is like some kind of specimen created just for my fantasies. I should probably stop eating donuts and start drinking protein shakes or something.

"I want that dress gone," he sort of growls against my neck with that voice that's so rough yet somehow soft it reverberates on my skin.

"That requires standing up," I tell him and start to try to sit up. But once again he manhandles me, flipping me onto my stomach before I know what's happening.

"God, I am never going to get tired of how tiny you are." I feel his fingers start to pull the zipper on my dress down.

"I'm letting you do this. Make no mistake, if I didn't want you to treat me like a blow-up doll, you wouldn't be," I advise him. "I have a blue belt in hapkido."

"That sounds like something you order at a sushi restaurant," he snarks, and I try to glare at him over my shoulder but it's impossible. My zipper is now at the base of my spine and I feel the fabric part as his hand slides up my back, palm flat against my skin. It's warm and rough because his hockey gloves have given him calluses. It feels like his fingers, spread out like they are, cover most of my back.

"Hapkido is a very serious martial art," I explain, even though the last thing I want to be doing is giving him a lesson in anything other than where I want those hands to go next. "My dad made my sisters and me take it for years growing up so we'd have self-defense skills."

"So you're a lethal weapon. Good to know," he replies and his fingers move to the clasp of my bra. "I promise not to sneak up on you in a dark alley."

I smile. "I'd love to flip you on your back. But I don't need a dark alley for that. I can do it here later. After."

"After?"

"After the orgasms."

He chuckles. It's a deep rumble that I feel like a bass drum between my legs. "How about you get to flip me if I don't give you an orgasm?"

My bra comes undone.

"Deal," I reply. "Of course, I might flip you anyway."

Suddenly his whole body is pressed into mine. I can feel his bare chest against my bare back and one of his thick thighs is between my legs and his cock is pressed into my left ass cheek. It's official. Everything about Elijah Casco is long, thick and hard.

"Sweet Dixie, the way I give orgasms, you won't have the strength to stand, let alone flip me," he promises before lifting himself off me and flipping me onto my back as quickly and effortlessly as he flipped me last time.

I stare up at him, with nothing but flickering candlelight and a faint glow from the street light outside pushing its way through my half-open curtains. He looks older in the dim light—rugged, confident and sexy. His hands move to my shoulders and start to pull my dress down, taking the straps of my bra with it.

Sleeping with Elijah feels risky, in an exhilarating sort of way, like I imagine bungee jumping or ziplining or skydiving would be. You're terrified, but you want to do it more than anything.

Suddenly I'm naked from the waist up, but I'm not self-conscious anymore because there is so much lust in his eyes as he stares at me that they've changed to a dark, mossy color. I feel like I should say something, make a typically Dixie-esque comment, but that look on his face is leaving me speechless. And then he's moving again, and moving me, before I have a chance to regain my senses. He lifts me by my hips and pushes me farther down the bed, and then I'm flat on my back and his lips are covering my left nipple and he's actually groaning as his tongue makes contact with my skin. My eyes flutter shut and I let out a loud sigh and arch my back into his mouth.

He moves to my other breast, and I lift my torso even higher off the bed. He chuckles and moves his head to the concave spot between my breasts; as he smiles his beard scratches deliciously against my skin and goose flesh ripples down my arms. "You're a breast girl."

I reach down and cup his head between my hands, tilting his fare to look up at me. "I'm an everything girl."

"Then let's do everything," he replies and pulls himself up so he's blanketing my body with his and our lips meet again.

It's intense—the way he's touching me, the feel of his mouth, the level of turned on he's making me. I need to bring it down a little, gain some control back even if it's just a molecule of it. So, as his mouth drifts from mine back down toward my breasts I use my martial arts training, carefully positioning my legs between his, and reach out with my arms and—boom! I flip him.

It's not graceful, and I almost fall off the bed when I do it and end up flailing a little, which I'm sure looks extra ridiculous topless, but I flipped him and he looks impressed. Stunned but impressed. "Cool. I've never fucked a ninja before."

I laugh—loudly. "You don't fuck ninjas. They fuck you."

I stand and he reaches an arm out as if to stop me until he realizes I'm just doing it to shimmy out of my underwear. His eyes follow the black lace as it drops to the floor. My dress is clinging precariously to my hips. I could shift my hips and be rid of it, but he's got way too many clothes on for me to be naked. So instead I get back on the bed and reach for his belt. He crosses his arms behind his head and watches me as I undo it and then pop the button and lower the fly. Before I can get any further he grabs both my wrists and with one quick, hard tug he yanks me forward and I land on top of him. He's smooth and warm and hard, except for where our breastbones touch, and he's got the sprinkling of hair that tickles my bare skin.

We find each other's eyes, and I can see the playful light in his green ones flicker and dim into something else at the same time I feel it happening to me. His hands move up my bare sides and stop just under my arms. The tip of his tongue makes a slow pass over his bottom lip. His voice gets even deeper and rougher as he growls, "Playtime is over."

And then he's pulling me up to press his lips to mine again. This kiss is all business, and that is such a paradox with who this man is in real life. Elijah is so playful and jovial all the time that the darkness and intensity that's driving this kiss is surreal and so sexy it's taking my breath away—and any remaining inhibitions.

We move against each other wildly—tongues dancing, bodies writhing, hands groping—for long, frantic minutes. I manage to get his pants and underwear down his legs but not before he grabs a condom out of his pocket and drops it on the bed beside us. I use the opportunity to take in his fully naked body. It leaves me more breathless than the kissing did. Elijah has one hell of a cock. It's long but also incredibly thick and perfectly straight and so damn hard right now it's throbbing—over me. That makes me flush and the ache between my own legs grows. It doesn't help that his eyes are riveted to my pussy, fully on display now. I watch motionless as he reaches out with one hand and, without a second's hesitation, cups it against his palm. His long middle finger bends and purposefully pushes into me.

I close my eyes and let out the softest, longest moan and tilt my hips, rubbing my clit against the heel of his hand. The fourth of July goes off behind my eyelids. "Sweet Dixie," he whispers roughly. "You feel incredible."

He moves his finger in and out and I rub my clit shamelessly against his palm again. It feels so fucking incredible. I have been giving myself orgasms for years now. And they're good. I have a great little vibrator and my fingers know how to get me off, but no modern technology or even my own familiarity can compete with this bliss. I could do this all night.

But Elijah has other plans. Suddenly his hand is gone and I'm air humping nothing. Before I can protest, he's got me by the hips and is effortlessly lifting me, pulling me up his body until my knees are resting just in front of his shoulders and now my pussy is inches from his face. "FYI, this is the only thing I think I'm going to love devouring more than fruity drinks."

In a millisecond his tongue is sliding up and into me just like his finger moments ago. The noise that leaves me this time is more of a whimper than a groan, and the minute his tongue slips higher, to my clit, circling it, my orgasm is clawing through me—visceral, scorching and fucking incredible.

"That was easy," he announces in a snarky whisper, and I want to respond with something even more snarky but I'm still completely lost in this orgasm and I want to keep it that way. I slowly, unsteadily move so I'm sitting on my heels beside his left hip. Through my fluttering eyelids I can see he's grabbing the condom and ripping it open. I watch him grab his cock firmly with one hand and sheath it with the other. He lets it go, props himself up on an elbow and reaches up and cups the back of my neck, pulling me down toward him. I crumble, still shuddering and breathing heavy. "Dixie, baby, look at me."

I open my eyes and find his. He smiles, kisses me softly and says, "You still want this? Want me?"

"Yes. I want you," I reply firmly, despite my shaking limbs. "I want you inside of me."

He kisses me again, less gently, and pulls himself to a sitting position, then I feel him reach for himself again. His other hand moves from my neck down my back and to my hip, then my thigh, and he lifts it and nudges me. I straddle him again, only this time directly above his hand holding his cock. He tilts his head to look up at me, I look down between us and gently lower myself onto him. He feels even bigger than he looks, and it's deliciously overwhelming with that incredible orgasm still wafting through me.

When he's settled completely inside me I expect Elijah to drop back on the bed and let me go to work, but he doesn't. He stays sitting, wraps an arm around my back and his lips around my left nipple. I start to rock. He starts to buck his hips under me and suddenly we've got this phenomenal rhythm going on and I can feel another orgasm starting to grow inside me. I like riding guys, a lot. I like to watch them watching me, and I get to control the pace and my orgasm usually. But with Elijah there is no control. He's still got his mouth on my tit and his hand has moved up into my hair and his hips are doing all the lifting, and it's sensory overload. Equal overwhelming parts erotic and intimate.

I feel like we're lovers—deep, passionate lovers intensifying our connection, our hold on one another—not flirting friends trying to work each other out of our systems. My lust for Eli isn't leaving. It's solidifying. I would panic about that, but suddenly I'm orgasming again. Hard. So fucking blissfully hard.

"Holy shit," I hear him groan into my chest and he roars like a fucking lion and comes just as hard as I do.

Moments later, when we're both on the other side, I feel his lips kiss their way across my collarbone to my shoulder. Both his hands are wrapped around my back, and he pulls me down and lays himself out on the mattress. I close my eyes as my head lands on the bed, and then I feel the soft chenille throw I keep at the foot of the bed cover me. A second later his lips are back on my shoulder and he's pulling me into his chest to spoon.

This side of Elijah is surprising too. It's so gentle and sweet, and I could get used to it…only I can't.

"I'm going to cuddle you to sleep and then I'm going to sneak out."

"Oh. Okay." And I can't hide my disappointment at the thought of him leaving.

I start to pull away but he doesn't let me. He turns me toward him. His green eyes look glassy and his full lips a little stained from my lipstick. I almost completely forgot we were all done up for a fancy work event. "I want nothing more than to spend the night here with you, but knowing Levi, he'll show up at the asscrack of dawn to take me to breakfast before he leaves with the team for their road trip, and if I'm not there he'll have questions I can't answer."

"Oh, right." I give him a tiny embarrassed smile. I just got all girlfriend-y and needy. I blame the fact that he got all boyfriend-y and sweet.

He curls me back into his chest and runs a hand through my hair. It feels like heaven. I sigh and it turns into a tiny yawn. He chuckles and kisses the curve of my neck. "I'm surprised you came so fast," I mumble sleepily. "I guess I'm good."

He chuckles again. "I was surprised too, but you chanting my name in that breathy little whisper of yours while you came was the hottest thing ever."

"What? I didn't do that." I swear I didn't do that.

Did I do that?

"I didn't think you realized it, which was what made it so much hotter," he whispers against the shell of my ear, and I smile. "You're incredible, sweet Dixie."

"You're pretty fantastic too, Elijah." I don't want to fall asleep. I want to stay like this, reveling in his warm, strong embrace and the feel of his breath tickling my shoulder and his lips on my neck for hours, until dawn, but I'm exhausted and long before I want, I fade to black.

7

ELIJAH

He pounds on my hotel room door way too fucking early just like I told Dixie he would. Levi is nothing if not predictable. It's hilarious that he and my parents are always at such odds, because he's more like them than either Todd or I could ever hope to be. Our parents are always calm, always punctual, never raise their voices or act brashly. I've never seen them cry, not even after my grandmother passed. Levi is exactly like them in that way. Or he was until he met his girlfriend, Tessa.

I fling open the door and come face-to-face with him. He grins—it's too big not to be sarcastic. "Hey! You're up!"

He knows I was far from up.

I leave the door open and wander back toward my bed, but before I can fall face first into it he's got a hand on my shoulder, keeping me upright. "Since you're up, throw on some clothes and let's go for breakfast!"

"What is it about dawn that makes you such a fucking

cheerleader?" I ask, but I stumble toward my open suitcase because I know he's not going to let me go back to bed.

"It's almost nine, Eli. Dawn was hours ago," he says to me, like nine a.m. makes him any less of a psychopath. "The team plane leaves at noon for Milwaukee. You'll be joining us soon, so get used to it, little bro."

I dig around for a clean shirt and the only jeans I brought.

"You look wrecked," he tells me. "Did you and Jasper go out after the event?"

I nod. I love when he makes up my excuses for me. "Just for a few."

"Find any chicks?" I glance over and he's cocking his dark eyebrow at me like a jovial sitcom dad. I roll my eyes.

"What, are you trying to live vicariously through me?" I grin as I pull on my olive-green Henley hoodie. "Sorry, big bro. I'm not kissing and telling just because you're tied down."

"I wouldn't have it any other way. You know, even when I was single I wasn't exactly into sowing my oats," he replies and leans his ass against the dresser. He glances at his watch as I head into the bathroom and try to calm my bedhead. "Come on, princess."

"Yeah. Yeah." I wet my hands and run them through my hair and then grab my coat off the chair and head to the door. "Wherever you're taking me better have bacon. I'm not getting my ass up at this hour for anything less."

The streets are pretty quiet because the rest of San Francisco isn't insane enough to be wandering around so early on a Saturday morning. I follow him left down the street the hotel's on and then right down another street, which is more like walking down a cliff. I'm totally cabbing it back. There is no way I'm climbing this later.

He tells me about the road trip he's heading out on, which is three games in three cities over five days. And then he does what I know he's going to do and asks me about my upcoming games. I tell him we have two at home this week and one away on the weekend in Vancouver, Washington, against the Winterhawks' farm team.

"You starting?" he wants to know.

I nod tersely. "The two home games, probably."

"Not the away one?"

"I don't know yet. I'm assuming it'll depend on how the two home ones go." I try not to sound too annoyed. These questions are his job, not just as my brother but as the captain of the team that drafted me.

"It's good they've gone back to starting you." I already know this. "The more ice time you get with them, the closer you are to getting ice time with us."

"Only if it goes well," I remind him as we stop in front of a place and he reaches for the door. As soon as I step inside I'm greeted by the smell of bacon. Thank Christ. "And it's been going okay."

Levi seems to absorb that information and the look on my face. As the hostess leads us to a table near the window he says, "Is this one of those situations where you hold yourself to a higher standard than you should?"

I shrug out of my coat. "No. I'm average at best right now. Why do you think I'm not already in Eddie's spot?"

Okay, there was no hiding my annoyance in that. Levi's dark brown eyes soften, and that makes me more annoyed. He must see that too, because as we sit across from each other he clears his throat and sets his expression into something more neutral. "You think it has something to do with the accident?"

"Nope," I say firmly as my phone buzzes and I reach to dig it out of my coat pocket. Man, I hope it's Dixie. "I think I need to adjust to the level of play. It's different than college. Here, these guys are all trying to prove something every game, so they can get moved up to their NHL team. It's fine. I just have to work harder, and I am."

"Okay." Levi rubs his jaw as the waitress says hello and asks us if we want coffee. "Black coffee and a large orange juice, please."

I look up at her and smile. "Do you guys have lattes? I would kill for a vanilla latte."

"We don't. But we can make a mocha with the hot chocolate and coffee."

"Then a large one of those and also a large apple juice," I say and glance at my phone, disappointed it's only a text message from Jasper. The waitress scribbles down the order and trots off. "Jasper wants me to meet him for breakfast."

"Invite him here," Levi says and gives me the address. I text Jasper back. "You know, if the accident is still bothering you the team has access to a—"

"If you say 'shrink' I will pour my mocha over your head when she brings it. Whipped cream and all," I warn him seriously.

Levi looks a little stunned but recovers. "I was going to say sports psychologist."

"Same difference," I return and frown. "I'm not a head case. I'm fine. This doesn't have to become a thing. It happened. It's over. I'm fine. Lots of players get cut by a skate and keep playing just as well as they did before. My slump is not skate related."

"You know this because...?"

"I know this because I researched the fuck out of this injury when it happened." I'm so over this conversation. "And seven players in the last twenty years have been severely cut by a skate blade during a game. Two of those were neck cuts, one of those got the jugular like me. And that goalie, Casey O'Rourdan, played for two seasons after the injury."

Casey O'Rourdan had started out as my inspiration, but now he haunts me. He really did recover immediately, like it was nothing, and even used to joke about it with the press. I'm desperately and completely irrationally jealous of him now. But of course I leave that part out.

Levi seems to think about this, or what to say to me next, and the waitress comes back over with our drinks and asks for our orders. Levi orders an egg white omelet with spinach, turkey sausage and whole wheat toast. I get a three-cheese omelet, a double order of bacon and an English muffin. Then I explain to her that we have a friend coming and order Jasper a coffee, a cheese omelet and pork sausage with sourdough.

When she's gone Levi is staring at me with an open mouth. "How the fuck do you play a hockey game filled with grease and fat?"

"Pretty well, actually." I shrug. "Now can we talk about something other than hockey? Like how has Tessa not left you yet?"

He laughs sarcastically. I take a sip of my apple juice and then realize I'm way more dehydrated from last night than I thought and promptly chug the rest. Dixie gave me quite the workout, and not just physically. That girl got under my skin.

"Why are you smiling?"

"I'm just happy for you." I'm not lying. I am happy for him, but I'm smiling over Dixie. I reach for my mocha and a spoon and scoop up the whipped cream and stick a heaping spoonful of it into my mouth. I swallow it down. "Seriously, though, I mean, you just never wanted to do the crazy, wild, no-strings sex thing?"

"It was never appealing," he replies and shrugs his broad shoulders. I love bugging Levi about being an inch taller than him, but I try to ignore the fact he's a little bit broader. "I mean, it's not like I was a monk. I had a few girlfriends and everything. I still wanted to fuck, just not with people I didn't like…or even know."

I nod and play with my spoon in my mocha. "I loved random drunken hookups in college. Going to the bar with the guys, finding some hot girl to flirt with and dance with and then…"

Levi laughs. "Yeah, and that's not abnormal. But why are you using past tense?"

"I don't know…" I pause. "Maybe I'm open to, you know, trying the relationship thing."

He lifts that damn eyebrow again.

"Don't do that. You look like Dad," I say.

The eyebrow drops. Before he can ask a question, though, Jasper is dropping his giant body into the chair beside me with an exasperated sigh. "Hey! I'm starving and the only thing that will fix this about-to-be raging hangover is serious sausage and eggs."

"That's what I ordered you."

"You're a godsend." He side hugs me like a total girl, even dropping his head onto my shoulder for a second. I can't help but laugh.

Levi is amused too as he sips his boring black coffee. "How come you're more hung over than Eli?"

"Because Eli didn't go out with Eddie Rollins after the event," Jasper explains and runs a hand through his disheveled white-blond hair. "That guy took me to like seven different bars trying to score."

Levi looks confused, and I know I look guilty. "I thought you said you were with Jasper last night?"

"*You* said I was with Jasper. I didn't correct you."

Jasper smiles. "Wait a minute, your brother doesn't know about Julie?"

"Julie?" Levi repeats and that fucking eyebrow goes up.

"Yeah, Dad." He drops the eyebrow. Thank God I had the good sense to store Dixie's number under a fake name in my phone. "There's a girl named Julie. Would you like to meet her parents? Maybe drive us to the prom?"

"Okay, relax." Levi rolls his eyes. "Is she the reason you're thinking of a relationship?"

"Yeah." I wish I could bite back my smile, but I can't. "But it's complicated."

"The best ones always are," Levi says, almost under his breath.

The waitress brings our meals and we eat in silence for a bit until Jasper finishes his last chunk of sausage and asks, "So speaking of complicated, did you really sleep with Braddock's girlfriend during playoffs?"

Levi stops chewing mid-bite and gives Jasper his infamous captainly glare. "Really? That's your question to the guy who leads the team you're going to join one day? Maybe not that soon, if you keep asking those types of questions."

Jasper's pale Swedish skin starts looking sunburned, and I bite the inside of my cheek to keep from chuckling. Jasper is too new to know that Levi's death stares aren't as deadly as they appear—most of the time, anyway.

"I…I just…I mean, there's just a lot of talk…and I thought…" he stammers.

"He wasn't dating her anymore when we hooked up. But I didn't tell him about it, and it was stupid and, yeah, the team could very well have lost playoffs because he, rightfully, could barely share the ice with me. There's rules, on and off the ice. I broke them. Don't be me."

Jasper nods. I feel this need to stick up for Levi even though I know Jasper isn't judging him. "Jude and Levi worked it out. Jude's happier now than he ever was with Tess."

"Oh, cool."

"Yeah, he's going to be a dad and everything."

"Anyway, the point is, no fucking with other players' girls," Levi repeats and puts his napkin down on his empty plate. "These guys are your brothers. Treat them that way. And no fucking with the staff or the ice girls."

He stands up, grabbing his wallet out of his back pocket. "And no fucking with the staff's friends or family for that matter. Or the friends and family of teammates. Sounds like a lot, but San Francisco is a big city. I'm sure you'll find someone not off-limits. Eli clearly did."

Jasper nods and I pretend not to be paying attention because he not only just told me not to fuck around with staff, which I've already done, but he added family of players to that list and, fuck, Dixie is that too.

"I gotta run. Want to swing by Tessa's salon and say good-bye before I head to the airport." Levi dumps more than enough money on the table to pay for all three meals. I could protest, but the dude's a millionaire, so I'll let him get it. He points to me. "I want more info about this Jessica later."

"Julie," I correct. "And I'm gonna spend another night, can I stay at your place?"

"Really?"

"Coach says I don't have to be back until Sunday afternoon practice."

"So Julie is local?"

"Yeah."

He seems to think about it. "Tessa is there, remember, so don't bring your girl there and make a shit ton of sex noises."

I laugh. "No sex noises. Julie has her own place. I just need a place for my bag." I think about it. Dixie doesn't know I'm coming. She might have plans or maybe not want a round two...especially after what I have to say, but I have to try.

He smirks. "I'll let Tessa know. You still have your key?" I nod. "Here's hoping you just need it for your bag. Oh, and wear a condom."

"What? Yeah! Of course. Shut up."

He laughs deeply, waves to both of us and heads out the door.

"Casco is intense, Casco," Jasper says and leans back in his chair.

"Yeah. I know." I grab my phone and start texting Dixie. "I didn't really want him to know about Julie yet."

"Why not?" he asks as we both grab our jackets and get ready to leave.

"Because it's complicated, and I'm honestly not sure how she feels about things," I explain as we make our way to the door.

"Are you kidding me? You two have been texting each other a billion times a day for over a week," Jasper says as we step out into the blustery late October morning, the streets much more bustling than they were before. "What happened last night? Was the sex bad?"

"Fuck no. Far from it." I button up my coat and try not to groan because we've started climbing that damn mountain of a hill. "It was the best sex I've ever had."

"So…?"

I look at Jasper and then shrug. "It's complicated."

"Yeah. You said that. I get it. She's here and you're in Sacramento, but not forever," Jasper reminds me. "But it could be worse. She's not your teammate's girlfriend. I mean, ex-girlfriend, or any of that other shit that Levi mentioned. Holy smokes this hill is a bitch."

"Yeah, the hill is a bitch," I huff. I take a minute to get up the thing before adding, "And you know Levi's right about those rules he listed. But he also broke them intentionally, and it all turned out okay."

I don't know why I'm saying these words out loud. They're not for Jasper, they're for me. "I'm betting if you asked Tessa, Levi and Jude, they'd do it exactly the same if doing it differently meant the results would be different."

"True." Jasper checks his phone for the time. "My flight is in a couple hours, and I want to catch a nap before I pack."

I nod and follow him into the hotel. "I'm just going to throw my stuff in my suitcase and head to Levi's. See you back at our apartment tomorrow before practice."

"Sure thing. Good luck, buddy." Jasper smiles. "She's lucky to have you."

I grin. "I hope she feels that way."

Inside my room I stare at my screen. She hasn't responded to my text. Weird. She's always pretty snappy. Up until last night I thought she slept with her phone in her hand. I'm beginning to worry my text was too typical for us. Like I should have sent something better—something more—after last night. Maybe I should have sent something other than Hey my name's Microsoft, can I crash at your place tonight?

But seriously, what am I supposed to say? *Sex with you just made me like you more. I want to have a secret long-distance affair while I'm in Sacramento because I can't quit you. Are you in?*

I mean, even that isn't really the truth. Sex with Dixie was fantastic, but being with Dixie in general was amazing. I could have stayed there last night and watched her sleep until dawn. She looks like an angel when she sleeps. I know this can't go on forever, but it can go on a little longer, and I need it to. I hope she does too.

8

DIXIE

I'm fighting back tears that are so intense my nose burns and my eyes sting profusely. I refuse to look at my sisters or my mother and concentrate on my dad—just his face. Just look at his face and nowhere else. "Daddy!"

I bend and he lifts his arms and engulfs me the way only he can. It always makes me feel safe and loved, even now. Oh God, I'm going to lose him. Don't think about it. Don't think about it. Do. Not. Think. "You look too thin, Little D. Have you been eating?" he asks.

"She's eating me out of house and home, as usual," Jude interjects, and I look up and see him by the front doors to the condo that is about to become my parents' and sisters' home. My eyes connect with my brother's, and I know that they've kept the severity of my dad's decline from him too. On the outside he's smiling his typical mischievous grin, but I can see beyond it to the pain in his eyes.

"Jude's still a drama queen, in case you were wondering," I tell our dad, and he chuckles. "Zoey loves having me over all the time. You can ask her when she gets here after work."

"I hope that's not too late," our dad announces, his voice a little slurred, which has never happened during the day before, only late at night if he's tired. Please may it be the long red-eye that's making it happen. "I can't wait to see her."

"She'll be here early afternoon. She's working half days right now," Jude promises.

"Let's get you upstairs, Dad," Winnie says and grabs the back of his wheelchair. Our eyes lock as she pushes past me. She knows I want to murder her.

We get Dad up to the apartment along with all their bags. Their furniture and most of their belongings arrived the other day, and Jude paid a company to unpack everything and set it up, as per Zoey's orders. She's consulted with our mom, and they'd picked out exactly where everything should go via multiple emails and Skype calls.

Jude bought the family a three-bedroom penthouse a block from his and Zoey's house. The building is fully accessible by wheelchair and still has that old-world charm of a classic San Francisco building—bay windows, crown moldings, hardwood floors, built-ins. It's beautiful, the best of the best, but for everyone it has been made ugly by the reason he had to buy it. Originally we were going to wait until the last possible second and move our dad into a fancy nursing home when it was impossible for him to stay at our family home in Toronto. But then Zoey got pregnant and both Mom and Dad wanted to be nearby for their first grandchild. So Jude decided to get them a place in the city. Dad's spot in the nursing home is still on hold, but for now they'll live in luxury a block from their future grandbaby with a part-time nurse who will be coming by every morning to help Dad with tasks like showering and to monitor his health.

I'm huffing like a chubby kid with asthma after lugging the second of Sadie's two suitcases into the room that will be hers. She requested it be painted a very pale, slightly smoky blue, and it's incredible. She bought herself a brand-new bed with a gray velvet tufted headboard with bling in each tuft. "I want this."

"I figured you would," she replies and smiles. "Tough luck."

I turn to her, glancing down the hall, but no one is on this side of the apartment but us. "He's in the chair full-time now?"

She nods. "Pretty much."

My heart clenches. "And the slurring?"

"That's not all the time," she replies and sighs. "But it's a lot of the time now."

"Why didn't you tell us it had gotten this bad?" I demand, trying to keep my voice down.

Sadie frowns. She looks so much like Mom when she does that. They have different smiles but identical frowns. I didn't notice that until recently, because neither of them frowned a lot while I was growing up. Now it's much more common. "Mom's idea. She didn't want to spoil Jude's happiness over the baby. And she wanted you to enjoy your job. She said you'd find out soon enough, and you did."

"What a way to find out," I mutter and lean against the doorframe. "I felt blindsided when you guys had to help him from the cab to his chair. He's always been able to walk a little bit, even this summer."

"I know. It sucks." Sadie reaches out and hugs me. "Just don't act like it in front of him, okay? When the doctor first told him he shouldn't use the walker anymore and should stick to the wheelchair, he melted down. Swearing and raging and even throwing things."

"What?" I feel a shudder of horror ripple through me.

"I know. It was bad," Sadie confirms. "He locked himself in the bathroom and basically destroyed it. Mom was frantic and in tears. Winnie busted down the door, but by then the damage was done. I was at work and they called me and I left my shift and came home. We actually had to give him Ativan."

"Fuck," I whisper, my heart twisting painfully in my chest. The unfairness of it all is overwhelming, and not just for my dad. But we, the kids, made a vow long ago to suck it up. We can fall apart when he's gone, but for now we are rocks. Braddock rocks.

"Tell me something good," Sadie begs, running a hand through her long, sandy-blond hair and releasing it from her low ponytail. Sadie is the no-frills one out of us, probably because of her job as a nurse. I'm wondering now that she's on a leave and living here if I can convince her to do a girls' day with me—mani-pedis and massages sound great. "How did things go with the goalie? Did he like the outfit?"

I flush and smile instantaneously. "Yes. A lot."

"Did you get some?" Sadie looks so damn excited it's almost sad.

"Yes," I say, because clearly she's deprived and needs to live vicariously through my sex life. "But you can't—I mean it—tell Jude. Or anyone. Ever."

"Jude who?" Sadie quips and winks. "Was it good? It was great, wasn't it? Goalie sex is the absolute best. They're remarkably flexible and so damn crazy. God, I miss crazy sex. Or any sex."

I laugh at her. "He was all those things and also insanely intimate."

She looks pleasantly surprised at that. "Nice."

"But it's a one-time thing," I say firmly. "Has to be. Once he makes the team, it's completely off-limits. We're bending the rules the way it is, and that's dangerous."

Sadie moves past me, out of her room and into the hall. I join her. I can hear our parents, Winnie and Jude talking somewhere at the other end of the condo, probably in the master bedroom, which Jude had renovated with wider doorframes and a shower Dad could roll his wheelchair into.

"Good sex is harder to find than a good job," Sadie announces as she swats my ass playfully. "Remember that."

"You need to get laid," I remark and she nods emphatically.

"Does goalie boy have a friend?"

"Shh!" I command as we get closer to the voices. She lifts her index finger and makes a cross above her heart on her chest.

We turn the corner and find everyone except Dad in the large kitchen.

"Jude, this is more than we could have ever hoped for," Mom is saying and she reaches out and grabs her only son in a bear hug.

Jude rubs her back and kisses her cheek before pulling back. "It's nothing."

"I hate that you're blowing your money on us when you have Zoey and the baby to think about now," Mom confesses softly with that same frown Sadie had earlier.

"Mom, Jude has more than enough money to take care of the baby, Zoey, and you and Dad. Two times over," Winnie reminds her of what we all know. Jude nods in agreement.

"Besides, Zoey has enough money to take care of herself and the baby without his help," I add and smile. "So do not feel guilty. I don't when I eat his food or use his Netflix or hack into his Amazon and order myself Jimmy Choos."

"You do that?!"

I shake my head. "No, but now I know I can, because you clearly don't check."

Mom chuckles at our banter. Good, that's what I was going for. Jude ignores me and takes Mom by the hand. "Let me show you Winnie's and Sadie's rooms down at this end. Away from you and Dad, so you have some privacy."

I watch them head out into the hall and walk down to the other end of the condo. I glance up and watch Winnie's face fall instantly as she pulls out her phone. "Fucking hell, Tyson! It's been less than twenty-four hours."

"That sounds like a good start to a long-distance relationship," I remark as I watch her angrily type something into her phone. Winnie and Tyson have been dating since high school. You'd think they'd be married with babies by now, but the fact is, they don't seem to really like each other all that much. I think her deciding to move here with the rest of the family is finally going to be the nail in their long overdue coffin.

"He is pissy because I didn't tell him when we landed." Winnie rolls her eyes. "And I haven't told him what weekend to come visit yet. He wants next weekend, but hell, we just got here, and I don't even know where my room is. I just need some time to get used to everything before I have to make him get used to everything."

"Ah, true love," Sadie quips, and I try not to giggle. In all honesty, this is serious. And it's a perfect example of why Sadie and I aren't in any rush to bring anyone else into our lives permanently. Winnie looks up and stares at both of us with a mix of annoyance and something else, like frustration. She bows her head again and goes back to texting, but Sadie isn't done talking. "Dixie scored the goalie."

"Shh!" I command harshly and stick my head out into the hall. Mom and Jude are nowhere to be found, thankfully. "Where is Dad?"

"He said he was going to lie down."

"Does he need help?"

Sadie shakes her head.

"He's okay with that stuff for now, especially because Jude got him one of those adjustable beds like in the hospital. He can lower it and raise the top or bottom." Winnie is finally done texting and sticks her phone in her back pocket. "Now what's this about nailing the goalie?"

"Shh!" I hiss. "I hooked up with that guy from the junior team. It was hot, and now it's over. And no one—especially Jude—can know."

Winnie shrugs. "I love keeping shit from big brother, so no worries. But why is it only once if it was so good?"

"I just wanted to do it to get him out of my system. That was our plan."

Winnie looks like she'd have more faith in the existence of unicorns than in anything I'm saying. She's always had a way of seeing right through my bullshit. "So you've worked him out of your system? He's no longer attractive and charming now that he's given you what I can only assume is great sex?"

"Fantastic sex," Sadie pipes up and instantly lowers her voice before I can shush her. "It was also insanely intimate. Her words."

Winnie's smile grows at that. "Okay, you have to figure out a way to keep this going, Dix."

"It's impossible," I reply and sigh. "And I may be up for a promotion at work, so the last thing I need to be doing is anything that will screw that up. I have a five-year plan, and he isn't in it."

They both roll their eyes simultaneously. "Ah, right. You are conquering the male-dominated business world one press release at a time," Winnie chirps, and I flip her my middle finger.

"She's going to be the next Ryanne Bateman," Sadie adds, her tone dripping with annoyance. She thinks I'm too OCD about my career. "A rich, successful businesswoman with no one to share the empire with."

"I don't need a man to be complete."

Sadie nods. "Of course you don't. But you also can be successful *and* have a man in your life. The two aren't mutually exclusive."

"Not this man. He's a fun time, but that's all," I reply. They both look completely unconvinced, but I don't want to debate this anymore, mostly because I know I can be easily defeated. If they push me just a little bit more I'll break down and call him, like I've wanted to since I woke up this morning. I decide to change the subject. "Are you finally going to break up with Tyson now that you live here?"

"I don't live here," Winnie corrects. Her gray eyes, the exact same shade as my mom's, hold a stern glint, and I can tell she's not just trying to convince me of this. "It's a temporary situation. Tyson will adapt, and I'll move home eventually."

"Or he can move here when we all decide to stay," Sadie mutters under her breath, but Winnie still catches it.

"He's not dual like us," she replies. "He can't just move to the US."

"Unless you marry him," I add in a perky, helpful tone I know is anything but helpful. They've been together almost ten years now, and somehow she thinks we're the ridiculous ones for bringing it up.

"I'm not marrying him right now," Winnie says flatly. "I'm scared to plan it and then something happens to Dad and…I just don't want to at this time. And he's too needy right now. Could you imagine how needy he'll be if we get married?"

She stomps out of the kitchen. Sadie rolls her eyes. I point in the general direction Winnie just went. "That is exactly why I don't want a relationship right now. Winnie is miserable trying to be what Tyson wants and deal with all this family stuff. Better to just stay single."

Sadie shrugs. "Maybe. But Jude and Zoey make it work."

"Yeah, but Jude is different. He always defies the odds."

"You do too," Sadie replies and smiles.

"Whatever. The fling with my goalie was perfect. Fun, satisfying and all the sadness and stuff about Dad doesn't have to be his problem." I walk over to the front door, just across from the kitchen, and grab my purse, which I dumped there when I was schlepping the luggage up.

"He doesn't know about Dad?" Sadie questions.

I shrug. "He probably does, because the team knows, but he didn't bring it up and I wasn't about to," I explain to her. "It's nice to be with someone who doesn't talk about it, you know?"

I watch her nod as I instinctively grab my phone out of the front flap and start to check my emails. The team is flying out for a road trip today, so things should be relatively quiet at work.

"Jude! You need to get to the airport, like five minutes ago!" I yell and notice I have a message.

It's Elijah. My heart instantly flutters even before I read it, and then when I read it, my heart adds flipping to the fluttering. It's another cheesy pickup line, but it's about hooking up again. "Can I crash at your place?" Is he serious?

I must be biting my lip when Jude walks into the hallway because he chuckles at me. "You look like you're trying to solve a math problem."

"Get your ass to the airport," I reply, my eyes never leaving Elijah's text. "They aren't going to hold the plane, golden boy."

"Are you okay?"

I move my phone to my chest so he can't see the screen, then look up at him. I know instantly he's talking about Dad. "Why didn't anyone tell me he wasn't walking at all anymore?"

"I didn't know until last night. Mom called me to warn me," Jude replies. "And I couldn't exactly break it to you at work last night. I'm sorry."

"It's okay." I sigh. Our eyes meet, and my pain is reflected back in his. "Now go. I'll come over every night to help them settle in and make sure Zoey isn't overexerting herself."

He reaches out and hugs me. "Okay. Thanks. Call if you need anything."

"I will." I give him a quick squeeze and then pull back and shove him. "Go."

"Guys!" Jude calls out. "I'm heading out."

Our sisters call out good-byes and our mom comes scurrying down the hall to give him a hug. I take the opportunity to reread Eli's text. As I'm reading another one pops up.

I want to see you again. Tonight. You free?

I'm smiling so large it distracts my mom from the waving she's doing as Jude heads out the door and down the stairs. She looks at me, perplexed. "You could light the sky with that smile, Dixie. What's causing it?"

"No one," I reply and side hug her. "Just happy you're here."

She kisses my forehead and pats my hair. "That's a load of hooey, but I'll get his name out of your sisters, don't you worry."

I laugh. "When it's important, I promise I'll tell you. This is nothing but a little fun."

"Well, go have your fun." My mom motions toward my phone as she pulls away. "I'm going to go check on your dad. Maybe catch a little nap next to him."

I nod and watch her go before glancing at my screen again. I should tell him no, I can't see him again. I can't because my parents are living here now and my dad is dying and my work is about to get really intense with the prospect of this promotion and I don't need his antics, as charming as they are, to distract me. But there's time to be an adult later. I text him back.

You might not be Fred Flintstone but I'll let you make my bed rock (again).

9

ELIJAH

I take the stairs two at a time but stop and give myself a second before I knock on her door. I can hear her inside as I run my hands through my hair and try to get my heart to stop hammering. She's singing. Badly. Oh my God, so badly. I smile and try to make out the song. Selena Gomez, I think. Jesus, she soOunds like a dying cat, and it's fucking awesome. I cover my mouth with my hand to keep from laughing out loud.

Dixie is such a dynamo and seems to be good at everything, but her singing proves that's not true. Somehow, though, I'm totally attracted to her off-key silliness, which makes my heart hammer even harder. What the hell is with me that I am so flustered by a woman? I've never had this problem before in my life. I don't know what it is about her, but she makes me so off-balance, and yet when I'm with her, I feel more grounded than I have since the accident.

She told me to come over at about seven and it's six forty-five. I was sick of pacing her block, and I was getting strange looks from the barista at the Starbucks on the corner for milking my tall caramel macchiato for two hours. I should have just hung out at Levi's, watched some sports or surfed the net, but I was antsy. I had this weird sensation like we were racing against a clock. If I didn't see her as soon as I could, I felt like I wouldn't get the chance. I would have been here the second she sent that Fred Flintstone text, but she said her family was in town and she needed to be with them until now.

I listen to her sing just a little bit longer and then try to cover the smirk on my face as I knock. She yells that it's open, which I need to talk to her about. I don't know San Fran well, but I know enough to know this isn't a high-end area. Not horrible, but she should be keeping her door locked, even if she's expecting company. I open the door and look around her apartment, something I didn't do much of last night.

She's got candles lit again, giving the place an intimate, warm feel. The bed is exactly where it was last night, in a nook by the window. There's what look like two brand-new wide, comfortable armchairs across from the minuscule kitchen area, but no TV. Instead on the wall are a bunch of framed posters—words. Slogans or motivational sayings, I guess you'd call them. Things like "Celebrate Every Victory" and "If You Can't Beat Fear, Do It Scared." They're all in simple dark wood frames, printed in different fonts on different-colored paper. They'd be crazy in any other chick's apartment, but for Dixie, it works. Especially the one that says "Throw Sass Around Like Confetti."

I'm smiling when she comes trotting out of her bathroom in nothing but heels and red lacy underwear and matching bra, holding a feather duster and a DustBuster. Holy shit. As my jaw drops, her smile grows. "Sorry. I was just tidying up."

"No you weren't," I reply, my own smile starting to grow.

"You're right. I wasn't." She laughs. "But you seem to like the hot housewife or naughty maid thing, so I thought I should run with it."

"You're incredible." I shrug out of my coat and let it fall to the floor and then start toward her.

"I'm also a complete slob," she confesses. "If you open my closet it's just piles of clothes and junk I shoved in there last night so you wouldn't know."

"You're also a terrible singer, and that wall of words says you're a Tony Robbins wannabe too," I tell her as I motion toward her wall.

She blinks but doesn't look the least bit offended or embarrassed, which I love. "I believe in the power of positive thinking, and you were eavesdropping."

"Hard not to hear that voice," I quip.

She feigns indignation and points the feather duster at my face. "You don't like it, you can buy earplugs."

"But then I'd miss the way you pant my name when you come," I say casually, but it gets the very uncasual reaction I'm looking for—she blushes.

I use her moment of astonishment to reach out and grab her, pulling her body flush with mine. It's crazy how she fits, that petite frame of hers curls into me, rubbing and bumping all the right places. I dip my head, our lips brush. "I don't do that," she protests faintly, and it makes me pass my lips over hers again, teasingly.

"Oh, you do that," I promise her. "And I want to make you do it again."

"Well, hurry up then," she goads, a smile on those naturally rosy lips. "I've got cleaning to do."

My arms tighten around her waist, closing any gap between us, and my lips take hers. The kiss is deep and hard, and she gives as good as she gets, matching every pass of my tongue and every push of my lips against hers. She drops the feather duster and grabs my belt instead, twisting and yanking until it's undone, never breaking the kiss or letting go of the DustBuster in her other hand. I move my lips to her ear, biting and sucking the lobe before telling her, "You might want to put down the vacuum."

She smiles playfully and turns it on for a second, filling the room with a roaring sound. Then she steps back, out of my arms, and says, "If you insist."

She bends right there in front of me, dropping to her knees, one hand undoing my button and pulling down my fly while the other gently places the mini vacuum on the floor. But she doesn't stand up right away. Instead, she pushes my jeans over my hips, and then she does the same with my underwear, careful not to catch my completely solid dick, which is now level with her pretty blue eyes. She's going to give me a blow job. I can tell by the smile curving the corners of her mouth and the way her tongue wets her lips. I somehow get harder at that revelation.

I move my hands to curl into her silky, straight hair and force my eyes to stay focused on her as she wraps a hand around the base of my cock and starts to slide her warm, wet mouth over the tip. Sweet mother of everything, this is incredible. Her mouth is firm, and her tongue swirls deliciously around my shaft as she goes straight for it—taking all of me in one long, unhurried movement.

"Dixie," I groan as I let my head tip back.

She responds by sliding back up from base to tip, only this time her hand tightens around my shaft and follows her lips, creating an unbelievable friction. She pauses at my tip, rubbing the flat of her tongue up and down the sensitive underside, and it takes every ounce of willpower I have not to snap my hips and shove myself into her mouth. It's so damn hard because her mouth feels so fucking good. But I don't want to control this, I want her to. And she's doing an incredibly hot job. In just a few short minutes my muscles are taut and I'm swimming in that tingling feeling, my orgasm set to launch.

I'm not ready. I want to drown in these sensations a little longer, but then I look down. Her eyes are shut, eyelashes fluttering, and the hand that's not on my cock is inside her own underwear. She's playing with herself. Holy fuck, that vision lights the fuse and my orgasm is inevitable now. I pull back, ready to come in my own hand, but she pulls me back into her welcoming mouth and I roar and see stars.

She makes a noise like a whimper and her mouth tightens around me and I watch her body shudder as she has her own orgasm. I reach down and pull her up, right up off her feet. She wraps her arms around my neck and her legs around my waist and I walk her toward the bed, kicking off my pants and underwear as we go since they were around my ankles. I carefully drop her down onto her back on the bed and lay myself over her. She likes it, I can tell by the smile. And I like her. A lot. More than I'm allowed to.

I run a hand over her forehead and into her hair. "I actually thought we could talk."

"Oops." She sighs it more than says it. "So you didn't want my lips on your cock?"

"I did. Just after the talking part." I smile.

She lets out a whiny sound and her tiny nose wrinkles up. "Talking will get us in trouble."

"Why?" I should keep my mouth shut, but I want to hear her concerns, because I need to know they're the same as mine.

"Because if we talk I'll have to tell you that I like you," she confesses and a blush creeps over her cheeks as she closes her eyes to avoid looking at me. Her bluntness despite her obvious insecurity makes my heart swell. It's so simply and totally Dixie. She has a way of being fearless and vulnerable at the same time. It's something I've never seen in anyone else. "And liking you is like driving full speed into a brick wall. It's gotta end, and it's gonna be bad."

"Not necessarily," I reply and gently let my lips ghost the curve of her neck. "I mean, I like you too, so that's something in our favor."

She opens her eyes at that and looks up at me tentatively. "You do?"

"Fuck yeah," I reply enthusiastically, and she laughs. "What's not to like? Other than the singing."

She slaps me playfully on the arm. I press my palms gently to the sides of her face and kiss her softly. She holds on to my biceps as I do it. "Seriously, Dix. I don't think we need this to end tonight. I don't think I can."

"I know," she confesses. "But the alternative is…impossible. Even if we kept this going long distance while you're on the Storm, you'll be on the Thunder soon, and then it's got to stop and we'll be in even deeper by then."

I know what she's saying is the truth, I just don't care right now. "We don't know when I'll be called up. Why should we stop having fun now because of something that might or might not happen?"

I hate admitting that I might never make the team, but sadly it feels like the truth right now. I feel a deep burn of humiliation at that, but I push those thoughts from my head and focus on what I think I can win—her.

"You'll make the team. One day."

"But until then…let's keep having a good time," I reply, moving us back to the subject at hand. "I think we both need something fun in our lives."

"Eli, the whole point of this was to work each other out of our system," she reminds me softly.

"I think that's going to take more time, though."

"I just…I don't think it's a good time for anyone to be in my life," she mumbles and I feel like, for a second, this isn't about her job, but then she adds, "I'm up for a promotion and stuff."

"We're not breaking any rules right now," I remind her. "I just think we'd be stupid to deny ourselves more of this."

She reaches out and wraps her arms around my neck, moving under me, and gently pushes her thigh up to rub against my cock, which is growing again. "More of this."

"Not just the sex," I reply firmly. "You. Me. More of us."

She cranes her neck, reaching up to kiss me. I kiss her back, but her phone starts ringing just when it's getting good. She pulls away, wiggles her way out from under me and scurries over to the coffee table. I can't believe she's going to take a phone call when we're about to get naked again.

"Sorry," she tells me as she glances at the screen, her finger poised to swipe Accept. "It's a work thing."

She answers and I sit there and watch her pace the room talking with someone named Kelley about a meeting on Monday. I don't know a Kelley in the Thunder organization, but that doesn't mean there isn't one. She talks about marketing strategies and a presentation or something, but honestly, I'm totally distracted by the way her tiny, perky little butt looks in those lace boy shorts and the curve of her breasts spilling over the cups of her bra. And the way her hair glows a golden color in the candlelight is pretty fantastic too.

She must have ended the call because suddenly I hear her say. "You're flat-out staring at my ass."

I blink and force my eyes up. "Not exclusively. I was staring at your chest too for a while."

She smiles. "Oh good. You didn't leave the girls out."

"Can you put that thing on silent? Because I'm about to do things to you that should not be interrupted," I say and casually stroke my now hard dick.

She watches me do it. "I can't put my phone on silent."

"You're that dedicated to work?" I have to ask because it seems insane.

"No. My family just moved to town this afternoon and Jude is on a road trip, so I want to be reachable if they need anything." There's this sudden serious glint in her eyes that makes me think that's not the whole story.

"They moved here permanently?"

"Yeah. Kind of. It's a long story." She shrugs. "But I won't answer if it's not my family."

"You just did."

She looks sheepish. "That was because I'm trying to get a meeting with the ALS Foundation here in San Fran. I want to volunteer to build a social media campaign for them. That was my contact setting up a meeting."

"ALS?" I prop myself up on my elbows and watch as she drops her cell back on the coffee table. "What is that again?"

"It's amyotrophic lateral sclerosis," she explains. "Also called Lou Gehrig's disease. It basically destroys your body, then kills you. It's horrific and I hate it and there's no cure. I volunteer with them, and the team has done charity events for them before. Now I'm trying to do a little more than the regular volunteer stuff at their annual walk."

"Why?"

She hesitates. I can see her step falter as she walks toward me on the bed. And that same serious glint slides over her eyes for a second, then she smiles seductively and climbs up on the bed, straddling my hips again. "Because I'm not just a kick-ass communications genius and the best sex you've ever had. I'm a good person too."

I grin. "And modest."

"Hard to be modest when you're staring at my ass like it's the eighth wonder of the world," she quips.

"And your tits," I remind her and place my hands on her hips. "But you know what the real wonder of the world is?"

"What?" she asks in a breathless whisper.

I use my hands on her tiny hips to hold her tight, standing up. I turn and before she can wrap her legs around my waist I toss her onto the bed. She lands on her back with a laugh. I quickly drop down and then slide my body on top of her. The sex last night was fantastic. I'm a huge fan of the girl being on top. Hell, I haven't met a sex position I didn't like, but right now, I want to be on top of her. There's something kind of intimate about missionary for me, and I crave that with her.

I lean down, rubbing my beard against the curve of her neck as I move my lips to her ear. "The way it feels to be inside you," I finish my thought. "That's the real wonder of my world."

"Oh my God…" she says in a breathy, almost moaning voice.

I cover her mouth with mine, kissing her hard and deep as I move a hand between us and push it into her underwear. "Watching you make yourself come was pretty wondrous too."

She probably wants to respond, but I've slipped two fingers inside her and curled them just right and she can't speak at all. She lets out a perfect little mew and pushes her head into the mattress. I balance on my forearm to give me more room to move my hand. She's panting and writhing in less than two minutes—and she's wetter than ever.

I feel my dick start to throb with need as she clenches around my fingers and bucks her hips with the pulse of her orgasm. I love watching her come. The way her skin turns all pink. The perfect arch of her back. The circle her mouth makes. The way her nipples harden. I cover one with my mouth now because the temptation is too strong. Then I move my hand from her pulsating core and I can't help but grind myself into her thigh. God, I need my own release so much I'm almost shaking.

I glance around the room, trying to locate my pants because that's where my condoms are. She blindly gropes for the night table drawer and pulls it open. Inside is an unopened box of condoms.

"You're the best," I whisper gratefully. She rips open a foil, then slips her hands between us to roll it on. The feel of her hands sends ripples of pleasure up my spine.

All I want with every fiber of my being is to slide into her wet, warm, welcoming heat, but there's one thing I want more—for this not to be the end. So I nudge her gently, entering her with just my tip, and then I hover there. She shifts under me, nudging her pelvis lower, trying to take more of me, but I move my hips back as soon as more than the tip slips deeper. She looks at me with such despair over not getting what she wants it's almost comical. "Elijah. Please."

"Tell me this isn't the end," I demand, my voice so damn low and gritty even I don't recognize it. "Promise me."

She doesn't respond, or react, her body still, her eyes locked on mine, her bottom lip caught tightly between her teeth. She still has that look of wanton desperation on her face though, so I know this is torturing her. Good. It may be playing dirty, but I'll do whatever it takes to get what I want—her.

"It's not the end," she finally replies in a heated whisper.

I push just a little bit deeper. My entire body quivers as I stop from fully immersing myself in her perfect pussy. "Promise," I demand.

"Oh God, I promise," she moans and writhes with need. "Now fuck me, Elijah. *Please.*"

I'm deep inside her before she finishes saying my name. Her back arches and she sighs with pleasure, or relief. Probably both. But I don't give her time to relax. I'm too riled up, too needy, for that. So I start to move, fast, long strokes, keeping my whole body low, against her body. I want to touch all of her at once. I'm desperate to feel her skin against mine.

She doesn't seem to mind, wrapping her legs around my thighs and her arms around my neck. Her hands dig into my hair roughly, and the delicious sensation her nails on my scalp send down my spine has me pushing deep, harder into her.

"Eli…Oh God, Eli…" That breathy voice sends me into overdrive. I wrap my fingers around the back of her knee and pull her leg forward. Her ankle lands on my shoulder and I twist my hips just a little bit as I push into her. It makes her gasp and arch her back. I kiss her recklessly, tongues, teeth and lips battling.

She gets tight—so damn tight—around my cock. And warm. So unbelievably warm, and then, as I push and twist for the third time, slower and harder this time, her hands grip my hair and she does something unexpected. She opens her eyes and locks them with mine as she comes. It's intimate and hotter than hell, and it sends me catapulting over the edge with her.

My body melts into hers and I bury my face in her shoulder and close my eyes and just absorb the fading sensations of both our orgasms. Her grip on my hair lessens, and after a minute she's gently running her fingers through, her nails grazing soothingly across my scalp.

"Why is it so good?" she ponders aloud, and I smile against the soft skin of her elbow. "I thought I'd had good sex before, but clearly I was mistaken."

"We're just getting started, sweet Dixie," I promise.

10

DIXIE

So why do your parents hate hockey so much?" I ask as the bartender slides fresh strawberry Margaritas at us and plops two umbrellas in each drink, as per Eli's request for extra umbrellas.

The question is blunt but he doesn't flinch. Our already easy
chemistry has gotten even easier as the night has progressed. Eli
was starving and the canned soup and sourdough bread I keep in
my apartment wasn't going to cut it. So we threw on some clothes
and I took him to Bert's, an old-fashioned diner renowned for its
killer milkshakes. He was stunned and fascinated by the amount
of food I consumed. A large roast beef sandwich with extra mayo
and extra sharp cheddar, curly fries and a chocolate cake shake that
they make by dumping a slab of chocolate cake in the blender with
chocolate ice cream and chocolate syrup. He ate the exact same
meal plus a piece of apple pie for dessert, which he said was to get
his fruits in for the day. It made me laugh.

I didn't have the heart to tell him his eating habits would have
to change as soon as he got on the team. They have a dietician

and strict rules, plus the food they serve on road trips is steamed everything—chicken, fish, broccoli, you name it, they steam it. Jude and the guys cheat every now and then but not a lot. Probably because they're older than Eli and they need all the help they can get to keep in shape.

After we ate we decided to walk off the food and spent hours roaming the streets of San Fran. He's excited about moving here, I can see it in his eyes. We ended up sneaking into a tiny dive of a bar near Haight and Ashbury, which is where we are now, drinking some strawberry Margaritas, extra umbrellas.

He ponders my question for a minute, twirling an umbrella between his fingers, and then he levels his green eyes on me. "My uncle, my mom's only brother, is paralyzed because of a sports injury."

I almost gasp. "Oh gosh. That's horrible."

"It was." He nods and drops the umbrella on the bar in front of us and then stares into his frozen drink. "It happened in a high school football game. He was this all-star quarterback with a scholarship to Penn State and everything. My mom's whole family was devastated emotionally and financially from it."

"I can imagine," I whisper and sip my drink to take the edge off my feelings. I know all too well about being blindsided by a loved one's health, or lack thereof.

"He's great now," Eli tells me, his mossy green eyes finding mine with an earnest look. "He's an architect. He's married and has two kids. He lets them play sports, and he's really proud of Levi and me. But my mom still holds a grudge against sports."

"I get it," I reply, and he looks a little taken aback by that. I place my hand over his on the bar, curling my fingers around his palm. "I'm not saying she shouldn't work through it. She should. I mean alienating your children because of your fears isn't the answer. But I get how devastating it can be to watch someone you love lose everything and then watch your children do something you think could leave them the same way. And it almost did with you."

His eyes cloud over and he swallows hard. The bobbing of his Adam's apple makes my eyes fall to the scar, the result of what I'm talking about. He seems like he's pulling away from me emotionally, and I worry I've overstepped, so I try to explain further, tightening my grip on his hand. "Eli, I didn't even know you. But to hear about your accident from Levi and see the video was gut-wrenching. She's your mom. That must have been flashback central for her."

He smiles at that, but it's pained, like it's more of a grimace. I worry again that I'm overstepping, but he finally turns his hand over to hold mine. "It was scary. It didn't just look like I was dying, I thought I was dying. But it didn't make me think playing was a mistake. It made me think wasting time playing at the college level was the mistake. I almost lost my chance to play professionally because I was trying to please my parents."

"That's why you went to college?" I ask, stunned. I had no idea.

"Yeah. I've always been the kid who, despite pushing their buttons like it's my job, tries to give them what they want," he explains, his eyes on our joined hands. "They wanted all three of us to get a college education. Todd, my oldest brother, did, but he became an entertainment lawyer simply so he could party in L.A. Not what they had in mind. Levi ditched school for the draft, which, as you know, had them disown him for a couple of years. I thought if I went to college before playing professionally it wouldn't give them a reason to disown me."

"But you changed your mind?"

He nods. "That accident changed my mind. Yeah. And they didn't disown me, but they are still pushing me to go back to school. They think I'm not playing well enough to justify my decision, and they're right." He looks frustrated.

I'm about to ask him if he thinks the accident is the reason he's not playing so well, but I stop myself. This is getting way too deep—for both of us, I think. We're supposed to be having fun, and there's no room in the plan for deep revelations and sharing. I sip my drink. "I guess big moments like that can cause you to re-think things."

His face hardens for just the slightest second, and I instantly regret saying it. But then he smiles jovially. "Yeah, but like I told you when I met you, it's a hell of a conversation starter."

I force myself to smile back, but honestly, I think he's full of shit. I don't want to call him on it right now, but knowing me I'll do it at some point, if he doesn't figure it out on his own.

He leans in further and kisses my cheek softly. It's more of a brush really. It's a habit of his, and I definitely could get used to it. "So tell me about your childhood with the notorious Jude Braddock," he urges.

I take another sip of my drink and smile. "We grew up in Toronto in an area called the Beaches. We had a super tiny house, but because Jude was the only boy he got his own room. He started playing hockey before I was even born, so my childhood weekends were spent in rinks watching him play. He'll tell you our parents spoiled my sisters and me, but the fact is Jude was always priority one."

Elijah stares at me for a minute with an expression I can't

decipher. "It's weird. You actually don't sound bitter when you say that."

"I'm not," I reply easily with a shrug. "Jude was a hockey prodigy. We needed to cultivate that. I didn't really have anything I loved the way he loved hockey. Don't get me wrong—my parents still made sure we girls got to do things like gymnastics and figure skating, and Winnie even played girls' hockey. But none of us loved anything the way Jude loved hockey. Sadie finally settled into art classes, which she was great at. I got really good at the piano, and Winnie took dance. But Jude, as much as I hate to admit it—and I will never admit it to him—is something special."

He smiles this soft, gentle smile that looks absurdly intimate on his rugged face and tells me in a raspy whisper. "I think you're something special too."

I take another long sip of my drink, hoping it will cool the blush creeping over my face. He gulps back half his drink and then says, "Are you close to your parents?"

"Absolutely," I say and think of my dad. I haven't told Eli about his illness. I think he knows because Jude came out last year and told the media at a charity event. And Levi has known since Dad was diagnosed, so he could have told him. But he's not mentioning it or forcing me to talk about it, which I appreciate. I spend enough time thinking about it that I hate giving it more energy by talking about it. It sucks the joy out of a lot of aspects of my life, and I'm not ready to let it suck the joy out of this. "I'm a total daddy's girl and proud of it. My parents are amazing. Been madly in love since they were eighteen. They never had a ton of money or even a lot of luck, but they were always madly in love, and they love us madly too."

The look on his face is pure longing. I realize this is nothing like his relationship with his parents, and I feel how much that sucks deep in my gut. "So they moved here from Toronto?"

I nod. "My dad is actually an American citizen. He was born and raised in Detroit and moved to Toronto to be with my mom after he met her in Niagara Falls."

He smiles. "That sounds like a cute little love story."

"It is," I admit. "And I want that too."

Except for the tragic ending, I add to myself. He smiles at me. It's sure but not cocky. And then he leans in and gives me another one of those brush kisses on my cheek, stopping near the shell of my ear. "I'd say we're off to a good start."

"Last call," the bartender interrupts, which is perfect timing because I don't know how to react to that last statement. He's right. We're off to a great start. But how can it go anywhere?

Eli asks for the check and takes his jacket and drapes it across my shoulders. I try to protest but he won't hear it. "It's the middle of the night and it's probably damp and chilly. Humor me."

So I do, but not because I can't handle the cold. Because his jacket smells like him—earthy and crisp—and being engulfed in that makes me warm everywhere.

I pull out my wallet to pay the check, or at least my part, but just like at the diner Eli pays it before I can. I want to protest but I know it's no use. I just make a mental note to pay him back another way—like naked. And hopefully tonight.

He guides me to the door, his hand firmly spread across my lower back. I can feel its heat, even through the thick fabric of his coat. Outside his hand falls from my back and tangles with mine, our fingers interlacing. I'm shocked at how empty the streets are and how quiet the world seems to be. It's almost two in the morning by the time we turn onto my street, and the craziest part of it all is I'm not tired. I'm wide awake and I'm blissful. There is no other word for it.

Before I can put my key in the lock to my building entrance he turns me to face him and pushes my back against the ancient door. He takes me in a searing kiss, and when he's done he says in his dark, velvety voice, "This is going to work, sweet Dixie."

"This is going to be fun," I correct him. "But the clock is ticking."

"Dixie Braddock, always about the rules and the deadlines." He smiles and kisses me again, quicker this time but just as deep. "So we should probably get inside and take full advantage of our limited time."

"You're pretty smart for a guy who takes pucks to the head," I joke, and he laughs.

I turn back to the door and slip the key in the lock.

Six and a half hours later we're catapulted back into reality by the shrill sound of both our phones ringing at once. We just finished showering—together—and are both wrapped in towels. I was rinsing off my toothbrush and putting it back in the holder, next to the new one I gave him, when he started kissing my neck, and then we were on our way to getting dirty again, but the ringing stopped everything instantly.

The first thing I think of is my dad. But then why would Elijah's phone be ringing too? In such a hurry to make love again last night, we left our phones in our clothes, which were by the front door, so we both rush out of the bathroom. Eli finds his phone first, grabs it and his underwear, and lets his towel drop, stalking naked across my apartment to answer it in the relative quiet of the bathroom. I find mine on the floor next to my sweater and see Ann's name flash across the screen.

"Dixie speaking," I say. My voice is a garbled mess, so I clear my throat and try again. "Dixie speaking."

"Dix, honey, I am so sorry to wake you so early," Ann confesses, and she sounds fully and completely awake. "We have a minor work crisis, and I need you on it. I know it's Sunday, but it really can't wait."

"Okay. Yeah. No problem," I reply swiftly, running a hand through my damp hair. It's the first time they've called me on my day off, and it's a good thing. Usually Ann handles weekend crises on her own, but she's calling me in, and I know it's because she wants me to show off my skills to the powers that be when her job is available. "What's going on?"

I grab Eli's shirt off the floor and fumble to pull it on. It's chilly in here because I'm still wet from the shower, and his hooded Henley is gigantic on me and covers all my important bits. I tug the long sleeves up, bunching them at my elbows, and walk toward the open bathroom door. My towel falls off and I leave it on the living room floor.

Elijah is in his boxer briefs standing in the middle of my tiny bathroom. His posture is rigid, shoulders up near his ears and hunched slightly forward. He looks up and our eyes meet, and I know seconds before Ann even says it. And then she does.

"They've called up Elijah Casco."

11

ELIJAH

Elijah?" Coach Schneider prompts.

All I can think is that this isn't how it's supposed to go. This wasn't the way I wanted it to happen. I can't take my eyes off her, and so I see every moment of realization flash across her face. I watch her features tighten in shock and then slowly fall in defeat and then I watch the hard bitter resignation take hold. Her phone is still pressed to her ear and she turns away from me as she talks into it. "So press release? And announcements on social media?"

"When do you need me on a plane?" I ask, working hard to keep my voice confident and upbeat so the mixed emotions I'm currently experiencing aren't evident. This was supposed to be the best day of my life, and now it's not.

"You'll get a call from management," he explains. "I think they're trying to book you on a noon flight."

Coach pauses, his tone getting gentler but still firm. "You're going to have to hit the ground running, kid. It's a lot of pressure and unfortunately not a lot of room for error. We're clinging to that last playoff spot, and we want to keep it that way, if not improve. I'll be honest, I'm not sure you're ready, but we need you. We don't have another option right now, and we drafted you for a reason so…prove me wrong, Casco."

"I will. I'm ready," I confirm and lean against the sink. "I can help get us there. I promise."

"Good. See you tonight," Coach says and hangs up.

Holy shit, I'm an NHL goalie. I take one small moment, push away everything else—the fears over my injury, the sadness over what this means for me and Dixie—and just let that accomplishment fill me with pride. I've played one game for the Thunder so far, but it was preseason and so it doesn't count, stat-wise. The game tomorrow night in Quebec will be my NHL debut. I've worked for this since I was eight and first strapped on goalie pads.

But then I step out into the main room of Dixie's apartment and the rest of my feelings—the dark, depressing ones—come to the surface again. Dixie is still on the phone, bent over her desk in the corner writing something down on a notepad. Her back is to me, and my shirt that she's wearing has risen up, revealing just the edges of her perfectly round, firm ass cheeks. It's sexy as fuck. But then she hangs up and turns around and looks at me like I'm a stranger.

She smiles. It's lovely and it's bright but it doesn't reach her eyes. "Congratulations."

She steps forward and hugs me fiercely, but she pulls back before I can even return the hug.

"Thank you," I reply and feel hopelessly awkward.

She walks away from me toward the bed. She drops her phone there in the rumpled sheets and then turns and heads into the closet. I watch her go. When she starts to speak her tone is cool. Friendly but distant. "So I'm going to run into work and write up the press release. It'll be out before your plane lands in Quebec City. And then I'll handle the list of media requests. You're probably starting tomorrow night, and everyone with a hockey blog will want to interview you post-game, so we preapprove certain media for—"

"Dixie. Stop," I command.

She pulls on a pair of underwear and grabs a sports bra. I watch longingly as she turns her back to me, pulls off my Henley and pulls on the red sports bra. I step closer, but something stops me from entering the closet. Instead I put my hands above me on the thick wood doorframe and lean my body toward her. "Can we stop acting like this doesn't suck?"

She turns, clutching my shirt to her chest like she's trying to cover herself up. Like she doesn't want me to see her naked. No, actually like I'm someone who shouldn't see her naked. My chest feels tight.

"Your dreams are coming true. It doesn't suck," she reminds me. "And honestly, the timing is probably the best possible thing that could happen. The longer we let this go on, the harder it would have been to stop. And it has to stop."

I want to argue with her. I want to give her a million reasons we can keep seeing each other. Fuck, I just want to be able to give her one. But I can't think of any that won't jeopardize her career or even mine. She waits a heartbeat for me to say something, but I can't. There's nothing to say. I have to catch a plane and she has to go to work and this has to end.

Knowing I've got nothing to add, she finishes dressing, pulling on a pair of skinny jeans and a black-and-white sweater. Then she starts to try to walk past me, but I'm blocking the whole doorway and I can't seem to make myself move. She reaches out, my shirt still bunched in her right hand, like she's going to physically move me. But that would mean putting her hands on my bare flesh, and she seems to realize that inches before she actually touches me and she pulls back. Instead she holds up my shirt between us.

"Take it. Get dressed," she demands. "We have things to do, like pretend this never happened."

"I know," I reply firmly, but I still don't move or take the shirt.

She looks up at me, emotion finally seeping into her face. Now she looks desperate, like a wounded animal. My chest feels like there's a truck on top of it. She pushes the shirt out closer to me. "Take it and go. Please."

I reach out but instead of grabbing the shirt I grab her wrist and pull her to me. She struggles to push me away but I push her up against the frame of the door and hold her there with my body against hers. I move a hand under her chin and force her face to angle toward mine. Then I kiss her. It's long and slow and painful because I know it's the last one.

She breaks the kiss first, pulling back and slipping out from my hold, dropping my shirt as she goes so it's in a pile at my feet. My phone starts ringing again. I know it's Levi without looking at it, so I ignore it. She glares at it and then at me. "You can't ignore calls anymore. Especially if that's team related."

I pick up my shirt off the floor and pull it over my head. "It's just Levi."

"If so, he's calling as your captain, not your brother," she says pointedly. I really don't like this. She sounds like a lecturing mom. "You have to answer his calls." She shoves her feet into knee-high black boots and then grabs her coat off the hook on the back of the door.

"Until I skate across the ice tomorrow night to the net, he's still just my older brother," I reply and walk over to the couch where my pants ended up last night. "I'll call him back in a sec."

"He takes priority," she tells me sternly. "I'm just a PR girl. My job is to help you avoid scandal, not create one. And it's my only role in your life now. You need to remember that."

I don't speak. I kind of ignore her because I'm just not willing to admit that yet, to her or myself. That seems to anger her more because as I tug on my pants she huffs and waits impatiently by the door while I finish dressing.

Without speaking I step into the hall and wait while she locks her apartment. My phone buzzes again, and again I send it to voicemail and shove it in my jacket pocket. Once she's locked the door she turns and brushes by me, scurrying down the stairs without even looking up to see if I'm following. It takes me a minute, because I'm so stunned, but I follow, making it out to the sidewalk a second before the door to her building shuts in my face. She's already several feet up the street.

"Dixie!" My voice sounds raw and anguished.

She waves without turning around. "Have a safe flight! Knock 'em dead out there, Casco."

She picks up her pace and makes it to the corner just as a trolley is stopping. She hops on, and in the faint morning light I watch the trolley take her away from me.

I walk back toward Levi's place, which is too far to be walking to, but I don't care. I don't feel like being in an Uber or cab right now. I just want to stumble along, trying to get a grip on everything. For the hundredth time I think this is not how I thought it would be.

My phone rings and this time I pull it out. It's Levi, just like the call log says it was the last two times. I sigh heavily and force my voice to sound upbeat. "Hey! Need a goalie?"

"Yes, I do. And I'm so proud it's you, Elijah," he says. I know this means almost as much to him as it does to me. He's been my biggest fan, my biggest support and my biggest inspiration. "Tessa says you aren't at home. You spend the night with your Julie girl?"

Right. The fake name. I clear my throat. "Yeah."

"Hope she gave you a good luck blow job before you left." He laughs at that and doesn't notice that I don't. "So you going to keep seeing her now that you're going to be local?"

"Nah." I have to force the word from my mouth, like it's a piece of food lodged in my throat.

"Oh." He sounds a little surprised. God, may he still hate talking about feelings because I'm not sharing these. "Well, it's probably best if you focus on the game anyway. It's a tough time to come into the season. Helping us make the playoffs is going to take all your energy and attention."

"Yeah." I pause on a corner waiting for the light to change. "You're right."

"Everything okay, Eli?" he asks. He's gotten more intuitive since settling down with Tessa, unfortunately.

"Yeah. Of course. I'm just…It's a lot," I mumble and cross the street when the light changes. "I have to call an Uber and get my ass back to your house and pack."

"Okay. I'll let you go. See you in a few," Levi says. "Eli, this is going to be fucking great."

"It will be," I say with conviction because it has to be. If I'm giving her up it has to be.

12

DIXIE

I don't know why I'm crying. I'm not sobbing or anything, but from the moment I jumped on the trolley and left him on the sidewalk, tears kept randomly slipping from my eyeballs. It's ridiculous. I knew exactly what was going to happen. Sure, I didn't expect it to happen this soon, but it was going to happen. I've only spent thirty-six hours with him, technically only the last twelve in the relationship zone, and yet I feel heartbroken. I broke up with my college boyfriend of a year and a half with less ache in my chest. Seriously, I'm insane. It's probably a great thing it ended before it began because I was way too invested, clearly.

The tears stop before I get to the office, thankfully. Not that anyone will be there besides the security team, but still. I flash my pass at the guard sitting behind the large marble desk in the lobby. He hits a button and the door buzzes and I pull it open. "Working on a Sunday, huh?"

"Hockey never sleeps," I quip and smile, but it feels forced. He doesn't care and neither do I. He just nods as I make my way to the elevator bank.

I'm a selfish idiot for being this depressed. It's very hard to even get drafted in the NHL. I remember when Jude was in high school he told me like 0.16 percent of all teenagers who play hockey would actually make it to the NHL. And now Elijah Casco is one of them. This is amazing. It's incredible. But it still hurts like hell.

Last night was the biggest mistake of my life. I let him lull me into this false sense of confidence that we could somehow keep this going. Ugh. I knew better, but I let it happen anyway. Because I've never felt such a strong connection to someone before.

I push open the glass door that leads to my department and make my way over to my desk. It's not as weird as I thought it would be, being here all by myself. It's actually kind of calming. I'm glad I opted to come in rather than work on this at home. I could have done it on my laptop, but I needed to get out of there. Even if I had somehow convinced Eli to go without leaving myself, the whole apartment smelled like him and everything in the place was a memory of our thirty-six-hour lovefest. I had to get away from that.

I drop into my chair and start up my computer. Forty minutes later I've drafted the press release and sorted through the interview requests that have already come in and listed them in order of priority. I send my draft to Ann for a quick once-over, and as I wait for her response I pull out my phone and find myself looking at the last half-naked selfie Eli sent me back when he was in Sacramento. It was hard to have these pictures in my memory and remain professional when I saw him at the event this weekend. How the hell am I going to do that now that he actually means something to me?

My phone buzzes in my hand, startling me so badly I almost drop it. Fumbling, I see Jude's name and number pop up on my screen. I hit Answer. "Hey, Jude."

"What's wrong?" he asks instantly. "You didn't sing that. You always—annoyingly—sing my name when you put a 'hey' in front of it."

"Nothing is wrong. I'm just busy. Working," I explain and swivel my chair around so I'm facing the window. The sun is filtering in and it warms my skin. I hadn't realized I was chilled, but I guess I am because it feels damn good. God, I wish I were on a beach somewhere. "I'm writing up the press releases about Noah's injury and Eli being called up permanently."

"They assigned that to you? I thought your boss handled the big announcements," he says.

"She wants me to handle this one," I explain.

"That's as good as a promotion," Jude says proudly. I smile. It's nice to have a brother who is so supportive. Honestly, he could have made this a nightmare for me because it's his team and his sport, but he's done everything possible to make it a positive experience, including lying about being my sibling.

"Let's hope so," I reply vaguely, because I can't spill Ann's news. "So why are you calling from the road? I know it's not the usual reasons, like some puck bunny put your dick on the internet."

He huffs his frustration into the phone. "For fuck's sake, Dixie, that happened once. Let it go."

I laugh lightly and he huffs again. "Have you checked in on everyone yet? I want to know how the first day in the new place is going. I would bug Zoey to head over there and check on them, but it's her day off, and I just want her to rest and take care of my boy."

"Girl," I correct him, even though I have no idea, but it's too much fun to annoy him. "I will go over there when I'm done here. I'll text you with intel. I'm sure they're doing fine."

I'm hoping that some alone time with my family will get my mind off Eli.

"I texted Sadie last night, and she said Dad went to bed early because he's getting a cold," Jude says. "If they need a doctor, I've had all his records transferred to one our team doctor suggested who is supposed to be the best neurologist in the city. Mom has her name and number."

"I'm sure it's nothing to worry about," I say, trying to calm him down. The one downside to having Dad here is that Jude is going to make himself even sicker than he already does with worry. "But email me the contact info too."

"Will do." Jude pauses and then adds, almost reluctantly, "Is it too much to ask you to check on Zoey too? I just worry being so far away. But don't tell her I sent you. She'll hate that."

The ache in my heart over Eli is temporarily replaced by a warm, fuzzy feeling over my brother, the manwhore-turned-lovesick-about-to-be-dad. "Don't worry, Zoey will never know."

"Thanks," he says gratefully. "You're my favorite youngest sister."

I laugh. "I love you, Jude." I never say that to him. Like hardly ever, but I'm feeling weak and vulnerable.

"Love you too, Dix."

I end the call and am turning around to check my open inbox on my computer to see if Ann has responded when something catches my eye. Trish is standing by the door staring at me. I'm so startled I jump and nearly fall off my chair. Gripping my desk with one hand and my chest with the other, I gasp. "Hey! Jesus, I had no idea you were here."

"And I had no idea you'd be here," she replies with a big smile as she walks toward her own desk.

"What are you doing in on a Sunday?" I ask.

"I heard about Noah and that they're bringing up Elijah Casco, and I wanted to get a jump on the press box requests," she explains. "You know it's going to be through the roof for the first home game."

I nod. Right. Trish is in charge of assigning press box seats.

"I take my job very seriously," she adds.

Okay, that was a weird declaration. I try not to frown. "I'm here helping Ann with the press release."

I feel like I need to explain that to her so she knows I take my job seriously too and I'm not just here stealing staplers or something. She smiles her typical smile that is so big it looks fake. "That's great."

She gives me one last smile and turns to her computer.

I wish I knew why I find it so hard to hang out with her. I try not to sigh as I check my email. Ann responded that my release is good to go, so I spend the next fifteen minutes uploading it to the press section of our website, then grab my bag and stand up. "See you tomorrow, Trish. Don't work too hard."

She smiles. "Yeah. You have a great night, Dixie."

I wave, overenthusiastically like she would to me, and I'm out the door before she can respond.

Sadie buzzes me into my parents' new place, and as soon as I walk in the front door my mom hands me a key. "Use this whenever. Also, we have a pull-out couch in the living room, and we can put another bed in Sadie's room if you'd like."

"Make it Winnie's room!" Sadie calls out, wandering down the hall toward the kitchen.

"I don't need a bed. The pull-out is fine," I promise and hug my mom, taking the key and slipping it onto my key ring. "I probably won't spend the night anyway."

"Is that Little D?" I hear my dad call out. I smile. The older I got, the more I disliked the nickname for a multitude of reasons, including the fact that I really was the littlest in the family, in age and height and weight, and also because it felt like it kept me in the baby zone and no one would ever think of me as an adult. I never told him that and now I never will. He can call me whatever he wants. I'm just grateful I still get to hear the sound of his voice.

I follow the sound down the hall to the den, where he's watching hockey on the biggest TV I've ever seen. Jude must have bought that, because their TV in the family room in the Toronto house was half this size. This TV is even bigger than Jude's.

He's in his wheelchair with his feet up on the tufted ottoman coffee table in front of him. He's got a mahogany TV tray next to him that I recognize from my childhood, with a big green smoothie beside him. I smile. My dad would never be drinking that if he weren't sick. Now he lets Jude talk him into all kinds of weird health foods, and he doesn't complain at all. I throw myself dramatically on the couch to his left, sprawling out across it. He smiles. "What have you been up to today that has you so wiped out?"

"Just work," I explain. "They asked me to write the press release for Elijah Casco's call-up, and the press requests are blowing up my inbox."

I see the pride in my dad's face I heard in Jude's voice and it makes me smile. "My Little D is a PR rock star," he says and winks. "I bet the Thunder needs you even more than they need Jude."

I laugh. "Please tell Jude that. And make sure I'm there and my camera is ready to catch his reaction."

Dad chuckles at that, his blue eyes glancing back to the screen. He lifts his right hand and points at the game. I look over. I think it's Brooklyn versus Seattle. "These games get so much hype, the Barons versus the Winterhawks, because the Garrison brothers play each other. I assume the hype about Eli and Levi being on the same team is just as big."

"It is." I nod and take a deep breath. "It's a lot of pressure for Elijah."

"Levi is tough. I haven't met the kid brother yet, but if he can bounce back from that neck injury, he's got to be tough too," my dad says.

"He's not quite the player he was before the injury," I reply softly because I hate admitting it. It's like his struggles are mine. "Not yet."

"He got back in that net after an injury that could have cost him his life," my dad says, his voice serious. "That alone makes him a tougher player than half the guys out there."

I smile and file that nugget of wisdom away in my brain to tell Elijah later if he needs a pep talk. Maybe I can give it to Jude to tell him, because I probably shouldn't be giving Eli pep talks, or talking to him at all unless it's work related, now.

Dad coughs. It's deep and wet. I sit up in concern as Sadie wanders into the room, eating a bowl of cereal in her pajamas. Our eyes meet as the last of Dad's cough rattles out of him. Sadie chomps quickly and swallows down a mouthful of Cinnamon Toast Crunch. "Daddy, is the cough getting worse?"

"I don't think so," he replies, eyes focused back on the game on the TV. "Jesus, that Deveau kid is a hell of a defenseman."

Sadie looks back at me. "I think we're going to swing by the doctor tomorrow, Dad. Just in case."

He sighs loudly but doesn't argue. I know he loathes doctors, and he's had them up in his face for over two years now. I lean forward and drop my hand over his. "Humor us, Dad."

He grimaces. "Fine."

Sadie swallows the last of her cereal and then yawns before tipping the bowl to drink the remaining milk. "Are you just waking up?" I ask.

She nods. "I woke up when you buzzed. Winnie's still asleep. We went to a wine bar last night to celebrate the move. We called you to join, but you didn't answer."

Right. I didn't.

"Figured you were with the boy again," Sadie says right in front of Dad.

He pulls his eyes from the game and looks at me with a smile. "There's a boy?"

I groan and throw Sadie a vicious glare before turning to my dad. "No boy."

"Sadie doesn't lie, Little D, and so if she says there's a boy…" He lets his sentence fade, and when I just shake my head no, he continues, "What are you embarrassed to tell me? Why? You don't think I'll approve? Is he like my age or something?"

"Ha!" I squawk and grin. "God no."

"Good. Guys my age that hit on girls your age are all pervs," my dad announces, and I can't stop cringing inwardly over the slight slur to his words. "So why won't you tell me about him?"

"Because it's not anything," I promise. "It was over before it began."

My dad seems to ponder that a moment, and then he gives me a wistful smile. "Okay, Dixie, if you say so. But I worry about you. You work so hard, but there's more to life than the office, honey."

"I know," I say. "But I'm focusing on my career right now. Besides, women have to work twice as hard as men to move up the corporate ladder just as fast."

"Just don't forget to enjoy life, Little D." He pats my hand and goes back to watching the game. I stand up and stretch, leaving my bag on the couch. "I'm going to grab some of that cereal Sadie has."

As I walk out of the room, I grab my sister by the arm and drag her out with me. Before I can even yell at her, Sadie says, "I'm sorry! I'm a little hung over. I wasn't thinking. I shouldn't have brought him up in front of Dad."

"What if he brings up the mystery boy in front of Jude?" I snap and tuck my hair behind my ears as we enter the kitchen. "Jude won't let it go until he figures out who it is."

"Don't worry, Dad knows better than to say something in front of Jude," Sadie says and goes over to the sink to rinse her bowl. "You know he just wants to feel like you've got someone to take care of you."

"Jesus, what is this, 1842?" I gripe and open the cabinets, looking for a bowl and cereal since I have no idea where anything is in this house. "I can take care of me. He doesn't hound you like that about men."

"I'm not his Little D," Sadie responds, and when I turn to glare at her again she laughs. "Dix, you are his baby. And you were a sick baby. He's always going to want to have someone looking out for you. Deal."

"I wasn't sick. I was a preemie." I always have to correct everyone in the family. "I just needed more time to cook."

"The preemie thing had them coddling you to begin with, but then you had to turn out the most like Jude, who he adores." Sadie rolls her eyes in jest.

"I'm nothing like Jude."

She laughs. "You two not only look alike, you're both insanely driven, unbelievably hardheaded and could tie for gold in the sarcasm Olympics."

Sick of watching me hunt for the bowls, she turns and opens a cabinet next to the sink and hands me one. Then she points to what looks like a door to another room. "Pantry. Walk-in."

I walk over and open it. Wow, it's already fully stocked. I grab the Lucky Charms instead of the Cinnamon Toast Crunch and pour a heaping bowl full. When I step out of the pantry Sadie already has the milk in her hand. "So, were you with the goalie last night or what?"

"Shh!" I command and sigh before taking a mouthful of cereal. "Yes. I was. But I won't be again. They called him up."

"Already? Really?" She looks appalled. It's kind of hysterical. "Did you at least get to orgasm again?"

"Yes. Four times." I chew and swallow another spoonful of cereal. "Four glorious times."

Sadie looks skeptical. "And now you're both going to walk away? From all those free and easy orgasms. Just like that?"

"Yup," I reply flatly. "He needs to focus on his career, and I need to work on getting the promotion."

"Okay," Sadie says slowly, running a hand through her tangled bedhead. "I trust you know what's best for you, Dix. I guess."

"Thanks," I reply and finish my cereal. I glance at my watch. It's almost three in the afternoon. I should get going and check on Zoey. I rinse my bowl and hand it to Sadie, because Jude or whoever designed this kitchen gave the dishwasher a front panel that matches the cabinets, and I'm not about to hunt around to try to figure out where it is.

"And even if you're as big an idiot as Jude, he eventually figured it out, and you will too," Sadie adds as she pulls down the dishwasher door next to the sink. "Or die alone with a lot of cats."

"I'm allergic to cats," I remind her.

"Then let's hope you figure it out."

I flip her the bird over my shoulder as I walk out of the kitchen. I head back into the den, grab my purse off the couch next to where my mom is now sitting and kiss my dad on the cheek. "I'll be back for dinner. I'm just heading over to see Zoey."

"Invite her too, baby," my mom says. "I made a giant lasagna. Just need to pop it in the oven."

"I'll invite her," I promise.

"Oh, and your phone rang. A Bieber tune," my dad tells me, and I want to laugh at the fact he knows what a Justin Bieber song sounds like, but that ringtone is just for Elijah.

"Thanks," I say and head down the hall and out the door. As I wait for the elevator I look at my phone. Sure enough I have one missed call from Eli. My heart flutters and aches at the same time, especially when I see he left a voicemail.

The whole ride down in the elevator I vacillate on whether I should listen to the message. But I can't not. So as I step outside I hit the button to listen to my voicemail.

"Hey." His voice is low and extra scratchy and deep, and hearing it makes me feel good. "I'm in Vancouver. I have a flight to Quebec City in half an hour. I'd say call me back but I know you won't. I get it. I don't even know why I'm calling except to let you know it's going to be hard to pretend I don't think you're the most incredibly sexy and amazing woman out there. You've left one hell of an impression on me, sweet Dixie, even if I'm not allowed to act like it. See you in a few days when we get back from the road trip."

I'm filled with such a light, airy happiness I feel like I could float. It's the worst possible reaction because we're still doomed. Our flame was extinguished before it even got to glow. But damn, I can still feel its warmth, and it's nice to know he can too.

13

ELIJAH

Eli leads us out!" Levi calls out to the team as we make our way down the tunnel toward the awaiting ice.

I know what they're doing. I've dreamed about it my entire life. A new player always leads the team onto the ice for his first game, only the team doesn't follow right away. They let the player skate out there by himself for a lap or two. It's tradition and a rite of passage. The announcer hollers out our team name and I step onto the ice. I can't contain the grin on my face. I skate a circle slowly around our side of the ice, all by myself, and look up at the stands. There are more than a few Thunder jerseys lining the glass even though it's the Royales' arena. They're clapping wildly and slapping the glass. I make sure to skate along the boards, smiling at all of them.

This is it. I fucking did it.

I turn, expecting to see the rest of the team skating onto the ice, but only Levi steps through the gate. The crowd roars and I know they've singled us out on the jumbotron. He skates right up to me as I stop in the crease in front of the net. He taps his helmet to mine and I can see that his dark brown eyes are more watery than normal. "Kill it, Eli."

He skates away and the rest of the team floods the ice. Warm-up is great. They pepper me with pucks and I stop almost all of them. I'm feeling incredible, completely on my game. It helps that on the bus on the way here from the hotel Dixie texted me. Just three words. Go Eli Go! Knowing she's supporting me gives me a jolt of serenity when chaos has been creeping in. Now adrenaline is pumping through my body and so is confidence. I'm ready. I'm hungry. Let's do this.

The first period goes okay. Not great. I stop six shots but let one in. So does the Royales goalie, though, eight minutes after me, so we're tied. We're halfway through the second and my adrenaline has turned to nerves and I have no idea why. It's supposed to get easier, not harder. I can't stop a wrister from one of the Royales defensemen who stole the puck from Duncan Darby a foot from my net. It slides right through my five hole.

Not a big deal, I remind myself. No one gets a shutout on his debut. I didn't expect to, even though I wanted to. It's not a weak goal. It's not a reflection on me…but it feels that way. And now we're down by one again.

The game starts to get more aggressive. There's a fight, and both guys are given penalties so we're four-on-four and the face-off is just to the left of me. We don't win it and someone takes a shot on me. I block it but don't get the rebound. There's two guys in front of me—one of the Royales trying to block my view and Duncan Darby trying to shove the Royale out of my way. I can't see the puck. I frantically dart my head around trying to catch a glimpse of the play. Duncan and the Royale are spearing and cross-checking the heck out of each other. I hear a stick slap the puck. Duncan shoves the guy in front of me, hard. He starts to fall back, grabbing Duncan's jersey to take him with him.

It's a mass of limbs and jerseys, and I can't take my eyes off their stumbling feet. My attention is riveted to the gleam of their skate blades. They're less than a foot from me, and as the two fall their feet fly up and I finally move—sideways, away from them and away from the puck sailing over my left shoulder and into the net. I never even saw it coming.

The goal buzzer rips through the arena, rattling me even further, as if that was fucking possible. Braddock skates by. "Shake it off," he commands.

Levi is staring at me from center ice. I can feel it, and when I look up, even though he's too far away for me to make out his features, I can feel the concern radiating off him. It's not helping. I don't know what the fuck will settle me, but that's not it.

Six minutes later they score again on a tip I should have caught, and then, when they do it again not even thirty seconds later, I see Coach Schneider point to Rollins and he gets up from his perch on the bench. I'm being pulled from the game.

I don't talk to anyone between second and third periods. I keep my eyes glued to a chunk of black tape stuck to the matte gray floor between my skates. No one talks to me either. No one is really talking to anyone. The mood is dark and the coach's speech is short. "Get it done. We are better than them. Prove it."

Eddie lets in two more goals in the third and we only score one more. We lose to a team that's not even in playoff contention. I'm the first to make it into the locker room, and I have to use every ounce of frayed restraint I have not to hurl my equipment to the ground as I take it off. I don't get to throw a tantrum. I haven't earned it. I haven't earned anything.

The coach enters the locker room as we start to undress. "We won back-to-back Cups, and if we want to win one more and have three in four years we need to not do this again. It's dynasty or fluke. Take your pick."

"Dynasty," Levi replies firmly. A bunch of other guys repeat the word too. I say nothing, but I nod.

Coach walks toward the door but turns back. "The PR department shortened the media scrum tonight. It'll be five minutes and only five reporters." He looks at me. "Heads up high. Answers positive. This too shall pass if you want it to."

He leaves and two minutes later, as I pull off my jersey, the reporters file in and head straight to me. I grab my gray team hoodie. Lots of guys give interviews half naked, but I'm already feeling too exposed, so I throw it on, leaving it unzipped but pulling the hood up. I sit on the bench as they form a semicircle around me and start peppering me with questions. Stuff like: Was it nerves? What threw me off my game? How did I plan to improve? Did I think I should start the next game? What did it feel like to play with my brother professionally for the first time?

I answered everything with the most positive spin I could muster. I did have some nerves but it's no excuse. I need to be better. Nothing threw me off my game. I'm just adjusting and I need to do it faster. And I will. They're lies but the reporters seem to believe me. The only thing I don't lie about is playing with my brother. I look at the NHL Network reporter and say, "It's a dream come true."

"Just gotta work on that nightmare ending, buddy," Eddie pipes in with a cool smile and slaps my back as he comes to sit beside me. It's not even his fucking spot. He just wants to get the reporters' attention, which he does. I don't give a shit. I don't want to talk to them anymore anyway, so when they turn to him I finish unlacing my skates, stand up and walk to the other part of the room, by the showers, to finish undressing there.

I head into the showers, the water on cool because I'm trying to dull the hot sting of humiliation coursing through me. I just want to get on the plane, take a seat at the back by myself, throw in my earbuds and ignore the world. We're headed to Toronto tonight for a game tomorrow night. Then Michigan and then home, where we'll be three days off before our first home game back.

When we get on the plane, I slip into the last row, put in my earbuds and stare out the window. No one sits next to me because I'm pretty sure they realize my shitty mood is taking up the whole row. But twenty minutes into the flight, Levi drops down beside me. I pretend not to notice, my eyes still glued to the black abyss outside my window. He hands me a pack of Reese's Pieces he must've grabbed from the snack bin they keep stocked for us in the galley. They've been my favorite candy since I was six. I take them without meeting his eye. "Thanks."

"I know it's cliché and fucking annoying as all hell, but you have to shake it off," he says in a low, calm voice.

I turn to him and give him an Oscar-worthy smile. "I know. I'm good. I just wish my off game didn't have to be tonight."

"Was it nerves?" he asks. "I remember my first game I was so nervous I thought I was going to piss myself the entire first period, and I almost did the first time I got the puck."

I smirk at that. "I wish you had so we could make adult diapers a standard part of your gear," I joke. He laughs and flips me the bird at the same time. "And I wasn't that nervous."

"So was it the injury?"

I try not to grit my teeth and ask him in a clearly confused tone, "What injury?"

"The neck," he says, frowning because he has no idea why he needs to elaborate.

"Why would I suddenly get antsy about something that happened a billion years ago?" I ask him and shake my head before giving him another easygoing grin. "It was an off game. One of those days where nothing goes right no matter how hard you try. We all have them. Remember that game last season where you scored on your own net?"

His dark eyes get darker. "I accidentally deflected the puck toward Noah. Total fluke."

"Yeah. I have the clip of it on my phone if you want to see it again." I laugh as he scowls. "Anyway, that's my point. This game was a total fluke for me too. And like you said, I will shake it off and move on."

"Okay." He's not convinced and he's not even trying to hide it. He scratches the back of his head and leans forward. "Well, if it's not a fluke, then you need to figure out what it is. And honestly, Eli, as your captain, I have to tell you, you don't get a lot of time before they'll write you off."

"The team?"

"The team, the fans, the league," he says and sighs. "Everyone."

The league isn't forgiving. And it's even harder on goalies. I know this, but hearing Levi say it makes the reality feel even heavier. I stare at the unopened Reese's Pieces bag. Levi nudges me. "What can I do? Do you want to talk about it? To me or someone else? Do you want me to practice with you one on one?"

I shake my head. "I don't need help. I'll be fine. I'll be great. I promise."

"Eli…"

I finally look up. I know my face is still pink with shame and now it's turning red because of anger. Not at him, at my life. "I know you want to make this into a big deal for some reason, but you need to stop. It was a bad day. The end. And I can't shake it the fuck off if you won't let it go."

"Okay." He backs off instantly and without offense. I tear open the Reese's Pieces, pop a handful into my mouth, then offer him the bag. He takes some, which is surprising because he's such a health nut during the season. "Okay, well, your brother will back off, but your captain can't."

I grit my teeth for a second but I nod. "So, Captain, what do you suggest I do?"

"Focus," he replies, swallowing the Reese's Pieces. "It's not a bullshit word. You have to live, breathe, eat hockey and only hockey. No distractions. No women. No booze. No nothing. If it's your entire life you'll fix it because living in the failure will be unbearable. Because you're not a failure, Elijah."

Then he stands up and strides down the plane aisle to his seat next to Jude near the front.

I don't know if he's right, but it's worth a try. That means cutting out Dixie. Completely. I've been thinking about her nonstop since I left her, fantasizing about ways to get her to break the rules and start seeing me anyway. If Levi is right, then I need to stop doing that. Not only do I need to stop thinking about her, I need to avoid her when I get back to San Fran instead of finding ways to run into her, which is what I was planning on doing. The thought is uncomfortable and even painful, but I will do anything to make this work. I've risked my life for this career. I've alienated my parents. I've given up my education. I have to try anything to make it work.

14

DIXIE

I walk into the office just before eight, which is early, but Ann requested I get here before the normal nine o'clock start time. I assume it's because she knows there's going to be a ton of media requesting locker room interviews for the game tomorrow night and she wants to make sure I get an early start. The Thunder again last night in Michigan. Elijah started again and he was pulled again. I have to get official confirmation from the coach when he comes in today, but I know Eli isn't starting the game tomorrow night.

I watched both games Eli played, my eyes riveted to the screen like I was watching a train wreck. And my heart ached for him. But both games I saw the point where it happened—where he froze up. Being obsessed with him has paid off. I watched a lot of his game videos from his college website and I know how he moves—intimately. The way he controls his limbs. Despite being six foot four and as wide as a brick wall, Elijah Casco moves like a panther on and off the ice—slow, methodic, sure. He started both games like that, you could see it, even under the pads. But in both games, after a serious scuffle in front of his net, everything changed. His motion became spastic, his reflexes delayed. It's subtle, but if you know him you see it. I can only hope someone else noticed it too, like the goalie coach or even Levi, and brings it up to him. I don't think he's aware of the change, but if he knows about it I know he'll figure out why, like I have. It's the accident. The jostling in front of his net, the players falling and the skates flying, is pushing him back to that incident.

The team flew back late last night, but they don't have practice today. I'm dying to see Eli again. I know we can't interact, at least not the way my heart and body want, but I feel like just laying eyes on him will bring some relief to that ache I have for him. And of course, the other side of me, the rational one, knows it's for the best he's not here. Seeing him and not touching him, having to pretend he's just another rookie on the team, is going to be brutal. Also, there's this weird vibe in the office this week, and I don't need to add to it.

Yesterday everyone was running around in closed-door meetings, which I couldn't find on our shared Google calendar, so I know they were unplanned. What I don't know is what they were about. I hope it wasn't Elijah.

I drop my coat on the back of my chair and put my latte and my breakfast burrito down on the desk. I swung by my parents' this morning instead of Jude's, figuring he needed alone time with Zoey. Mom was making her amazing breakfast burritos and made one for me. I haven't had one since this summer when I visited them in Toronto, and they're my favorite thing in the universe. I'm about to sit down and savor my last bite when I notice Trish's jacket is also on her chair. I pop the last of the burrito into my mouth and look over to Nadine's desk. Her jacket is there too. But where are they?

Mr. Carling walks in as I'm swallowing the last of my mom's culinary masterpiece. He sees me and smiles. "Morning, Dixie. Everyone else is in the conference room already," he says with a smile, even though that fact leaves me nervous. Why am I not there too? They told me eight thirty. He walks briskly to his closed office door. "Just let me dump my coat and we can walk there together."

"Sure thing," I say calmly, but I'm anything but. Something is up, and I don't know what it is. I hate not knowing things. It causes my mind to run a million miles an hour in the worst possible direction.

I stand, shove my purse in my desk, and grab my phone and slip it into my pocket before taking a notepad and pen. He comes out of his office in just his dress shirt, having removed his suit jacket too. I scoot around my desk and slip through the door with a grateful smile as he holds it open. He falls in line beside me as we walk down the hall toward the elevator bank. The conference room is a floor below us at the other end of the building, the side attached to the arena, and it has a glass wall that actually overlooks the ice.

"I'm sorry about Noah," I tell him. Noah, the goalie Eli was called up to replace, is Mr. Carling's son.

"Thanks. He'll be great after the surgery and recovery. It's frustrating for him, but this is better than playing injured and risking the rest of his career," Mr. Carling explains. He himself was a player and had a lengthy successful career, so he knows injuries and time off are part of the game. I'm walking faster than normal, and Mr.

Carling pats my shoulder. "Relax. We're not late. I asked Ann to bring everyone to the conference room early because I needed to talk to you alone."

"Okay. That doesn't help me relax," I admit lightly but inside my nerves have escalated to almost a panic-attack-inducing level. What the hell is going on?

"Ann is leaving," Mr. Carling tells me. "I'm going to announce it now, which is why I had the whole team come in early."

"Oh wow!" I say, drawing on my high school drama class skills.

"Yes. I'm happy for her career, but it'll be a real loss here, as I know you know," he continues as we reach the elevators and he punches the Up button. "Luckily she hired some great people to keep the ship going while we interview for her replacement."

I nod and smile because I'm one of the people she hired. He smiles back, and it gives me confidence. But then, as we step into the elevator and the doors slide closed, he clears his throat and says, "Dixie, someone went to HR yesterday and told them you're seeing a player."

Everything in my heart plummets so quickly I have a moment of dizziness. I subtly reach out and grab the railing. He's smiling. Why is he still smiling? Is he going to be happy about firing me? Oh my God, my career is over. No hockey team will ever hire me after this. My dad is going to be so disappointed. I'm humiliated. And what will this do to Eli? Will they send him back to the Storm?

"We protect whistleblowers, as you know, so I can't tell you who it was. But we know it's a false claim," he explains calmly as the elevator doors swish open, bringing air back into the elevator that had suddenly felt suffocating a moment ago.

We both step into the hall, but my legs feel shaky. "How do you know it's false?"

He chuckles. "Because we know you would never do that. You're one of our most dedicated employees." He smiles again and adds, "And the person they think you're romantically involved with is Jude."

"What?!" I say that way too loud and instantly cover my mouth. "I'm sorry."

He chuckles again. "It's fine. I understand why that would be horrifying to you. And of course we had to explain to this employee why it's a false claim. The fact is we have a strict policy against fraternization with the team, and if we weren't going to fire you immediately the person had to be told the truth."

My heart plummets again. "So this person knows I'm Jude's sister?"

He nods and smiles reassuringly. "We knew this day would come eventually. I'm actually shocked that we kept it in the bag this long."

"I just...I don't want this to affect my role or any future role I might have with the organization," I tell him, which I know he already knows because it's what I told him when he offered me the internship in the beginning and I had to give him my real last name.

"It hasn't and it won't," he assures me as we reach the doors to the conference room. "We're not making any kind of announcement or anything, but you can start using your last name if you'd like."

"No. I'll stick with Wynn," I say quickly. This person knows, but that doesn't mean I want everyone else to know. Others might find out eventually, but it won't be with my help. I like my anonymity. I really want to know who knows. And I know they did what was expected of them, telling on me, but at the same time I feel betrayed. They should have just talked to me and I could have explained it myself. It feels like whoever did this has it out for me.

He opens the conference room door and I thank him and step inside. The whole PR team is there. My eyes scan everyone—Nadine, Ann, the two guys Ron and Dave who work with our corporate sponsors, and Trish. As soon as my eyes land on her face, she immediately looks away and I know it's her. And then a light bulb goes off. Sunday when she showed up at work, she must have heard me on the phone making plans with Jude. And I told him I loved him.

I feel a wave of animosity toward her, but I fight to push it down. She did what she was supposed to do. I need to not blame her for this, but I'm definitely not going to go out of my way anymore to force myself to like her. She's one hundred percent just a co-worker and not someone I need to bond with. I walk around the table and sit next to Nadine, away from Trish.

Mr. Carling announces Ann's departure and that her last day will be at the end of the month. In that time she's going to help select her successor. He goes on to say he encourages applications from within. Ann subtly glances over to me when he says that. I don't react externally, but my heart beats harder.

"Okay, let's get back to work," Mr. Carling says. "Elijah Casco is the big topic of the day for obvious reasons, but we also have the NHL Network here doing promos. It was a last-minute request we're honoring. Dixie, can I ask you to escort them around? I'll email you the list of who they'll film."

"Sure." I nod.

"I can help too if you'd like," Trish pipes up.

Mr. Carling doesn't even blink. "That's okay, Trish. We're going to need you to handle the media requests while Dixie works on this."

"Oh. Okay. Sure thing!" She sounds chipper and she's wearing a helpful smile, but her arms are crossed and her shoulders are rigid. If anyone else notices, they don't react.

We all stand and start out the door. I'm grateful I don't have to go back to my desk right now. I'm still filled with anxiety and feeling antsy. Walking around and guiding this TV crew will be good for me.

Everyone gets on the elevator going up to our floor, but I wait for the other one going down and then make my way down the hall that leads to the arena. I swipe my pass card, which is dangling on a lanyard around my neck, and enter the arena. Just as I knew they would be, the halls are empty. Not even the coaching staff comes in on the day after a long road trip.

My heels click down the curved concrete hallway that circles the arena. My phone bings and I pull it out. It's an email from Ann with the details of who and what the network wants to film. Apparently they're doing new promos for the team and some players are coming in to be filmed. As my eyes run down the names listed on the email I start to hear muffled voices coming from just up the hall, in the team dressing room. Levi Casco. Jude Braddock. Duncan Darby. And…

Elijah Casco.

15

DIXIE

Fuck," I mutter under my breath as my heart starts slamming against my rib cage and my anxiety levels peak again.

"Potty mouth at work?" I hear my brother's voice and snap my head up from my phone to see him standing in the doorway to the locker room. "Classy, Dix."

"Sorry." I clear my throat and shove my phone in the pocket of my blazer. "I need to go meet the crew. Welcome back."

I brush past him without looking inside the room because Eli is in there. I need a minute to make sure my game face is in place before we make eye contact. If I looked at him right now, with no time to prepare my poker face, I'm pretty sure everyone would be able to see the desire in my eyes and know that I've seen him naked.

"No quip about how it's a miracle I'm here early?" he calls out after me. "No barb about our losing streak?"

I don't answer him. I just pick up my pace. Man, today is turning into a clusterfuck.

The NHL Network crew is at the door chatting with the security guard when I get there. I've worked with the producer before and it's gone great, so I can only hope today will be the same. I lead her, the camera guy and the lighting guy, who is pulling a dolly full of equipment, back the way I came. The producer, Celine, hands me her shot list. It's pretty straightforward. The guys will take some shots on the ice in their uniforms and pose together for a few stills. This is the stuff the network plays to promote games or in between periods as filler. I'm guessing the need for new footage has to do with Eli being called up for the rest of the season.

The door to the locker room is visible again. He's in there. I know it. I can feel him. The anticipation of seeing him again creates a tingle down my spine. My brain may know it's over, for now, but my body clearly didn't get the memo.

I point down the hall. "You guys can get set up on the ice, and I will make sure the guys are ready. Who do you want first?"

"Darby would be a good start," Celine responds and continues toward the tunnel to the ice.

I take a deep breath and step into the locker room, shielding my eyes with my hand. "Are we all decent?"

There's a mix of affirmative answers so I uncover my eyes. Levi looks amused, Darby looks baffled, Jude looks concerned and Eli looks goddamn beautiful. He's hunched over wearing his goalie pants and a gunmetal-gray Under Armour shirt. He's looking up at me with those dark green eyes through his thick, almost black lashes. His expression is hard and tense, but it softens as soon as our eyes connect. I look away—I have to—and move my focus to Duncan. "They'll take you as soon as you're ready, Duncan," I say.

"Honey, I was born ready," Duncan proclaims. He finishes tying his skate and stands, grabbing his stick and winking at me on his way out the door.

"The rest of you can make your way over to the ice once you're geared up," I explain and turn to leave.

"What's wrong with you?" Jude asks, stopping me in my tracks.

I turn back to face him and nervously push my hair back. "Nothing. Why?"

"I don't know…" Jude cocks his head and his eyes sweep over me. "You're acting weird."

"No, I'm not."

He gives me one of his cocky grins. "You have never covered your eyes coming in here before. You've just barged right in."

"Yeah, well, I've decided if I want to see your penis, I'll Google it," I reply tartly and Levi laughs. I don't hear a sound from Eli's corner of the room, and I don't look over to gauge his reaction.

"There's the Dixie we're used to being horrified by," Jude announces and acts relieved. I smirk.

"Get dressed and get out there, please." I turn and walk down the hall toward the ice.

The crew set up quickly and are already positioning Duncan for the shoot. I lean against the boards and watch. Levi and Jude join me a few minutes later. Celine goes through her list with speed and accuracy. Levi and Jude do some drills, taking slap shots and posing as requested. I keep glancing behind me, waiting for Elijah to show up.

"Okay, now let's get some footage of Levi taking shots on Eli," Celine announces and looks at me.

"I'm sure he'll be here shortly," I reply and glance behind me again.

"Go yell at him like you do at us every time we're late," Jude suggests.

"Levi, do you know what's taking him so long?" I ask, ignoring my brother completely.

"No idea." Levi shrugs. "Probably his hair. It's high maintenance."

Everyone laughs except me. Jude is looking at me with that confused head tilt. My brother is too good at reading people. I force myself to sigh, like I would if I was annoyed with any of the players for being late, and I make my way back to the locker room.

Elijah has his back to me, pulling his jersey over his chest protector. I watch silently as he picks up his neck protector and stares at it. I clear my throat. His head snaps up, but his eyes cloud over even more when he sees me. "They need me?"

I nod. "They want Levi to take some shots on you."

He nods. "Of course. They want to see me make him look like a rookie. I can do that."

He's chipper and his snarky comment is definitely typical Eli, but for some reason I feel like something's off. "Are you okay?"

He looks up, and there's a blankness in his eyes. "I'm great."

He's looking at me like I'm nothing more than a Thunder employee...and it almost knocks the wind out of me, which makes me a hypocrite because it's exactly what I told him to do. I take a step back and struggle to fill my lungs, but I keep my shoulders back and my eyes squarely on him, refusing to admit it.

"Let's go," he says swiftly and marches past me.

Holy shit. He's doing exactly what he should do, so why do I feel so hurt right now?

I try to look unruffled as I watch the rest of the shoot. Levi and Jude both take shots on Elijah, who blocks them effortlessly. Celine gets more footage of each of them skating and stopping and of Elijah scuffing up his crease, as goalies do, and then they start with the still photographs. Just when I think they'll wrap up, the cameraman picks up his camera again and Celine turns to Elijah. "So any thoughts you want to share on how things are going so far?"

Oh no. Just fucking no. "This isn't an interview, Celine," I warn her and step onto the ice.

"I know, I just wanted a little quote from the newest NHL goalie," Celine says breezily, blowing me off completely. She turns back to Eli. "Are you starting tomorrow night, and if you are, are you ready for the pressure of playing in the home arena of two-time back-to-back Stanley Cup champs? These fans are unforgiving."

"Okay!" My voice is hard and loud. "Thanks for coming out! That's a wrap, guys."

Eli glares at me. Levi skates forward and turns so I can't see his face. He must say or do something because Eli instantly looks away from me and his expression softens. He pulls off his mask and turns to face Celine with a much warmer look than he gave me. "I'm ready for whatever role the coach gives me. I don't want forgiveness from the fans. I fully intend to earn their adoration."

Everyone smiles at his charmingly cocky answer. Hell, even the cameraman looks enamored. I clap my hands once to get everyone's attention. "Okay! That's a wrap!"

Celine and the crew start to pack their things. Twenty minutes later they're leaving the building and my phone buzzes. It's a text from Jude.

Need to talk.

I text him back a fine and force myself to walk toward the locker room again. God, I hope everyone else is gone. The door is closed, which is strange, but I know if I knock Jude will think I'm acting weird again so I just push it open and step inside. The main room, lined with benches and the players' stalls, is empty.

"Jude?" I call out and begin to walk toward the back, where an archway leads to the bank of sinks and beyond that, the showers. "Jude?"

Suddenly Elijah appears from the shower room. His dark hair is wet, droplets of water dripping from the tousled tips to his bare shoulders and then sliding down through his damp chest hair. He meets my gaze with a stormy expression. A hand moves to his only covering, the white towel around his waist, as if to ensure it stays on. "He's not here."

His words are clipped and so cool I almost shiver. "Oh. Do you know where he is? He wanted to talk."

"It's not my job to keep tabs on your..." He catches himself. "On Jude."

He brushes past me so quickly the air lifts my hair. I turn and watch as he stalks over to his stall and reaches up for something on the shelf. It's his underwear. He doesn't put it on. Instead, he glares at me again. He wants me to leave so he can get dressed, but right now, I don't care what he wants. I put my hands on my hips. "Did I do something?"

He huffs out a frustrated breath. "Actually, yes, you did. I can handle reporters and their asinine questions. I don't need you to protect me."

God, why is he being such a douche? Well, two can play at that game. "For the record, it's not your job to handle reporters unless I say so. I set up the interviews, and today wasn't one of them. They were trying to bend the rules, and I don't bend rules. The Thunder management doesn't either. I wasn't protecting you, I was doing my job. And it'll go down the same way next time, so you better get used to it."

His jaw is clenched, but he manages to spit out a "Fine."

"Now what else is bothering you?" I challenge.

"Can you leave so I can change, please?" His tone is so cold and he looks so uncomfortable right now just because I'm in here with him.

"I've had what's under that towel in my mouth, so stop treating me like I'm an awkward virgin," I snap. God, I hope his brother and Duncan have already left. I didn't ask.

"Then stop acting that way," Eli snaps. "Because if you're going to keep walking in here covering your eyes and turning seven shades of pink, someone is going to figure out that you know what's under this towel and you like it."

My eyes drop like they're bungee jumping—straight down to the bulge under his towel. Forcing my eyes up to his face is as hard as lifting a hundred-pound weight. He must see that, because he swallows hard and softens his tone just a little. "Look, you can't have it both ways. You want to pretend this didn't happen? Then I get to treat you like you're just some incredibly hot, unbelievably uptight Thunder employee."

His words hurt. It's like he's breaking up with me, only we both agreed we aren't together. This is crazy. This is exactly why we never should have touched each other. And great, he isn't done talking. "I need to focus on my career right now anyway, just like you."

"Good." Only it doesn't feel good. But I say it anyway and then walk away, ignoring him when he calls after me to wait. I take a step into the hall and Jude is coming toward me with Duncan. They both look up as I step into their path. Duncan gives me one of his typical goofy smiles. "Hey! Are Eli and Levi still in there? I need to invite them to my party."

"Eli is," I mutter, and Duncan thanks me and wanders into the locker room.

Jude slows to a stop in front of me with that curious look on his face again that is starting to annoy the hell out of me.

"What do you want?" I demand.

"Are you going to tell me what's wrong?" he counters. "You've been acting strange all day, and now you look like you might cry. Why?"

"You're nuts. I'm fine," I reply tersely and cross my arms. "Now I need to get back to work, so what did you summon me for?"

"I just wanted to know why, when I walked by that intern Nadine a few minutes ago in the hallway, she stopped me and said"—he pauses and switches into a high-pitched voice, his impression of Nadine—"Oh my God, I don't know how I never noticed the resemblance before! Of course you and Dixie are related. You look totally alike!"

He stops his ridiculous impression and gives me a confused shrug. I sigh and shake my head. "Fuck," I groan and hang my head for a second in defeat. Of course Trish told Nadine. Obviously she's going to tell everyone. I look up at my brother. "They know."

"That you're my sister?" Jude clarifies, and I nod. "How many people know?"

"I'd guess just about everyone by now," I reply. Could this day suck any harder? "One of my co-workers went to HR because they heard me on the phone with you and thought I was sleeping with you."

Jude looks like he might vomit. He actually turns green. "That's disgusting."

"I know!" I agree wholeheartedly. "Anyway, Mr. Carling told her the truth, and I guess he didn't say to keep it under wraps so…my cover is blown."

"Oh." Jude looks at me with sympathy because he knows this is the last thing I want. He reaches out and pulls me into a hug. "It's not the end of the world. I mean, the management knew anyway. And they also know that you're awesome at your job, and it has nothing to do with the fact that your brother is the best player on the team."

I pull out of his arms. "No. I said they know I'm related to *you*, not they think I'm related to Levi."

I grin and Jude looks annoyed. "I'm trying to be a good big brother, and you're ruining it. Fabulous."

"Big brother? Who is a big brother?" I turn at the inquiry and see that Duncan and Eli are now in the hall too. I turn back to Jude, giving him a pleading look: *Please don't tell the team too.*

Jude moves his eyes from me to his teammates. "I am. To my sisters."

"Right! Your family moved to town." Duncan nods and

scratches his curly red hair. "You should invite them to my Halloween do-over party too. The more the merrier!"

"Okay. I'll invite them." Jude looks at me. "We had a road trip for Halloween, which is Duncan's favorite holiday, so he's throwing a do-over party this weekend."

"You should come, Dix," Duncan says enthusiastically.

"Thanks, but I'll pass," I say. "You guys have a blast."

I walk away, careful not to look at Eli as I go.

16

ELIJAH

You are the happiest gladiator I've ever seen," Levi tells me.

"It's a party, Levi. I'm supposed to have a good time," I reply.

"We've been here forty minutes and you've mixed cocktails for people, talked to every person in the place and just spent five minutes dancing in the living room. I feel like someone should give you a lampshade to wear on your head, Mr. Life of the Party," Jude quips, pulling up his sunglasses. He's wearing a referee outfit with sunglasses and a white cane. A blind ref. I have to admit I smiled when I saw him. His girlfriend, Zoey, is sitting on his lap wearing jeans and a white T-shirt with fake blood on it and plastic baby arms coming out of her pregnant belly.

The party is in full swing. Every player on the team is here and so are their friends and girlfriends, and everyone seems to be having a great time. I'm doing a bang-up job of pretending I'm enjoying myself too, although clearly I'm not.

I haven't talked to Dixie since the locker room five days ago. We played twice in that time, and I didn't start either game. The

Thunder lost both, but there was a sick feeling of relief that it wasn't my fault, and it superseded the feeling of humiliation at being benched. That had me toss and turn all night long. I should have been more upset that I didn't get to play than relieved by it. I'm sick of disappointing my team and myself.

I saw Dixie right after both games, directing the press for interviews. She never made eye contact with me or acknowledged my existence. This is exactly how we're supposed to act, like we barely know each other, but it sucks. Hard. And I told myself to stop thinking about her, but I can't. I still think about her all the time. I miss talking to her and texting with her, because it was so fun and easy, and nothing else is right now.

Levi stands up and reaches for his girlfriend's empty cup. She's dressed like a cat and she looks sexy and adorable. Then he turns to me. "You wanna come get drinks with me?"

I nod and stand up. Levi is dressed like Thor. It's his way of embracing his nickname, and judging by the long, sultry stares from the women in the room as we walk back toward Duncan's kitchen, it's being well received. I catch a couple women looking at me that way, but I ignore them.

"So how did your meeting with Lu Price go?" Levi asks as we enter the kitchen and make our way to the island that's covered in bottles of booze and mixers.

"Fine," I reply shortly. Lu Price is the goalie coach for the Thunder. The meeting didn't actually go fine, but I don't want to get into it tonight. I'm supposed to be having fun. I walked into the meeting jovial and upbeat, but Lu was all business and blunt. I need to improve and fast. He suggested the problem was related to my accident and that I see the team sports psychologist. I told him I would think about it. He told me to think fast and hard, and that I needed to take this more seriously—as serious as a heart attack were his exact words. Definitely not the beginning of a great working relationship.

Levi looks like he's about to keep asking me questions about it, but luckily Eddie walks over to join us. "Hey, kids!" he says happily. He's dressed like a shark attack victim. His top half is bare, except for his chest hair, which is in desperate need of grooming, and the rest of him is covered by a felt shark. Its mouth is around his waist, where's he's put fake blood.

"There is some serious talent here tonight," Eddie advises me as he leans on the island beside me and reaches for the bottle of Patron. "I figured it would be lame. Just a bunch of hockey players and their ball and chains and their ugly single friends, but there are hot chicks!"

Levi scowls at him. "Dude, you're a total pig."

"Yeah. So?"

Levi shakes his head and reaches for the vodka. Eddie just shrugs. "Hey. Did you know? You must have known."

"Know what?" Levi asks as he pours vodka into Tessa's glass and then reaches for the orange juice.

"That the hot piece of ass in the PR department is Jude's baby sister," Eddie announces, and my whole body bristles. Levi's head spins around so fast that his dark hair slides into his eyes.

He leans toward Eddie and almost growls. "Who told you that?"

"Someone else in the PR department," Eddie vaguely explains. "I guess she's been lying since she started. I mean, I know you must have known, because you grew up with Braddock."

Fuck. I know Dixie didn't want this to get out.

"It's not just me," Eddie says defensively because he can tell by our expressions that we're upset about this. "Everybody has been talking about it all week. Didn't you hear Marchie call her Baby Braddock when she brought the press in?"

He's talking about one of our defensemen, Vincent LaMarche. Levi's scowl deepens. "Is LaMarche here tonight?"

Eddie nods. "Over there by the fireplace. He's picking up a hot blonde dressed as a blind mouse."

Levi looks at me. "Bring Tess her drink for me? I have to ruin Marchie's night."

I nod. There is nothing I would rather do...except maybe call Dixie. This has to be upsetting her. I know it was really important to her to not be associated with Jude. She didn't want the team to think he got her the job, and I'm sure the nickname Baby Braddock must make her blood boil. I grab Tessa's drink and a beer out of a cooler by the island and weave my way back through the house to the living room.

I hand Tessa her drink and tell her Levi went to talk to someone. Then I take a sip of my beer before I turn to Jude and try to sound as casual as I can as I ask, "Did you know that the team found out Dixie is your sister?"

Jude frowns momentarily and stands up next to me. Zoey seems to have gone somewhere because I don't see her. "Yeah. One of Dixie's co-workers accused her of having an affair with me, so HR told this woman the truth and she told everyone."

"So did the chick get fired?" I ask because whoever did this to Dixie should have gotten fired.

"No. Dixie's secret wasn't an HR policy," Jude explains and

pushes his sunglasses up on his head again as he glances over at me. "Management doesn't care if she's related to me. Only she cares."

"The team is teasing her about it," I explain.

Jude smirks. "You don't know her well enough, but trust me, if they bust her balls long enough she'll break theirs. My sister is tougher than any guy I know."

He's right. I knew that even in the little time we were communicating and touching and everything else. Dixie is tough and brilliantly smart. Still, I know this sucks for her. I hear a bunch of people gasp and then I hear a laugh—loud and deep. It's Levi. I step around Eddie to look into the dining room, where the sound's coming from. Carla, Duncan's live-in girlfriend, is pushing her way through the crowd holding a roll of paper towels. Levi is still laughing. A girl dressed as a blind mouse in a short black skirt with a tail attached, a black crop top, big black mouse ears, sunglasses and a long white cane walks by me into the kitchen holding an empty plastic cup. Another one darts by with longer, slightly darker hair in the same outfit. She's obviously chasing the first mouse.

Levi makes his way back over and wraps an arm around Tessa. "I went over there to give Marchie hell for picking on Dixie. Turns out he was hitting on Sadie, and when she heard what I was saying about what he did to Dix she poured her drink on his head."

"Yeah, that sounds like Sadie." Jude smiles, and then he turns to me. "Dixie's not my only sister who can hold her own."

So Sadie Braddock is one of the blind mice. The other must be the other sister...Winnie, I think Dixie said. There are usually three blind mice. Is Dixie the third mouse? I glance around the room and take a few steps to get a better view of the people in the dining room. My eyes move down the hall, and I see Zoey at the foot of the stairs. She's looking up the stairs and talking to the third mouse. It's Dixie. Her back is to me, but I would recognize that petite body and that sleek blond hair anywhere. Seeing her fills me with an ache so deep it feels physically painful, and I have to move, shifting from foot to foot like I would to shake off a cramp, but of course it doesn't help. I don't know if she feels the weight of my stare, but something makes her glance over her shoulder. She's got the sunglasses from her costume on, so I can't see where she's looking, but I know it's at me. I can feel it. I'm frozen under her gaze, unable to move. Zoey says something, touching Dixie's wrist, and she finally turns away.

I continue to watch as Dixie hugs Zoey and then darts up the stairs as Zoey comes walking back into the room. Well, waddling is a more accurate description. The girl is almost as tiny as Dixie, so her frame is having trouble with that giant baby belly. Jude immediately reaches for her and helps lower her into the chair he'd been sitting on earlier.

"Dixie is in the bathroom upstairs," Zoey tells Jude. "I think she regrets letting Winnie and Sadie talk her into coming tonight. She said she was going to call a Lyft soon and head home."

I slip away and make my way down the hall and then up the stairs. I have no idea why I have to see her or what I'm going to say. All I know is she's not leaving here until I do.

17

DIXIE

I should not have let Winnie and Sadie talk me into coming. I was perfectly willing to sit at home and watch Netflix and eat Cheetos and rue the day I was born. But they resorted to guilt, saying that they'd barely seen me since they moved and they missed me. Finally Sadie said the one thing that changed my mind: "Your goalie will probably be there. I can't wait to meet him." I was terrified they'd bug Eli, and I was suddenly consumed with the need to see him in a costume. I didn't know what he would dress as, but I knew he would look amazing.

And he does. He's dressed as a gladiator in a leather-like skirt and a molded copper-colored plastic chest plate with leather cuffs on his wrists and a sword dangling absently from his left hand. His dark, thick hair is pushed back except for a piece that falls across his smooth forehead.

I noticed him almost the second he got to the party, but I made sure to watch from a distance. He was smiling, dancing and laughing and didn't seem to have a care in the world, which was the polar opposite of how I felt. It made me realize how incredibly different we really were and how doomed we probably were even if we didn't work for the same team. That made me feel hollow.

I know he knows I'm here now, and I can only imagine that he'll try to have some awkward conversation with me. Oh God, I have to get out of here. I push my sunglasses up on my head and stare at my reflection in the mirror. I grab my cane and open the door. And then I freeze as I cross the threshold. Elijah is standing there right in front of me in the dark hallway. His hair is still slightly askew and his lips are pink and his eyes are soft and sad. Basically, he's breathtaking.

He takes a step toward me. "Are you okay?"

"Yes."

"I heard everyone knows about you being a Braddock," he explains. "And that the guys are giving you a hard time."

"That's not your problem," I say softly, without venom. "I'm not your problem."

"I can't stop thinking about you," he declares suddenly in that voice that is impossibly low and incredibly rough and completely perfect. "I have to. I need to. I can't."

I feel a flood of relief at his words. It's so strong it almost feels euphoric. Without thinking about it I take a step closer to him. My free hand grips the doorframe. His eyes drop from mine and he stares at the sword in his hand. He looks desperate and defeated. This is not the guy I was watching downstairs. Suddenly I realize that must have been an act for his teammates. This Eli doesn't make me feel hollow, but he does make me ache. My fingers curl around the doorframe and my knuckles hurt with the force of my grip as I try to keep myself from reaching for him.

"I used to be good at things. Everything. Especially women and hockey," he admits in a soft voice just barely above a whisper. "Now I don't know which one I'm worse at."

"You were really good with me," I reply in a tone equally as soft and modest. "Really, really good."

His head tilts back up, his chin level and his eyes on me. He blinks. I blink.

Two blinks are all we manage before we both lose all sanity. I don't know if he kisses me or I kiss him, but we're kissing. His hands are in my hair and mine are in his and that stupid plastic costume slams into my chest as my ass hits the counter in the bathroom. I push back until his ass hits the wall beside the door. His hands move from my hair to the front of my costume—over my breasts and down my sides and around to my ass, which he grabs and uses to push me into him.

I hate his fucking costume. I can't touch any skin on his upper body except his arms. I cling to his biceps and let him hook the back of my knee and hitch me up so his hard-on fits solidly into the cleft between my legs. He pushes me back against the counter again. I wrap an arm around his neck and reach between us with the other. I want to get his costume off like it's the answer to world peace. It is the answer to my peace—or at least it feels that way.

And then a sound fills the air between us. A gasp followed by a giggle. But neither of us is responsible for it. I recoil from Eli like he's made of acid and spin to face the door we never closed. Thankfully it's just Sadie and Winnie. My eyes dart past them, but I don't see anyone else.

They've got their arms looped together and Sadie grins wickedly. "This must be the goalie."

"If he is so off-limits, then why are you so on top of him?"

I run my hands through my hair and glare at both of them before turning to Eli. He's wiping a hand across his mouth and looking frantic. He steps around me, careful not to touch any part of me, and slips by my sisters. "Sadie and Winnie, I presume? Hi. I have to go."

He blurts it all out in a tight but friendly tone at warp speed and then he's down the stairs before I can blink. Winnie frowns. "He's not one for pleasantries."

"He's a Casco," Sadie explains. "It's like in their genetic code to be aloof and abrupt."

"You know he's Levi's brother?" I hiss in shock.

Sadie nods calmly and steps into the bathroom to check out her reflection. "The minute you mentioned a goalie I did my research."

"You cyberstalked him," I reply flatly.

Sadie just shrugs. Winnie's eyes are so wide I'm scared they might fall out of her head. "Oh my God, how did we not know Levi had such a fine piece of ass for a brother? Well, I mean, Dixie knew, because she's banging him, but—"

I yank Winnie into the bathroom and close the door, shutting out the possibility of anyone overhearing us, I hope. I point my finger at my oldest sister the way Mom used to do when she was pissed. "Do *not* say that out loud ever again. Anywhere. For any reason. If people find out we hooked up, I lose my job and his struggling career gets even harder. Do you understand?"

Winnie looks offended. "Okay. Relax. I would never do anything to hurt you."

She's right, and I'm an ass. "I know. I'm sorry. It's just...this is a nightmare."

Sadie leans in and hugs me. "Dixie, we've got your back. Always."

"I'm glad you interrupted. We slipped, and I don't even know why," I explain and rest my head on her shoulder. "Last time we talked we were barely civil and then this. And nothing's changed. We can't be together right now."

"Your HR department is dumb if they're willing to lose you over a relationship," Winnie says.

I pull out of Sadie's hug and look at her. "It's a standard clause in sports organizations. And the team is already treating me with less respect after finding out I'm Jude's sister, so imagine how much worse it would be if they knew I was sleeping with their teammate."

"Levi told me the guy who was hitting on me had been calling you Baby Braddock, so I dumped a drink on his head," Sadie tells me with a bright smile.

"Vincent LaMarche?" She nods. I'm horrified but also more than a little impressed. That guy is a douche on a good day. And not the Eddie Rollins kind of creepy-but-harmless douche. Vinnie is an actual asshole. "You can't do that, Sadie. Although I'm kind of happy you did. Don't do it again to anyone else, okay?"

"Okay, fine. But you're here tonight as Jude's sister and not a Thunder employee, so I was defending my sister," she explains. "Now back to the important stuff. What are you going to do about tall, dark and unavailable?"

"How'd he get the scar on his neck?" Winnie asks as she jumps up to sit on the counter. "It's totally badass."

"He had his jugular cut open by a skate blade," I inform her and her whole face falls. "They've talked about it relentlessly since he joined the team. Do you watch anything Thunder-related at all?"

"Nope. Not a hockey fan." Winnie's face is draining of color the more she thinks about my explanation. "I didn't know that could happen. Could that happen to Jude?"

She looks terrified.

"Yes. But the odds are slim. Please don't worry about it." She nods reluctantly. I turn to Sadie. "I'm going home."

"Are you taking Eli with you?"

"No. I can't." I sigh, annoyed that she's not getting it. "I'm proud of my job. I'm on the verge of a promotion. If I get it I'll be the first person in Thunder history to go from intern to assistant communications manager in less than three years. That's a big deal."

"Okay," Sadie says and lifts her hands as if to say "don't shoot." "As long as you're happy."

"I'm not, but losing my job isn't going to make me happier," I retort. "I just need to get out of here."

"Okay. Do you want us to go with you?" Winnie asks.

"No. I honestly just want to go home and go to sleep," I tell her. "Stay and keep hitting on Jude's teammates. Make sure he sees so it drives him nuts."

They both smile at that. Someone knocks on the door. I hug them both and open the door and we step out, letting a tall, annoyed blond girl in to pee. We make our way downstairs together, but I dig through the coats piled on the hall bench as they head toward the kitchen. I find my coat and put it on, glancing into the living room. I see everyone but Elijah. He's nowhere to be found.

I slip out the front door. The air is cold and damp and it feels like it's the slap in the face I need right now, so I decide not to call a Lyft and walk at least a little bit of the way. I get to the corner and feel a hand wrap around my upper arm. My adrenaline surges and

I turn, free arm up, heel of my hand poised to go into the attacker's throat. But he grabs that one too. "It's me!"

I blink and stare up into Eli's perfect face. "Crap. Say something next time!"

He smiles, but it's sad. "Sorry. I just saw you leaving and…."

He looks back down the street toward Duncan and Carla's house. He lets go of my arm, but his stare pins me in place. It's lost and a total reflection of how I feel right now too. "Can I walk with you?"

The request is soft and raw and I can't seem to find my voice, so I just nod and we turn left down a side street that will take us away from possible prying eyes. We walk in silence for a couple blocks, slowly meandering through the bustling Saturday night foot traffic. It feels good to just be with him. It's probably a feeling I should fight, but I don't want to. Finally he stops and looks down at me with an expression that I can't read. "I'm starving. Wanna grab a bite with me?"

I glance down at my mouse costume and then let my eyes slide up his gladiator outfit. "Like go into a restaurant? Dressed like this?"

He just shrugs like it's no big deal. As if on cue two guys pass us on the sidewalk and start to chuckle. "You guys know Halloween was a week ago, right?"

Eli looks over and flashes them a bright smile. "That's your Halloween. In our religion it's today. And it lasts a week. Got any candy?"

The guys both look perplexed, shake their heads and continue to walk away. Eli smiles at me and winks. I can't help but laugh. "If anyone gives us grief in the restaurant we'll tell them the same thing. They won't bother to ask which religion, but if they do we'll tell them Flying Spaghetti Monster. It's an actual religion, believe it or not."

"You're nuts," I reply, still smiling.

"Yeah, and you need a little nuts in your life," he says and wiggles his eyebrows, which makes the comment instantly dirty. "Especially if it's my nuts."

"Oh my God. You never change," I say in mock exasperation, but I have to admit to myself that I've smiled more in the last three minutes than I have all week.

"Eat with me. Nothing more, I promise," he says. "Because the fact is I think we could both use each other's company."

I hesitate. This is just going to make my life harder. He dips his head slightly so his face is closer to mine, and then he says in a rough whisper, "Please."

"Only if it involves milkshakes." The minute I make that bad decision I feel a wave of happiness wash over me. I want to spend time with him more than I want to do what's right, and I've never felt that way about a man before. I think it would make me a little scared even if my career goals weren't at stake.

His handsome face lights up in a victorious grin and he wraps an arm around my shoulders. "Let's hunt down some milkshakes, sweet Dixie."

When we get to the diner they seat us in a booth at the back. The waiter comes over and Eli orders us two chocolate cake milkshakes and then turns to me. "Tell me what you want in life."

"Wow. That's a loaded question if I ever heard one," I reply.

"I find you fascinating, not just sexy and incredible in bed," he tells me with a smile that makes me warm. "I've never met a more focused or driven person my age."

"I'm not your age. I'm older."

"By one year. Sorry I forgot, ma'am." I glare at him for the "ma'am." He chuckles. "Seriously. How did you decide to get into sports communications and why?"

"I've been around hockey my entire life. I already knew how the business of it works thanks to Jude, and I thought that would give me an edge. And being a woman in this industry, I need all the edge I can get. Maybe part of me wanted to defy the odds and make a stand in such a male-dominated business too."

Eli runs a hand through his thick, dark hair and leans forward on the table. "Most people fresh out of college just want a job with health benefits, never mind taking on misogyny."

I shrug and pause as the waiter drops off the shakes. Eli orders a burger and fries and I ask for a bacon grilled cheese and onion rings. "Go big or go home."

Eli lets out a deep laugh that I can feel between my legs. I shift in the booth, forcing myself to ignore it, and take the maraschino cherry out of my milkshake and hand it to him. Instead of reaching for it by the stem, he leans closer on the table, opens his mouth and bites it off the stem. Holy fuck, he's hot.

When he's finished chewing and I still haven't continued speaking he grins. "So being Jude's little sister and having a front-row seat to his career was like free training in sports communications?"

I clear my throat and gain some composure. "Yeah, because every time he did something dumb, which was often, I could think of a hundred different ways to handle it that would have been better than how his team at the time handled it."

"So Jude is why you're with the Thunder and not some other team?" Eli asks and wraps his perfect lips around his straw. He sucks down what looks to be half his milkshake.

"Nah. Mostly I wanted to work with the one woman who has

made misogyny her bitch. Ryanne Bateman." His jovial expression dims a little at that. What is that about? "You look like you have something to say about her."

He shakes his head and drinks some more of his milkshake. "She just has a bit of a reputation with players. One that might even make your brother's past look angelic."

I frown. I'm disappointed he's being a typical guy here. The waiter brings our food over, and once he's gone I continue our conversation. "Don't tell me you believe the crap about her sleeping with players."

"Why wouldn't I believe it?"

I sigh. "Because it's just another bullshit rumor that always happens to women when they're successful. God forbid a woman just be considered a badass who's good at her job. They always have to be accused of sleeping their way there or abusing their power once they get there. It's so annoying!"

I'm genuinely irked and he knows it. He looks concerned, like he knows our fun evening is taking a bad turn, and he's trying to decide how to save it. I reach for the ketchup at the same time he does and our hands tangle. Neither one of us pulls away. "You like to have people to look up to, don't you? Role models?"

I'm flustered by that question simply because I've never really thought about it. "It's just nice to have goals and people who inspire you. It helps keep me motivated."

He nods slowly. There's something in his gaze that makes me think he's not saying something, but I'm too distracted by the tingle of our skin-to-skin contact to figure out what it is. He lowers his voice and says, "Sometimes putting people up on pedestals leads to disappointment when they can't live up to your expectations."

I finally pull my hand from his, taking the ketchup bottle with me. He stops talking and just watches me as I dump some ketchup on my plate. Our eyes connect and he flashes a smile at me. "Like you think you've met the perfect girl and then find out she puts ketchup on her grilled cheese."

"It's delicious."

"It's an act against God."

My only response is to pick up my grilled cheese, dredge it through the ketchup, and take a giant bite. He groans in horror like a drama queen and I laugh. This boy is so much fun. We eat our meal, exchanging cheesy pickup lines and making each other laugh. The horrendous week I've had feels so far away, and like it happened to someone else, all because of this green-eyed man with a devilish smile.

I grab the bill and pay it while he's in the restroom so he can't argue. Of course he then spends the next ten minutes, while we split a piece of coconut cream pie, trying to sneak forty bucks into my pocket. He finally gives up, and we make our way out of the restaurant. I open the app and summon a Lyft, then I glance up at him. "I've met Ryanne more than once, and she's never been anything but a badass professional."

His mossy eyes focus on me and he blinks. "Ryanne? We're talking about your boss crush again? I thought we'd moved on."

I nod. "Yeah, we have. I just…I hate that women get a bad rap in business."

"Not all women do," he says and looks serious for a moment. But the expression quickly dissolves and is replaced with a smile. "We're having a good time keeping it light. Let's not change that now."

I still want to push him on this issue, but I force myself not to. "You're right. You should distract me with another horrendous pickup line."

He takes a step toward me and gently wraps an arm around my back, his hand resting on my hip. "I would have taken you right there on the bathroom sink if they hadn't interrupted."

I feel a tingle between my legs, like my girl bits are agreeing with his statement. "I was hoping that would happen. But I'm glad it didn't. It would have complicated this already difficult situation."

"But it felt like it was worth it," he tells me quietly. "You feel like you're worth it."

And just like that, I'm breathless.

"I still want you," he tells me simply.

"I still want you too," I admit with just as much ease. God, it's so easy to say. Why can't it be easy to do?

"So what are we going to do about it?"

He's waiting for my response.

"There's nothing we can do about it now," I tell him. "My life is complicated right now, and I need to stay focused. You do too."

His beautiful green eyes bore into me, as if searching for something—a flicker of doubt, maybe—but he doesn't find any. As much as I'm attracted to him, I am not risking my career over him. I won't.

My Lyft pulls up to the curb, and as I walk toward it so does Eli. I turn and press a hand to the front of his gladiator chest plate. "You can't get in this car with me."

"Why not? I want to make sure you get home okay," he argues.

"Because we'll sleep together again," I say bluntly. "I won't be able to stop myself, and that's not going to make anything easier, only harder."

"Speaking of hard…" He grins.

"Stop," I demand but a smile is overtaking my face. "We can't. You know that."

"I know," he admits, growing solemn. "Can I at least get a kiss good-bye? On the cheek?"

I rock up on my tiptoes and press my lips to his cheek for an embarrassingly long time but it feels so good and he isn't complaining. But then his hands wrap around my waist and I can feel his hard length against my stomach and I'm instantly wet and there's a pulse like a snare drum between my legs, and that's when I know I have to walk away. I pull back and he doesn't fight me. But he does cup the back of my head and whisper, "I'm going to get off tonight thinking of you. Of what it's going to be like next time—because there will be a next time. Promise me."

"I promise," I whisper back.

I am a fool. Playing with fire and making promises I don't know how to keep.

18

ELIJAH

I barely got three hours' sleep last night. After Dixie got in the car I walked all the way back to my hotel, and then Jasper called to tell me about his night and how the team misses me and how jealous he is I was called up. He tried to ask a million questions about what it's been like and how it's going, but I know he watches the games and he knows how it's going. So I evaded the questions, and after we hung up I took a long hot shower and then ignored all common sense and unwritten rules and sent Dixie a selfie in the bathroom mirror. I'm naked and wet holding a towel in front of my cock, barely covering it, but I'm also standing sideways so the side profile of my ass is on full display. I cut my head off, though, so no one can identify me. I figured she wouldn't get it until she woke up, but fifteen minutes later I had a text from her.

Are you butt dialing? Because I swear that ass is calling me.

I'm still chuckling when she sends another.

Get some sleep or the Saints will hand that perfect ass to you tomorrow.

It was everything we both knew we shouldn't be doing, but for the first time since I joined the team I felt grounded and centered again.

Coach started Eddie, and for the first time since being called up, I'm enjoying being on the bench. Okay, *enjoying it* might be an overstatement, but I'm at peace with it. Eddie had a good first period, only letting in one goal. But we're only five minutes into the second and he's let in two more, and both of them looked weak. He should have stopped them—at least I know that's what the coach is thinking. As a goalie, I also know not everything is how it looks from the bench.

Levi finishes a shift and hops over the boards. I can hear him swearing all the way down at the end of the bench. "Jude, I need you to fucking score and get this thing back."

"Yes, Captain." Jude grins and winks at my brother. "I'm on it."

And he does score, two shifts later. But then Eddie fumbles a puck with seconds left in the second period. It bounces off his chest and he scrambles to catch it, but it hits his glove and bounces out, over his shoulder and into the net. Our net. He fucking scored on himself.

"What. The. Actual. Fuck!" Coach Schneider barks.

Levi and Jude both let out a "For fuck's sake!"

Beside me on the bench Duncan snickers, and I smack his helmet with my hand to get him to shut it. Seconds before the period ends, Coach shuffles down the bench. "You're in for the third, Casco. Be ready!"

That calm I was getting used to wavers a little, but I nod, and when the whistle blows I march down the tunnel first, and skip the locker room, heading to an empty medical room to give myself a minute to prepare. I concentrate on holding on to that sense of normalcy. That calm and control.

The locker room next door is pretty silent, as is usually the case when we're losing. I can hear people talking as they walk by—trainers and staff. I stay in there until I hear Lu Price call my name. I take a deep breath and step out into the hall. He looks at me with his hawklike features, his expression cool. "You good?"

"Yep."

"Good. Let's go."

The team starts filtering out and toward the tunnel, and I fall in step next to Levi. He bangs his helmet against mine. "Get us out of this mess."

I nod.

We're ten minutes through the period and I've stopped four shots. In that time Jude and Levi both score. We're one away from a tie, and our team definitely has the momentum. The thing is, the Saints know it too, so they're playing more frantically. Before I know it they've got the puck and they're back in our zone.

I block two more shots, and I dive to catch a rebound while a Saints player lunges for it. Darby cross-checks him in the back and he tumbles over me. The puck flies free and everyone scrambles down the ice except Duncan and the Saints guy, who have decided to continue their shoving match in my crease. I start to get up at the same time the Saints guy tries to punch Duncan, but he loses his balance and some part of him, I'm not sure which part, hits me near the bottom of my mask. Hard. I feel cool air waft against the skin where my neck meets my jaw. It's startling. I reach up. My plastic neck protector is off. I drop my stick and frantically search for the plastic piece in my crease.

I don't give a fuck about the game, I only give a fuck about my neck. Behind my eyes, as I look at the ice, I see flashes of the bloodstained ice from that day. I can almost feel the warm stickiness against my palm.

Luckily Duncan is in a full-on brawl with the Saints guy now and the refs have stopped play and are fully involved in trying to break it up. Hopefully the crowd and TV cameras are too, because I know I look like a panicked child right now. I see it. It somehow ended up inside my net. I reach down and grab it. When I stand back up I feel a hand on my shoulder. It's Levi, concerned brown eyes staring at me from under his visor. "You okay?"

"Yeah," I bark and shrug off his hand as I grab my stick and skate swiftly across the ice. I hold up the piece so the coach knows what's going on as I step off the ice. The equipment manager, Allen, rushes over and we stand next to the crowded bench trying to reattach the damn thing. I'm breathing heavy, like I've been skating laps around the ice. My heart feels like it's trying to crack my rib cage wide open.

"The fucking thing is broken," he announces. "Do you want to go without or—"

"He's not going without. What the fuck is wrong with you?" Coach Schneider snaps at Allen, and then he turns to Eddie. "You're back in while they fix his equipment, which better not take long."

Allen scurries down the tunnel, and I follow along as quickly as I can on skates. The whole time I'm struggling to breathe normally. It's so bad now I'm almost panting. Fucking hell. I wait in the hall, just next to the tunnel, while he runs down to the equipment room. My eyes are closed, but as soon as I hear the clicking of heels on the concrete they fly open. She's walking down the hall toward me in a tight black pencil skirt and a soft pink blouse, a bunch of papers in her hand. Her eyes are on me, absorbing every inch of my demeanor, which I know must be radiating chaos.

She pulls her eyes from mine and glances up and down the hall. It's empty. She stops directly in front of me, a few feet away. "You're okay."

It's not a question. She's stating it in a calm, even tone.

We stare at each other in silence. My eyes slide over her beautiful face, and the calm confidence of her expression seeps into me, making it possible to take a deep breath. I glance down the hall. Still empty.

I'm moving faster than I ever thought possible on skates and weighed down with pounds of equipment. I haul her into the empty, dark medical room and before she has time to stop me I press her back into the wall and cover her mouth with my own. She fights me at first, dropping her papers and pushing against my shoulders. But it doesn't last long and in seconds her arms are wrapped around my neck, pulling me closer. When I try to break the kiss, she bites my bottom lip lightly. I press into her and slide my tongue back into her mouth.

"Casco?!"

The voice in the hall is loud and panicked. We jump apart like a bomb has gone off, and I leave her there in the dark and walk out into the hall. Allen sees me and marches over with the new neck guard. "I thought you fucking went to play without it, and Coach clearly doesn't want you to do that."

"I don't want to do it," I reply as he hurriedly ties the guard onto my helmet. "If my jugular can be sliced with this thing on, imagine what would happen without it."

"Yeah, dude, I saw that video, and it was brutal." Allen finishes tying the guard, and I nod and rush back down the tunnel.

While I was gone Duncan scored and tied it up.

"Casco thirty-five!" Coach Schneider barks, using my number to differentiate between me and Levi. "You're in next whistle. Good?"

"Good!" I call back.

My breathing is normal, my pulse steady. I'm okay. Just like Dixie said.

I finish the game and we go to overtime, which remains scoreless. In the shootout I stop everything that comes my way—easily. Levi scores to give us the win. I am so happy I want to throw my equipment off and roar. But it's just a regular midseason game, and I'd look like a fool.

Instead I settle for the team coming over to congratulate me one after the other.

Back in the locker room Dixie breezes in, holding the same papers she had earlier. The ones I made her drop all over the dark medical room's floor. Her eyes sweep the room. "Levi, Brian and Elijah, you're doing interviews tonight."

"What about me, Baby Braddock?" She bristles at Eddie's condescending comment. He doesn't seem to notice. "I'm the game-winning goalie. No one wants to talk to me?"

"Eddie, don't talk to her like that," Levi says firmly.

"What? She's Jude's baby sister," Eddie argues and shrugs. "He scored her a job the way you scored Eli one. Hockey is renowned for nepotism. It's accepted. Nothing to be embarrassed about."

"I've told you, that's bullshit," Jude mutters.

"So, Baby Braddock, add me to the interview list," Eddie says to Dixie.

"No one wants to interview you, Rollins, because even when the backup doesn't have to step in to save the game you tanked, you leer at the female reporters like they're cheerleaders and you're a creepy school janitor at a pep rally," I tell him, pulling my jersey over my head. I run my hand through my hair because it's fallen into my eyes. "And if you keep being a disrespectful little shit, Dixie's never going to schedule you again."

Eddie gives me a cold, hard sneer. "You're mighty lippy for a kid who shakes when a skate gets too close to his precious face."

"My name is still Ms. Wynn to you," Dixie says, turning to face Eddie, towering in front of him with her hands on her hips. "If you call me anything else at any time I will not acknowledge you even if you're been set on fire and you're asking me for the glass of water in my hand. Do you understand, Rollins?"

"Listen, Dix—"

"Ms. Wynn," she cuts him off again. "And four reporters requested that lippy kid, as you called him. Not because he stood on his head in that shootout, but because he's a better interview than you. You're really fucking boring."

She storms out of the locker room.

"Fucking bullshit," Eddie grumbles and storms around the corner toward the showers.

I pull off my pads, and as I reach for my hoodie to throw on before the reporters come in I notice Jude staring at me. "What?"

"You like sticking up for my sister," he remarks.

"Yeah, well, someone has to do it. You didn't." Okay, I don't need to be defensive or insulting. That's not exactly playing it cool.

Jude smiles. "Oh, I will always defend and protect her. When she actually needs it." He stands. "Remember that."

I watch him grab a clean towel and scrub his face with it. I think he suspects I've got a thing for his sister, and that's a problem. As we start to strip down and wait for the reporters Dixie is sending in, Levi asks him if Zoey came to the game.

He shakes his head as he pulls off his jersey. "She's watching it on TV with my family at my parents' place. My dad has a bit of a cold, so everyone stayed with him, including Zoey, who said she was too exhausted to come all the way to the arena anyway."

"Too bad. Tessa was hoping you two would go grab dinner with us," Levi says and turns to me. "You wanna join? You could invite that Julie girl you're sort of involved with."

"Ha. No, I can't," I blurt out without thinking. Levi's eyebrows furrow and Jude stares at me, lifting his. I shrug. "I told you, it's not really a thing, and I'm not subjecting any girl to meeting you if I don't have to."

Levi flips me the middle finger as Jude pulls his phone out of his suit jacket hanging in his locker and checks it. I'm about to turn away, but the fact that his face just completely drains of color right before my eyes stops me. Levi notices too. "Jude? What's wrong?"

"Zoey's at the hospital. She's in labor."

19

DIXIE

I'm so angry I feel flushed when I walk out of the locker room. But I'm not just angry at Eddie for being an asshole. I'm angry at Elijah for jumping into it. I saw Jude's reaction to that—the way his eyebrows lifted and his stare narrowed. It made him suspicious, and it might have made other people suspicious. That can't happen. And neither can spontaneous makeout sessions in the medical room. If it's all or nothing for us, then it has to be nothing right now. And since he won't take that seriously, because he takes nothing seriously, then I have to.

I feel my phone buzz in my blazer pocket, so I pull it out and frown when I see it's Winnie. Again. She's called twice and Sadie called once in the last twenty minutes. I told them never to call me during games, and afternoon games are the busiest for me. I hit Decline and look up to see the reporters are coming down the hall toward me, so I plaster a smile on my face and greet them. "Hey, everyone. So you've got Brian Spaulding and both Cascos waiting for you in there. You've got ten minutes tonight."

I start to lead them toward the locker room. Tom Stoll, a local newspaper reporter I've gotten to know pretty well, gives me a big friendly smile. "How are you doing?"

I look up into his kind hazel eyes. "I'm okay. How are you?"

"I'm good." He glances at the other reporters walking behind us, chatting amongst themselves, and lowers his voice. "I just want you to know that you're the best PR person we've dealt with here, no matter what your last name is."

Great. Even the media knows I'm Jude's sister. And some of them must be doubting how I got the job and my integrity now, because Tom wouldn't have made that statement of support if he hadn't heard something derogatory. I'm trying to figure out how to respond when Jude comes tearing out of the locker room like his ass is on fire. He's wearing his equipment, no jersey and his Under Armour underwear, with the flip-flops he wears in the shower. Nothing else. I start to smirk, ready to make some kind of smartass comment, but then I look into his eyes. They're swimming with fear and paniç.

"She's having the baby," he tells me, oblivious to the reporters, who are listening intently. "It's eight and a half weeks early. Is it too early? It seems too early. I don't know."

Holy shit. Something heavy and cold instantly forms in my stomach and drops to my feet. "Go find out!"

"Come with me!" he demands.

Levi comes running out of the locker room, barely dressed. He's still damp with sweat, but he's thrown his suit on, and I mean *thrown*. His shirt is misbuttoned and untucked, he's wearing his dress shoes with no socks, and he's only got one arm in his jacket. He's also got an armload of Jude's clothes. "Tessa is already in the car waiting by the door. Let's go. We'll take you, and you can get dressed on the way."

Jude grabs me in a quick hug before charging down the hall with Levi.

The reporters start excitedly throwing questions at me about Zoey and the baby. "We don't answer personal questions about players," I remind them and stop at the locker room door. "Obviously it's just Brian and Eli now for questions. Someone will be by to walk you out in ten minutes."

They all head straight for Eli, and I turn and start to run down the hall, pulling my cell phone from my pocket to text Ann and tell her I have to leave. I can't believe Zoey is in labor. Oh my God, Jude is going to be a father. I'm about to be an aunt. I realize how surreal the whole pregnancy has felt now that the reality is here. I feel tears well up in my eyes.

I turn the corner, still running, and almost crash into Nadine, who is standing by the elevator with Trish. They both look up, startled, as I manage to slide to a halt without tumbling into them. "Zoey is having the baby."

"Who?" Trish asks.

Nadine isn't so dense. "Oh my God! Jude's Zoey?"

I nod. "He left a few minutes ago. Levi is driving him."

"Does the press know?" Trish asks. "Because it's going to get out, and you know how they love when we do an official announcement with a baby picture and everything."

"We can do that." I nod. "I can go to the hospital now and—"

"Right!" Nadine smacks her forehead. "He's your brother. I swear you hid it so well for so long even I forgot."

I can see Trish's face twist into a very unflattering scowl. "So you're just going to take off? Even though we still have tons of work to do?"

I stare at her like I'm looking at an alien life form. Because only some kind of alien with no heart or a black one would think I shouldn't leave right now. "My brother is about to be a dad."

She continues to stare blankly at me. "It's not like you're the one about to give birth. Besides, labor can last hours, even days. She could just be having those fake contractions."

"I should go find out," I reply tersely and turn to Nadine so I don't accidentally throat-punch Trish. "Have you seen Ann?"

"She asked me to meet her upstairs. I'm headed there now."

We all get into the elevator, but I hesitate and turn to Trish and regret what I'm about to ask before it even leaves my mouth, but I have no choice. "Can you finish up with the press for me so I can go see Ann?"

"No."

"Why not?"

"Because it's not my job," she barks back. "Unlike everyone else, I'm not going to give you special treatment just because you share a last name with the team superstar."

I'm so furious I'm shaking. "Trish, this isn't some kind of favoritism. I would do this for you if you had a family emergency."

She crosses her arms, and I swear she's trying to shoot fire from her eyes. "I have my own things to do. I had to draw the winner of that stupid contest you created. We said we'd announce it after this game, so now I have to call the winner and then set up the prizes and post it."

"If you help her out now, I will stay late and help you," Nadine offers, and I want to hug her.

Trish searches for a reason to say no to that. I can see the struggle on her face. I can't imagine how much work it takes to be this big of a bitch. I have to bite my bottom lip to keep from saying that out loud. The elevator starts to buzz because we've been holding the door open so long. "Fine," she huffs.

Nadine lets go of the Open button and smiles sweetly at Trish. "Thanks. I'll be upstairs ready to help you as soon as you're done."

As soon as the elevator starts chugging upward, I hug Nadine. "Thank you."

"No worries. I would want to be there for my brother too," she replies and smiles.

I text Winnie and ask her what's going on. She texts back a second later and tells me Jude just got there and he's in a room with Zoey and the doctor. They're all waiting for an update. The elevator opens and Nadine steps off before me, but her step falters as we turn the corner and I bump into her. I look up from my phone screen. In front of us through the glass door that leads to our offices I can see Ann standing with Mr. Carling. Their eyes are both fixed on Nadine and their expressions are so grim it makes my skin prickle with worry.

"Oh no," Nadine whispers so faintly I almost miss it.

"What's wrong?" I ask, but she doesn't answer. She simply walks into the offices.

Ann looks over at me. "What are you doing here, Dixie?"

"I needed to talk to you," I reply in a voice that sounds as confused as I must look.

Ann looks at Mr. Carling, and he nods and then looks back at Nadine. "Nadine, come with me, will you? We have a meeting in the conference room."

He walks briskly to the door, and Nadine hesitates but follows him. I have no idea what is going on, and I hate that. It fills me with dread and panic. As soon as the door closes behind them I turn to Ann. "Everything all right?"

"Fuck no," Ann hisses and I'm immediately on edge. I have never heard her swear at work. "But I can't get into it right now. What did you want to talk to me about?"

I blink. "Zoey is in labor."

Ann takes a second to register what I'm saying and then she grins. "Oh my God! Amazing! Is Jude on his way to the hospital? Thank God we weren't at an away game."

I nod. "He is, and I was hoping to leave early and be with him."

Her whole face darkens. "Right now?"

I realize that my ask just became impossible because Nadine is in this mystery meeting and probably won't be able to help Trish like she promised. I swallow and try not to sound as desperate as I feel. I just want to be with my family. "It's just Zoey is early, and Jude's kind of freaking out, and it's my first niece. Or nephew. And I just…"

Her expression isn't changing. "I really need you to stay and help Trish with this contest. It shouldn't take more than an hour with the two of you on it. I'm going to be tied up with this Nadine thing all afternoon."

I try not to sigh. Instead I just nod. Ann squeezes my shoulder. "I know it's not ideal, but we need you, Dix. And I'll make sure Mr. Carling knows you did this. It'll add to the reasons you should have my job."

I nod again. She rushes toward the door, off to join the meeting with Nadine and Mr. Carling. "You'll be out of here in under an hour. Nobody has a baby in under an hour!"

I hope she's right. I walk over to my desk and sit down, quickly texting Winnie that I'll be there as soon as I can but I have work stuff to deal with first. She texts back three letters.

WTF

I shove my phone in my desk drawer, swallow down my anger and frustration, and open my laptop. The faster I get this done, the faster I can leave. I can hear my phone vibrating in my desk but I ignore it. Trish walks into the office, sees me and looks instantly annoyed. "I thought you were ditching us?"

"Ann needed Nadine in a meeting, so I'm here to help you," I reply, trying not to let the depths of my disappointment show.

"Great. So I just did your job for nothing," she snipes and I lower my hands into my lap so she doesn't see they're in tight fists.

"Did you contact the winner yet?" I ask, my voice surprisingly sweet, even though I'm gritting my teeth.

"Yeah. They live in Toronto, so we should make this happen on the road trip next week," Trish says as she marches by me to her desk. "And they want to meet Eli because their kid is a goalie or some shit."

I bite my tongue so hard I swear I taste blood. "I'll book a dinner in the hotel. Are you going with to oversee? Do you want to book your own room or should I?"

I can feel her glare on my skin like she's thrown acid on me. I look up. "Mr. Carling said you should go. Since it was your idea."

"Oh." I swallow and nod and start pulling up the hotel information. I get to travel with the team, which means I get to travel with Eli. This news makes my heart flutter and ache in unison. God, I'm so confused over this boy.

My phone vibrates again and, worried it's news about Zoey, I open the drawer and look at it. I swear, if she had that baby before I could get there I will burst into tears. But it's Justin Bieber's name on the call display, which is what I have Eli's number saved under. I glance at Trish and hit Ignore. My phone goes silent and then I quickly text him.

Working. Can't talk.

He texts back immediately.

Aren't you going to the hospital?

I ignore him and go back to work. Forty minutes later, I've booked the restaurant for the winner of our contest and a hotel room for myself and proofed Trish's press release for her, which she posts to the team's Instagram and I post to our Facebook and website. The entire time I'm working I regret even coming up with the idea of the contest. We were asked to brainstorm ways to engage fans who weren't local. My idea was to have an Instagram contest where they post photos in Thunder jerseys at landmarks where they live, and the winner would get tickets to a game next time we played near them and get to have dinner with the player of their choice. Management went with it, and it was wildly successful. But right now I don't feel any pride in that. I just want to get to the hospital.

I text Sadie as I grab my stuff to leave, and she says no one has come out to tell them what's going on and she and Winnie are about to storm the nurses' station in search of answers. I'm hoping to beat Trish out the door and have the elevator to myself, but she's right behind me and gets in with me.

"I'm applying for Ann's job," she announces as the elevator descends.

Because this day can't get any worse. "Okay."

"I assume you are too." I nod and she does what she does best—frowns. "I suppose you'll get Jude to put in a word for you."

"Of course not!"

"Whatever," she completely dismisses me. "Just know I won't let you steal this."

The elevator opens and she storms off. I head outside and purposely walk in the opposite direction, fumbling with my phone to pull up my Lyft app since I carpooled in with Jude. As I make my way across the parking lot there's a loud horn honk directly behind me, and I jump a foot off the ground. If it's Trish, I swear I will kick her car so hard. But it's not. It's Jude's Tesla—and Eli is behind the wheel.

"What the hell…"

He leans his head out the window. "He left his keys in his locker. Levi asked me to drive it over to Jude's house for him. I figured I would wait and take you to the hospital first."

I don't even think twice. I don't care how it looks or what people will say or anything. I just run around the car and jump in the passenger seat.

20

DIXIE

The way Eli drives is turning me on. That's never happened to me before, and I have no idea why it's happening now. People have always said Jude had a sexy car, and I have to agree now that someone hot is driving it. Eli's pushing the speed limit, zipping in and out of lanes and handling the hills with this wild gracefulness. He looks over at me and winks. "I think I need to get one of these cars."

"You should offer to buy his," I reply. "Once he's a dad, he should have a minivan. At least that's what I keep telling him. If I had the money, I'd buy him one just to see his reaction."

Eli laughs. "You and Jude are exactly like me and Levi."

I nod absently and text Sadie to tell her I'm on my way. Then I realize a calendar alert has popped up. I was supposed to meet the ALS chapter director in forty-five minutes to talk about my social media campaign idea. Shit. I totally flaked. "This day can't get any more stressful."

I quickly dial her number. When she answers I take a deep breath and try to sound professional. "Hi, Kelsey, this is Dixie

Braddock. I know it's short notice, but is there any possible way we can move our meeting? A family emergency came up."

"Of course! I hope everything is all right," she says sincerely.

"Yeah. I mean, it's not a life-or-death thing." I pause and Eli snorts at that. "I mean, it's a life thing. My sister-in-law is in labor at the hospital, and I'd just really like to be there. I know that's not exactly an emergency."

"It's a new family member! That's important," Kelsey replies, and I can hear her smiling through the phone. "I mean, if we can't be with our family for events like this, what's the point? No worries at all about the meeting. Call me later this week when things settle down and we'll reschedule."

"Thank you so much." I am so relieved I could cry. Eli must see it on my face, because he reaches over and squeezes my knee gently. "Hey. It's going to be okay. All of it. Everything."

"The reaction at the ALS Foundation was a pleasant surprise compared to how the Thunder reacted to me wanting to leave," I mutter.

"It sucks they wouldn't let you leave."

"Oh, that's not the half of it," I reply and explain to him how mean Trish was acting.

He's smiling when I finish my story, which is weird, but at the same time it's soothing. "That's why I love hockey so much. If someone pisses you off, you get to beat the shit out of them, and the only punishment is sitting in a box for five minutes."

I laugh. "If only life were like hockey."

"The world would be a better place."

He slows and turns into the hospital parking lot, pulling right up to the front doors. "Go!" he commands and I start to open the car door but turn back around.

I grab his face in my hands and press my lips to his. I kiss him with every shred of energy left in me. When I finally let him go his eyes are dark and glassy and his lips full. "This job has taken a lot from me today. I wanted to take something back."

I jump out of the car and run into the building. I find my sisters in the emergency waiting room, but my mom and dad are nowhere to be found. Sadie stands up. "False labor."

"Thank God."

"Yeah, because if it were real, that kid would be here by now and you'd have missed it," Winnie remarks with a half smile on her face. "And you'd have lost any chance at being the favorite aunt."

"I got here as soon as I could," I reply defensively.

"Mom and Dad left already. Dad was exhausted and he's still under the weather," Winnie tells me. "Levi and that sweet girlfriend of his just left like a minute ago with Jude and Zoey."

"You should have told me it was a false alarm so I didn't rush over here." I follow along beside them as we make our way toward the front doors I just burst through.

"No, we wanted you to show up," Sadie explains with a wicked grin flashing across her features. "So we could take you out for drinks."

"I have to work in the morning. In fact I should be working now," I explain. "I canceled a pitch with ALS to come here."

Winnie rolls her eyes and grabs onto my arm. "Oh my God! Quit being Corporate Climbing Barbie and just come have fun with us. I know you know how. You used to be good at it."

"I still am." I fight the urge to say no to them because I really could use some sister bonding. "Okay, fine. Just a couple drinks. Not some late-night bender."

"Sure," Sadie says, but she completely winks at Winnie right in front of me.

"I mean it!" I bellow as they hook their arms through mine and lead me out the door.

They take me to some crazy Western-themed bar with a live band and a mechanical bull in the middle of the room. I have no idea how they found this place or why the bartender knows them by name. I would ask, but I'm sure I don't want to know the answer. Eli texts me as we grab a table.

Jude was home when I dropped off the car.
Explained the false start.
Did you get home from the hospital ok?

"Winnie, look! She's smiling."

"Oh! I know that smile," Winnie announces. "That smile is caused by a man."

"Shut up, you two," I mumble and start to text him back, but Sadie swipes my phone out of my hand and bolts from the table. "What the actual hell!"

Winnie cackles with laughter and as I jump off my stool to chase after Sadie, she catches my arm. "You know resistance is futile, Little D."

I sigh and sit back down. "Don't call me that. Only Dad gets to call me that."

"Of course." Winnie rolls her eyes as Sadie comes back to the table skipping and smiling ear-to-ear. She puts my phone down on the table and I grab it.

"What did you do?" I demand as she smiles coyly and flips her long hair over her shoulder.

"I told him to come join us," she announces. "Well, *you* told him, since it's your phone. I also told him…I mean *you* also told him you miss the feel of his mouth on your body."

She turns and high-fives Winnie as my eyes bug out of my head and I frantically pull up my text messages. I groan loudly because she wrote exactly what she said she wrote. I glare at her but it only seems to make her smile grow larger. "Oh and she's got some hot-as-fuck pictures of him on her phone. I sent myself a few so I could show you."

She holds up her own phone to Winnie, and I watch Winnie's jaw drop. She grabs Sadie's phone. "Holy crap, your goalie has one hell of a body, Dix. How can you walk away from that?"

"How can I not?" I counter. With the day I've had, I have to admit my job is losing a little bit of its luster. I know that will pass but right now…"I need a drink."

Winnie lifts her arm and waves at the waitress. As our second round comes, the bar starts to fill up, the music gets louder and Eli is suddenly standing next to my stool. He smiles down at me with his ruggedly handsome face and warm green eyes. "Hi again."

"Hi," I squeak out, embarrassed about the text he thinks I sent.

He looks over at Winnie and Sadie. "Which one of you two charmers lured me here pretending to be Dixie?"

Sadie raises her hand gleefully. "Guilty!"

"But I fully support my sister," Winnie pipes up, trying hard to look serious, but she keeps slipping into a grin. "I'm the oldest sister, and it's my job to look out for these two. And Dixie tends to get a little obsessive and hyper-focused when she has a goal in mind. We decided she needs to relax and get a little more of this in her life."

Before I can stop her, Winnie has reached for Sadie's phone, and she's holding up the bathroom selfie of Eli in nothing but a well-placed towel. He looks horrified for a split second, and then he bursts out in that deep, vibrating laugh of his that's so sexy it makes my pussy pulse.

"Let me buy you nosy Nellies a drink," he says and calls over the waitress, resting a lazy arm across my shoulders. Oh God, this is seven hundred kinds of wrong, but it's the best feeling I've had in ages.

I cut myself off after that round because I have to work in the morning, but we stay at the bar another two hours laughing and telling embarrassing childhood stories, mostly about Jude and Levi, so it's extra enjoyable, and daring each other to ride the mechanical bull. Finally I let rational thought take over. "I have to get to bed, guys. Work tomorrow."

"You and that damn job." Sadie sighs dramatically.

"We're not leaving until someone rides that bull," Winnie declares, slapping the table with her palm. "And if it's Eli, preferably shirtless."

"He can't get on that bull shirtless," I warn. "If you think I work a lot now, wait until I'm dealing with those photos all over the internet."

Eli shrugs and starts to lift his shirt by the hem. Winnie and Sadie start to whistle like they're at a strip bar. I grab his hands and stop him before he reaches his nipples. He gives me a devilish smile. "Trying to keep it all for yourself?"

I don't answer him. Instead I turn to my sisters. "Listen, Slutty Spice and Skanky Spice, I am going home, no bull, mechanical or otherwise."

I grab my coat off my stool and suddenly Eli is helping me put it on while my sisters pretend to fan themselves and sigh dramatically. I look up at Eli. "I am so sorry. Now I know why Jude wishes he was an only child."

"Come on, I'll walk you home," Eli offers and puts a hand on the small of my back as we weave our way out of the place with Winnie and Sadie following behind. It's raining now, so we huddle under the awning out front and I hug my sisters good-bye. The both hug Eli too before climbing in the back of a cab. As they drive away Winnie rolls down the window and calls out, "Hey, Dixie, save a horse, ride a goalie!"

Sadie lets out a "Woo-hoo!"

I bury my face in my hands as Eli's laugh rumbles up beside me. He holds my shoulders, giving them a squeeze. "Your family is amazing."

"That's not the adjective I would have gone with," I reply. He takes my hand and starts leading me down the street. I try to stop him, but it's impossible. "It's raining!"

"So? Are you made of sugar, sweet Dixie?" he asks and keeps pulling me down the street. "Live a little. Be a little reckless."

So we walk, on a Sunday night in the pouring rain, down the dark, almost abandoned streets. And somehow, for the first time in a very, very long time—since before my father's diagnosis, since before my double life working in PR, since before I decided I had to be a glass-ceiling-busting corporate badass—I feel completely at peace. And maybe it's the rain. Maybe it's slipping down over my soaked hair and dripping into my ears and drowning my common sense or washing away my very well thought-out life goals, but all I want to do is kiss him.

As we start to walk by an alley I step into it, pulling him with me, and then with all the strength I have I grab him by the front of his jacket, shove him against the damp brick wall, rock up on my toes and kiss him. My lips cover his the way they have since the elevator—perfectly. And our tongues move together with matching need and urgency. He reaches up and cups the side of my face as his lips pull away just enough to talk. "Do you know what you're doing here, sweet Dixie? What about the rules?"

"I've played by the rules enough today." I let my hand slip between us and palm the front of his jeans. "I think it's time to give this reckless thing a chance. Just for tonight."

I start to lower his zipper, and the way his eyes widen makes me smile. I kiss him again, tugging on his plump bottom lip for just a second as it ends, and I slip my hand into his open fly. My fingers brush against his shaft, and he punches his hips forward. "You should come home with me," I say.

He wraps his arm around my waist and lifts me, spinning us around so it's my back against the wet bricks. "We're supposed to be reckless here." His breath tickles my neck and then I feel his lips on my earlobe. "There's nothing reckless about fucking at home."

"Everything about us is reckless," I remind him in a whisper.

"Then let's act like it," he responds, his hand slipping up under my trench coat and skirt. He cups my pussy in his palm, his fingers grazing over my slit through my lace thong. "Let me have you now. Here."

A ripple of desire rolls down my spine. I pop the button of his jeans to give my hand more access, and then I reach for his cock again, wrapping my hand around it. He lets out the hottest deep, dark noise from the back of his throat. And it does me in. "Fuck me, Eli."

He doesn't need to be told twice.

As I walk into work the next morning, I try not to smile too brightly but I can't help it. Wild sex in a public place really leaves an afterglow. The way he tugged my underwear aside so forcefully they tore. The way I moved my skirt up my legs, just enough to show him where he needed to go. The forceful way he held me close, pinned between his body and the wall, and pushed into me as I rolled my hips. It was insane—we were insane—and it was insanely satisfying. We'd stumbled back to his hotel, which was closer than my place, and fell into bed soaking wet and exhausted. I woke up at four in the morning, quietly got dressed and headed home.

Now, as I make my way to my desk, I try not to think about last night at all. The less I think about it in the harsh light of day, the longer I can pretend it wasn't a colossal mistake. I hate letting people down or appearing unprofessional. I sit down at my desk, and as I shrug out of my coat I realize Nadine wasn't at her desk. Mr. Carling's office door opens, and Ann walks out. Our eyes meet, and she's wearing that same grim expression from last night. She walks over, smoothing the front of her gray slacks with her hands. "Thanks again for staying last night and getting things done. Are you an aunt?"

I shake my head. "False alarm. Is everything all right?"

Ann sighs heavily. "We had to fire Nadine last night."

"What?" I blurt out way too loudly. "Why?"

"She slept with Eddie Rollins." Her grim expression gives way to one of disgust. Ann and I have both talked about how creepy Eddie is. "He apparently confessed to HR, and judging by the look on her face yesterday, I know it's true."

"Why the hell would he tell HR?"

"I guess a trainer overheard him bragging about it," Ann replies. "He didn't deny it because he was probably done with her, and getting her fired is an easy way to get rid of her. Because he's pond scum."

"Shit." I feel sick. I love Nadine. But my stomach isn't just churning for Nadine. It's roiling with guilt and angst because—this could be me. "Do they have to fire her? I mean, they aren't firing Eddie, right?"

Ann frowns. "Of course not," she replies, her tone edged in bitterness. "The sports double standard is real, Dix. Our HR policy is zero tolerance and immediate termination. The players' policy is zero tolerance and immediate stern talking-to."

She's being sarcastic. It doesn't say "stern talking-to," but they must have worded it without the promise of termination for their policy. I get it. They're not as easily replaced as we are, but it still makes me sick. "I can't believe she would be so stupid," Ann laments and sighs.

I can. I am that stupid.

21

ELIJAH

She's fucking ghosting me. That's why I had a shit game. Because I've been trying to reach her for the last twenty-four hours, and she's ignored every text and every call. I even went to her place last night at almost midnight and she either wasn't home or wasn't answering. And today when she breezed into the locker room, she purposely stood with her back to my locker and stormed out without so much as a sideways glance. So of course my game was off. We didn't lose and I didn't get pulled, but there are twelve-year-old goalies who could have played better than I did tonight. Luckily Levi, Jude and the boys were on fire, so I might have let in three goals, but they scored seven. Still, I'm seething about my performance.

When she marches into the locker room after the game and announces the media will be in shortly and they want to talk to Jude, Levi, Duncan and me, but she still has her back to me and won't even glance in my direction, I lose it. I stand up. "I'm not doing press tonight."

"What?" Levi says, confused.

"Yeah. What?" Dixie echoes and finally looks at me. Her face is a mask of nothing—no emotion of any kind, and that fuels this frustration burning like coals inside of me.

"I need to see a trainer about my calf," I lie.

"You can do that after the media scrum."

"Yeah, but I'm going to do it now." I start to walk out of the room. "No press for me."

I head down the hall toward the training rooms. It takes a second, but I hear her heels clicking away on the concrete behind me. Good, she's following. She calls my name. I ignore it and keep walking. Her heels click faster. I slow down a little so she can catch me. As soon as I feel her arm on my bicep I turn and slip into an unattended medical room, pulling her in with me. I close the door behind us. The lights aren't on, so it's instantly dark.

"What the fuck are you doing?" she demands.

"What the fuck are you doing?" I counter. "You've been ignoring me. I fucking hate being ignored."

"So you're throwing a temper tantrum?" she says with a condescending look I've never seen before and hope to never see again.

"I had a shitty game, and I don't feel like dealing with a million questions about it," I tell her. I take a step toward her, turning on the light. "I didn't have a shitty game last time we were in here. In fact I had my best game."

She opens her perfectly glossed mouth to say something but freezes. Her blue eyes look startled and then they darken. Her hands move to her hips. "So, what? I should make out with you before every game? Make my lips part of some superstitious ritual?"

It's more than her lips. It's her. I want to explain that she's like a grounding force, that she's the only one who makes me feel normal since the accident, but I don't, because then everything gets heavy, and I fucking hate heavy. This doesn't need to be fucking ruined like everything else in my life. Frustration bubbles up and courses through my veins like adrenaline.

So instead I step closer. "Would that be so bad?"

"Are you going to pay me a salary with full medical coverage and a 401(k)?" she asks hotly. "Because that's what I'll lose, and I'm not willing to risk it anymore. I never should have to begin with."

She starts to walk past me but pauses just short of reaching for the door. She turns back. "You need to see someone about your PTSD."

"What the fuck are you talking about?"

"You don't need me, you need a shrink, Eli," she tells me firmly but with a gentle tone and softness in her eyes. "Traumatic events and near-death experiences like having your neck ripped open leave scars, and not just physical ones. I know you know this. Deep down. What I don't know is why you aren't doing something about it."

"It's not the fucking accident," I growl, and the sound is so foreign even to me it makes the hair on the back of my neck stand up. "I am not some basket case who can't take a goddamn hit. I've had a ton of accidents on the ice. I've had a concussion, I've had my lip split, my wrist broken, my—"

"You almost bled to death!" she says so loud it's almost a scream, and it startles both of us. My eyes fly to the door. If anyone heard that outside we're fucked. She must realize that too, because she takes a shuddering breath and lowers her voice. "Goddamn it, Elijah, you're still a man if you stop acting like everything is a joke and admit that it was fucking terrifying. In fact, it would make you more of a man."

"Well, at least I don't want to kiss you anymore," I snap. I can see the hurt splash across her face, but I storm for the door anyway.

"You do agree with me. You just won't admit it, because you have some ridiculous sense of pride that is going to tank your career before it even begins," she says tersely. "This is because of your parents."

That freezes me in my tracks like someone poured quick-setting cement into my veins. "Excuse me?"

Slowly I turn to face her again, rage and indignation flushing my skin.

"They're uptight. They're cold," she explains quietly, clearly hoping it softens the blow of reality. "They frown on emotions, and seeing a shrink would be like admitting you're defective, but guess what? We're all defective. No one is perfect. We're all fucked up, and we all need help! Perfect is creepy. Do you want to be creepy, or do you want to be an amazing goalie again?"

"Fuck. Do you even know the meaning of the word 'subtle'?" I bark and reach for the door handle. "It's a good thing your sister is the nurse, because your bedside manner would fucking kill people."

I storm out into the hall, but she's right behind me, nowhere near ready to let this go. She comes around beside me and veers me toward the wall. I stop and glare at her. She looks hurt and maybe even a little intimidated and a lot tired. She glances around the hall, making sure no one is in earshot. "I'm sorry, Eli. I'm not trying to be cruel, but I've learned that sugarcoating things or ignoring problems doesn't make them go away."

"You're not really a girl with a lot of problems," I say flatly. "You just have to stop screwing me and your life is fine."

Her face twists into pure disbelief and the hurt on her features slips into anger. "My father is slowly dying in front of me, little by little, every damn day, and there isn't a damn thing I can do but watch. That's a problem-free life to you?"

I am, officially, without a doubt, the biggest asshole on the planet. Such a big asshole I am at a complete loss for words, so I just stare at her with a stricken look.

"Yeah. I know you know about my dad's ALS. You just forgot for a second. It's fine. We haven't talked about it. Because we don't seem to talk about anything that matters," she whispers, her eyes glancing down the hall again before landing on mine. "And that's even more reason why this needs to stop. I shouldn't get serious about someone who doesn't take anything seriously. My career is serious. My life, the things I'm going to have to eventually face with my dad, are all serious. I can't let myself fall any further."

She takes a step back, straightens her shoulders and focuses those gorgeous blue eyes on something behind me.

"Okay! Let me take you in." She steps away from me and I watch her walk toward the group of reporters making their way down the hall toward us. "Eli is out tonight, folks, but Jude and Levi are available for questions and you know Jude loves to talk about any game he wins—incessantly—so I'm sure he'll give you an earful."

I watch her walk away. As the press enters the locker room she glances back at me. She looks wounded, but I'm the one who feels like there's a gaping hole in my chest suddenly.

22

ELIJAH

I'd say she broke up with me, but we weren't together to begin with—technically—so that's not what this is. It just feels like that. We've been avoiding each other. It's amazing how easy it's been to not run into her even though we spend a huge amount of time in the same building. I reacted badly—to everything—six days ago at the arena. I know that now that the anger has subsided. I just hate being ignored. My parents used this tactic on us growing up. If we had an opinion they didn't like, they didn't talk it out with us, they ignored us. If we did something they didn't like, they didn't ground us, but they gave us the silent treatment. That set me off, and then the way she ripped into me—accurate or not—about my injury and then my parents was too much. It was like she walked up and tore a Band-Aid off the gaping hole inside of me where I store all the bullshit I don't want to deal with. I wasn't ready for that, but I needed it. I know that now, as my second appointment with my sports psychologist comes to a close.

I have to admit to myself, it's not at all as painful as I thought it would be. The guy is relaxed and friendly. He doesn't make me lie on the couch—in fact, there isn't even a couch in his office. We sit in armchairs across from each other, and we've started both sessions just shooting the shit about hockey—how the team is doing, who played who the night before. Somehow, without me even realizing it, we talk about me—my feelings on everything from hockey to life and how everything has changed since the injury. It's the second session in five days and I'm already feeling a little more grounded than I have in two years. I'm sharing shit with him I've never said out loud to anyone. And it's not weird or humiliating. It actually just feels good to get it off my chest.

"Listen," he says as he glances at the clock. "I watched some of the footage from a game a couple weeks ago. I saw you kind of panic when that neck guard came off, but you didn't let that fear take you under like it seems to have in the past. When you came back out you had a great game. What did you do differently?"

I know exactly what grounded me. What gave me confidence. I just can't say it here. He apparently sees that on my face, because he smiles encouragingly. "I don't tell your coaches a word of what we say in here. Not one."

"Levi told me to give up everything else and make hockey my only focus," I tell him, rubbing my palms nervously on my jeans.

He looks skeptical. "And that worked?"

"No. I did the opposite," I say vaguely.

He waits patiently for more.

"There's a woman who means a lot to me. But our relationship is complicated, and we've been pushing each other away. I saw her while I was waiting for my neck guard to be fixed and…I didn't push her away. She makes me feel like the person I was before this bullshit accident took over my brain. And then I'm able to be that person again."

He nods. Just nods, like I don't sound at all codependent or insane. "It's not the woman. It's your instincts. You give in to them when she's around. You don't second-guess yourself or get caught up in the past. Don't rely on her for that. You need to start doing that when she's not there to remind you."

Huh. The little timer on his desk dings, signifying the end of our session. We stand and he shakes my hand. "I have you scheduled for next Tuesday."

"Yeah. Okay." I nod. "Thanks."

I feel really good as I leave the office. I think about what's happening with Dixie right now. My urge is to track her down and make her talk to me again, but my instincts are telling me to give her a little space and give myself some too, since the shrink told me not to rely on her. I'll go on the road trip and maybe talk to her when I get back. She'll still be here. And I'll still be falling in love with her. And hopefully she's falling in love with me.

So I go home, pack and am waiting outside the hotel when Levi picks me up half an hour later for the drive to the airport. He's in an upbeat mood for him, I can tell. Even though it would look like his goldfish died to the outside world.

"So when are you going to bring your car here?" he asks me.

My car is still in Sacramento. "I haven't thought about it."

"What about a place of your own?"

I shrug. "They haven't said I'm staying."

He looks at me like I just spoke a foreign language he doesn't understand. "Come on, Elijah, that's just a formality. You're staying for the rest of the season. Eddie's contract is up this summer, and I'm sure we'll let him go and keep you."

"Your brotherly love is blinding you, Levi," I tell him and smile. "I appreciate the support, but seriously, I've had one good game. Actually only one good period. I'm sure they haven't decided if they'll send me back down when Noah gets healthy or keep me here."

He waves a hand like he's dismissing my words. "You're staying. I know it. Get an apartment already."

"Remember, even if they keep me the rest of this year, my entry-level contract expires in June. I'll start looking when I know if they're going to give me a new one," I say, mostly just to get off the topic. "So I got a call from someone named Trish."

"Yeah. Trish works with Dixie in PR," Levi explains as he merges onto the freeway. "What'd she want?"

"She said that the winner of some contest the Thunder was doing picked me." I explain about the message that was on my phone when I woke up from my nap. "She said there would be a PR person coming on the road trip and they'd explain more, but that tonight I'm having dinner with this winner. Apparently his nine-year-old son is a goalie. A reporter will be there too. Have you done this type of thing before?"

"Yeah, all the time," he replies easily, taking the exit for the airport. "It can be tedious, but you're way more outgoing than me. You'll be fine. Especially if you score Dixie."

"What?" He wants me to score Dixie? What the hell...

"If you score her as the PR person on the trip, you're golden.

She's the best at making things comfortable," Levi replies easily. "I once had to give a rink tour to this girl who had my face tattooed on her chest and kept calling me Big Daddy. Dixie made sure to stand between us, because the girl was a little handsy, and kept the conversation light."

Would it be Dixie on this road trip? That itself is both a blessing and a curse. I have no idea what to expect. Will she talk to me? Is she still upset? Should I talk to her? It was easy to think I could beat the temptation of wanting to talk to her because I would be miles away, but now she's going to be on the same plane and in the same hotel. And we're going to have to have dinner together. Shit. I just hope I don't make this worse somehow.

When we get to the airport and clear security we make our way through the concourse to the private terminal where the team plane is located. A lot of guys hate the travel part of this job, but I definitely love it. A private plane sure beats a bus, which is how the Storm travels.

My eyes are darting around the terminal, but I don't see her. I do see a reporter I recognize from the post-game scrums. He sees us too and smiles and waves, walking over. Fan-fucking-tastic. I'll have to keep my guard up if he's around. Levi gives him an easy smile. "Hey, Tom. You hitching a ride?"

Tom smiles. "Yeah. Covering the game and doing a piece on the fan contest too."

"Eli is the player they picked," Levi tells him, and I want to kick him.

Tom looks over at me. "That's flattering, considering you're the newest addition and haven't played hardly a full game."

He means that as a genuine compliment, I think, but it comes across backhanded. Still, I smile and nod. "Yeah. I guess this guy is sick of Thor over here and wanted a younger, handsomer version. Anyway, I'm looking forward to it."

"This contest is a brilliant way of connecting with fans outside of SF," Tom adds.

"Dixie came up with the idea," Levi replies. Man, when did he become Captain Chats-a-Lot? What happened to the king of one-word responses? I miss him.

Tom's smile widens. "A brilliant idea from a brilliant woman."

I study his face and the way it lights up over Dixie, and I swear to God it's much more than professional admiration. He likes her. Asshole. I see Duncan standing by the door that leads out to the plane and I wave at him. "I've got to talk to Darby."

I march over there like a man on a mission. The mission is not to punch the reporter. Duncan smiles at me. "What's up, Kid Casco?"

"Don't nickname me that," I mutter.

"Did Thor have a brother?"

"Yeah. That asshole Loki," I reply and instantly regret it as I realize he's talking about Levi's nickname.

"Loki it is!" Duncan proclaims.

"Oh hell no," I bark, annoyed, and it just makes his smile get bigger. Damn it.

He turns to Jude, who is approaching with two Starbucks cups in his hands. "Eli's nickname is Loki."

"Really? I was thinking Hammer." Jude sips from one of the cups. "Because Thor needs his hammer to win, and we need our goalie to win."

Duncan is quiet for a moment and then he says in awe, "Wow. That was deep. And I like it. Hammer it is, kid!"

"Okay, fine, whatever. Just stop with the 'kid' shit." I follow Jude as he starts toward the door. "Are you freaked about leaving Zoey right now after the scare?"

"A little bit," Jude admits and his eyes cloud over. "But the doctor swears she's fine, and she hasn't had any more fake contractions." Levi and Tom are following a few feet back, but I can hear them chatting. The sound of the guy's voice annoys the crap out of me.

I enter the plane just behind Jude and follow him down the aisle. I don't see her, and I'm about to spiral into disappointment when she appears from the galley kitchen at the back. She looks past Jude and right at me. She doesn't smile, but I can see warmth in her eyes even though she's trying to mask it. Jude walks up to her and hands her one of the coffee cups. "They've launched the pumpkin spice lattes, so I got you one."

"Forget everything I've ever said. You're a great brother." She gulps down a big sip.

Jude drops down in a seat and I move to pass him, which means I have to pass her. The aisle is narrow, like on any plane, and I make a point of taking up more room than necessary so even when she turns sideways to let me by, our bodies connect, brushing torsos. Pink automatically starts creeping into her cheeks, and I bite back a smile of satisfaction at that. "I'll save you a seat."

"I'm sitting up front," she replies softly but with tension in her tone.

She turns and marches up the aisle away from me, aptly twisting and slipping past player after player as they board.

I shove my bag into the overhead bin and sit in an aisle seat so I can look ahead easily and see her. She's in the second row from the front, window seat. Tom drops down into the seat beside her. My fists clench again.

The entire flight was a nightmare. They chatted almost the whole time. I couldn't hear what they were saying, but she was smiling. A lot. When she finally pulled out her laptop and he pulled out a book and stopped yakking her ear off, I tried to sleep but couldn't, probably because instead of counting sheep I was counting ways to make Tom look like an idiot in front of Dixie. I was honestly worried she'd fall for his bumbling charm. After all, he's safe. There's no HR policy about dating reporters.

Now I'm in my hotel room unpacking and more frustrated than ever. I wanted to know what room she was in but I didn't get a chance to ask because Tom sat beside her on the bus to the hotel and rode with her in the elevator. They both got off on the seventh floor. My room is on the eighth. The idea that he has a room on her floor makes me crazy. Well, crazier than I already was.

There's a knock at my door, and I stalk over and swing it open. Levi is standing there and the smile on his face fades when he sees the look on mine.

"What's wrong?"

"Nothing," I mutter. "Come in."

He does, the door closing behind him, and he drops down on my bed, crossing his ankles and lacing his fingers behind his head. I walk over to the nightstand and check my phone to see if Dixie might have texted me and I missed it. She didn't.

"So…I wanted to ask how things went with the sports psychiatrist, but judging by your mood I probably shouldn't," he tells me.

"What?" I look up from my phone. "No. It's fine. The sessions went well."

"Oh. Good." Levi's jaw is tight and his eyebrows are pinched together, which proves he's unconvinced. "So you think it helped?"

"I guess we'll find out next time I play," I mutter. I decide to text Dixie and ask her what her room number is.

"Coach told me you're starting tomorrow night," Levi reveals. I press Send on the text and look over at him, dropping my phone back onto the tabletop.

"Really? For sure?"

Levi nods. "I'm not supposed to mention it, but I wanted to tell you."

"Thanks." I give him a quick smile.

"So if it's not the shrink that has you looking like you want to punch something, what is it?" Levi pulls himself to a sitting position, his back against the headboard.

I walk over to my suitcase as I debate what to say to him. I need to talk to someone. Dixie's sisters know about us, but I don't have anyone to bounce things off of, and I really feel like I need it right now. I sit down on the chair next to the luggage rack and run a hand through my hair, then rub the back of my neck. The shrink's words float back into my head. Instincts. Trust them. My instincts are telling me I can share this secret with Levi.

"Nothing major. Just the fact that I'm falling in love with Dixie."

It takes a minute for him to react. It's like someone presses pause on his face—it's frozen in a curious, patient expression like he's still waiting for me to tell him something. Then his reaction is like an explosion. He sits up straighter, leans forward, mouth falling open and eyes widening almost comically.

"I'm sorry, what? Dixie? Braddock?"

I nod.

"The blond girl with the smart mouth and smarter brain who is—"

"Fucking beautiful and sexy and brilliant?" I finish his sentence with my own adjectives. "And the fellow employee of the San Francisco Thunder. Yes. Her."

"In love?" He looks as skeptical as he would if I told him I had had an anal probe by aliens.

"Falling. Hard and fast," I admit, and it feels fantastic to finally say it.

He leans back and then leans forward again. His brows pinch together then pull apart, then pinch together again. It's like watching some weird eyebrow foxtrot. "But how? I mean, do you guys even talk outside of work?"

"We've been talking and texting since that charity auction before I joined the team. Actually we kissed last year when I was in town to play that preseason game."

"You kissed her? Way back then? Why?"

"Because we were stuck in an elevator." I shrug and sink back into the armchair. "Anyway, we knew that when I started on the team we'd have to cut it out, so we decided to have sex to really work it out of our systems," I explain. I tip my head back so I'm looking at the ceiling instead of Levi as I finish my confession. "And that didn't really work because I still want to have sex with her again. Indefinitely. And we have kind of been slipping up. She helped distract me."

"From?" Levi demands.

"From my problems on the ice. But I made her feel like this

isn't a big deal, that she was nothing but a distraction, and she's more than that." I sigh heavily. "She's just this…amazing force, you know? From her career to harassing her brother to telling me off, she does it all with this bold, fearless energy. And she's the only thing that got me through this PTSD shit from the accident by forcing me to face it."

"I wanted you to face it," Levi says earnestly. I look over at him and can see the hurt on his face.

"Don't get all pouty, big brother, you fucking diva muffin." I grin at him. "You know I wouldn't listen to you if you were the last man on earth."

"Because you're a fucking tool," Levi replies.

"No. Because you're a pod person sometimes," I retort with love. "You try to be perfect and emotionless all the time, like Mom and Dad. This was an emotional problem."

"So you admit you're an emotional train wreck?"

I lean forward and very slowly, very carefully flip him the bird. He lets out a hearty laugh.

"Back to the important stuff," Levi says, and I glance at him. I don't think I have ever seen him look more befuddled. "Does she know how you feel?"

"No. I told you, I fucked it up. But I want this to continue, regardless of all this shit it'll cause." I sigh and lean forward, my elbows on my knees. "And that makes me a selfish asshole, because if we get caught, she's the one who loses her job and ruins her career, not me."

"Yeah…" Levi agrees and then bites back a smile. "But you'll end up with two black eyes, at minimum, because Jude will attempt to kill you, so she's not the only one who'll suffer, if that helps."

"It doesn't," I reply in a clipped tone.

"Sorry. I don't mean to make light of this." Levi pulls himself off the bed and stands, arms crossed as he ponders my shitastic situation. "How does she feel about you?"

"The same. At least she did. But she's just fighting it," I explain. "Her co-worker got fired for messing around with Eddie."

"Yeah, I heard they let someone go." Levi nods. "It's not the first time it's happened, and it won't be the last, I'm sure."

Our eyes lock, and he instantly looks flustered. "I'm sorry. I don't mean Dixie."

"But it will happen to her if they find out." I swear under my breath, a long, low stream of expletives. It doesn't make me feel better. I stand up. "Look, I'm going to go down to the pool and do some laps, burn off some stress, before I have to go to this dinner thing with the fan and Dixie and that tool reporter."

Levi laughs. "Tom's a great guy."

"Yeah? Would you be saying that if he hit on Tessa in front of you, but you couldn't do a damn thing about it?"

"He's interested in Dixie?" Levi looks stunned again. "Dude, is your life always a soap opera, or is this a new thing?"

I flip him two middle fingers this time. "Very supportive, dick."

"Sorry. I honestly wish I had advice for you, Eli," Levi says as he walks toward me. "She might have feelings for you, but giving up her job is a lot to ask."

"I know." I nod. "That's why I'm not asking."

He nods. "If I think of anything helpful, I'll let you know. And not to add to your list of problems, but make sure when it's time, Jude finds out from you and her and not someone else. He's not going to forgive you otherwise, and as much as they love to annoy each other, the Braddock kids would kill for each other. Remember that."

"Kind of like you would kill for me?" I joke.

"I wouldn't kill for you, but I'd help you move a body," he quips back as I open the door and he leaves. I close the door behind him and drop back on the bed and close my eyes. How the hell am I going to make this work?

23

DIXIE

I pick a soft, loose, long white blouse, fitted black ankle pants and leopard-print heels. Pants are the key to getting through this night. I need to have minimal exposed skin so Elijah can't touch it. I've missed him like he's a limb that's been severed. And seeing him on the plane, feeling our bodies brush, Jesus, I was on fire. That can't happen again, especially not with fans around.

I stare at my refection in the mirror as I apply my lipstick. I look healthy and relaxed with glowing skin and clear, glassy eyes. It's not just makeup tricks, it's the fact that as soon as I walked into my hotel room, I stripped down and touched myself, coming hard with his name on my lips. He had me that worked up, and I thought climaxing would clear my head and give me focus, but it didn't. I still want him. I still feel myself falling in love with him. I can't. Not right now. I have a lot to work out.

I smooth my hair and heave a big breath, exhaling slowly. I love my job, but I'm starting to love him too. Jude knocks on my door. I know it's Jude not just because I asked him to swing by but also because he's knocked in the same rhythm since he was a kid. I glance at the clock on the table as I walk past the bed to the door. I have half an hour before I have to be in the restaurant downstairs for the fan dinner.

I swing open my door. Jude is in Thunder sweats, flip-flops and a heather-gray T-shirt, and his hair is askew. He must have just woken up from a nap.

"Hey! Come in!"

He wanders over to my bed and falls back onto it like he's practicing a trust fall. His eyes are closed when he hits the pillow. I smirk. "Tired, princess?"

He lifts a hand and rubs his eyes, then yawns. "I can't sleep like I used to. I keep trying, but I mostly just lie awake and think about the million things that can injure babies or how quickly I can get home if she goes into labor again. Or the billion ways I might fuck up this parenting thing."

He looks at me, and I can tell he's not being flippant. He's serious. "FYI, just the fact that you're stressing out about all of that makes you great dad material. And this kid is a Braddock. It'll be tough and smart. And Zoey is tough too. She'll do just fine in labor, even if God forbid you don't make it back in time. Have a little faith in your woman and your DNA, Jude."

He gives me a small smile. "Thanks."

"About DNA, the reason I asked you to come see me is I need your help on something I've pitched to the ALS Foundation," I explain. "It's a social media campaign."

"Is this for the Thunder?" He grabs a second pillow to put under his melon.

I shake my head and lean my ass against the TV console. "No.

It's just me contributing on my own. I had this idea, something that might bring it more coverage, like the ice bucket challenge did."

"I didn't know you were doing that." He looks impressed. "That's great, Dix."

"Thanks. It started this week," I explain. "But big names are key to making this work. I know you know a few really well, like the supermodel Stella Ascott and that TV actor who you party with in Toronto. The one from the teen paranormal show that's so popular."

He nods, and I spend the next ten minutes explaining my campaign, which involves celebrities, like the ones he knows who have massive social media accounts, going dark, posting nothing but one written fact or statistic on a symptom from each stage of ALS every day for a week until, on the final day, they post nothing, or just blackness, to show how the disease robs you of everything. He listens intently, sitting up as I get to the end of my pitch.

"I don't know these people like you do, and I don't think I'd get anywhere cold-calling them, and I can't use my position with the team because it's not for the Thunder, so can you help?"

"Yeah, of course." He smiles and I see pride in it. "It's a great idea."

"Thanks!"

"Are you sure you're going to be able to take this on on top of all the work you do for the team?" he asks, standing. "Between this and your job and all the time you've been spending at Mom and Dad's, you're going to have no life."

"I'm okay with that for now," I reply vaguely.

He studies me. Jude is ridiculously intuitive, to the point that it's almost creepy. I used to think I just lacked the ability to have a poker face, but I've seen him read other people just as well, so it's not only me. He tilts his head a little. "You turn twenty-six soon. You should not only *want* a social life, you should *have* one. And be dating. A lot. I swear the entire sorority is in some kind of spinsterhood competition."

I'd be insulted, except it's amusing. When I was growing up, he used to tell me and my sisters we were too ugly and annoying for boyfriends, and then when we had them, he'd try to scare them away. Now he's worried we don't have boyfriends.

"Yeah, you caught us. The person who dies alone wins," I quip and roll my eyes.

"Well, it looks like it's going to be a three-way tie," he jokes back as I glance at the clock and grab my purse off the chair in the corner.

"Two-way. Winnie technically has Tyson," I remind him and grin. "And in the event of a tie the person with the most cats is the victor."

He laughs and follows me out of my room. As we walk down the hall toward the elevators I glance over at him. "I want what Mom and Dad have."

He looks over at me, his eyes searching for any hint of levity like I'm somehow going to turn this into a joke. I look back at him with serious eyes. "They met each other and they just knew. And the universe knew, and everything just fell into place for them. It was perfect, and because of that it was easy and simple."

Jude looks like he just smelled a fart. "In the words of my future wife and the mother of my unborn child, oh Mylanta! That's a load of crap."

We reach the elevators. I press the Down button and he presses the Up. "How do you figure? They got married three months after they met, and they've been together thirty years. They've had fights and financial and emotional ups and downs, but neither of them had to give anything up or suffer because they wanted to be together. The stars aligned."

"Dad picked up and moved to Canada—illegally—to be with Mom," Jude reminds me. "They got married quickly so he could stay legally. Yeah, they loved each other, but that wasn't the ideal way to get hitched. And Dad's parents weren't thrilled with him just leaving Detroit and his family like that. Things were tense between them until I was like eight. I remember it because I could feel it every time we went to visit them. And Zoey and I are soul mates and the perfect couple." I glance over as he grins at his own lack of modesty. "We have the perfect love affair, but it's not the perfect story, technically. She was married and in the middle of a vicious divorce, and I was trying to hide from all the women I'd banged. And then I knocked her up less than a year in, and we're not even married yet. Sounds crazy to anyone you'd tell it to, but yet, we're perfect."

"She's perfect. You're perfect adjacent," I reply as his elevator arrives and he steps inside.

"All I'm saying is don't look for someone who doesn't require sacrifice," he tells me. "Look for someone worth sacrificing for."

His words settle inside me all heavy and warm. He's fucking brilliant when he lets himself be, but I can't acknowledge that in front of him, so instead I smirk. "Have you been memorizing fortune cookie messages again?"

He rolls his eyes so hard it looks like he's passing out. "Another bonding moment down the shitter."

My elevator doors open as his close. I step inside next to two guys in golf wear and let Jude's words roll around my head. I wish this dinner tonight wasn't happening. I wish I could stay away from Eli long enough for us both to figure out if this is really as serious as it feels and what to do about it.

I'm supposed to meet Tom before the winner and Eli get here. He wants to go over some questions about the contest so he gets the details right in his story. The bar is fairly busy but I can see Tom at the end of the long polished oak bar. He's with Vinnie LaMarche and Eddie Rollins. I walk over but stop a few feet away to ask the bartender for a Pinot Grigio. I hear Eddie laugh at something, and then I hear Vinnie tell Tom, "He has a girlfriend. You could ask him about that."

The bartender slides the full wineglass across the bar. I scrawl my room number on the bill and walk over to the guys. "Who has a girlfriend?"

"Oh, hey!" Tom leans in and hugs me, which I wasn't expecting and, frankly, didn't want, so I kind of freeze up. When he lets go I pull back so abruptly some wine slops over the side of my wineglass. He doesn't seem to notice my reaction. "I was just asking Rollins and Marchie for ideas on some questions for Elijah," he says as I take a sip of my wine.

I swallow the wine in my mouth so quickly I'm surprised I don't choke. "He has a girlfriend?"

"I think so. He mentioned her when he was here for that charity event," Vinnie explains.

And I feel myself slipping into panic mode. Is it me? Was he talking about me? Oh God, do they know it's me? Wait, he thinks I'm his girlfriend? I want to smile at that thought, but then I realize Tom can't probe him on it if it is me. "We don't usually let reporters ask about personal lives, unless the player brings it up first."

"You can be subtle about it," Vinnie suggests, and I want to toss my wine in his face. "Ask him if he knows a Julie. That's her name."

Wait…what?

Tom laughs. "I don't think that's subtle, Vinnie."

"Ask him about college. He's got some wild stories about college," Eddie adds and sips his light beer. "Like having an affair with a teacher's wife!"

"What?" It flies out of my mouth before I can stop it, and it's hard and judgmental.

Vinnie glares at Eddie. "I told you you couldn't tell anyone, Eddie, you dick."

Eddie shrugs and smiles at my still horrified face. "Relax, Marchie. We all have secrets, right, Baby Bra—"

I step between Vinnie and Tom and right up into Eddie's face. "If you call me Baby Braddock ever again I will grab you by your tiny dick so hard you never have a Baby Rollins."

"You can't talk to me like that!" he replies, offended.

"Take it up with HR then. I'm sure you know their number, since you reported Nadine after you got bored with sleeping with her," I hiss back. "And FYI, everyone does have secrets, but the one about your tiny dick is out, thanks to the women you mistreat who don't have to pretend you have anything worthwhile down there anymore."

I turn to Tom. He looks astonished but also a little impressed. "Let's grab a table."

He nods and follows me toward the restaurant attached to the bar. I hear Vinnie tell Eddie, "She burned you so bad I feel like I should pour my drink on you to put out the flames."

I smile at that. Fuck Eddie. Let him go to HR. He told inappropriate personal information about a player to the press, and he tried to belittle me. Even if I get my wrist slapped, it will be worth it. I'm not even that furious with Eddie. I'm actually hurt by the information about Eli. Who the hell is Julie?

"Before you say it, don't worry. I won't ask Casco about the teacher's wife or even the girl named Julie." Tom smiles at me reassuringly. "I know how hockey players are, and besides, I don't write for TMZ."

I give him what I hope looks like a grateful smile. "I appreciate that, Tom."

The hostess has our reserved table ready, so she grabs the menus and asks us to follow her. Tom motions for me to precede him and puts a light hand on the middle of my back when I do. It's a simple gentlemanly gesture, but I don't like it, so I pick up my pace quickly so his hand loses contact.

We sit next to each other, facing the entrance. I open my menu to pretend I'm busy reading, but Tom ignores his and leans forward on the table. "So, you seeing anyone, Dixie?"

"No. Not really," I reply, not pulling my focus from the menu. "I don't have time."

"There's always time," Tom counters. "How about I show you by taking you for a drink after the next home game?"

"Hey." Eli's delicious rumble of a voice pulls both our eyes up. He's striding toward us, looking like an office-casual Disney prince with his shock of dark hair dropping over his forehead and his dark jeans and fitted gray cashmere sweater with just hints of his white-and-blue-checkered button-down popping out at the cuffs and collar. I notice people noticing him because of the fluid way he carries such a tall, broad body. It's mesmerizing, and I always have a hard time not staring, but tonight, looking at him kind of hurts, so I easily glance away.

Tom stands and they shake hands.

"Dixie."

I look up at him when Eli says my name. "The fan will be here any second. Have a seat and finish up your interview with Tom. I'll go meet him at the hostess station."

I push back my chair, grab my purse and walk away. I pull my phone out of my purse and glance at the time. The guy was supposed to be here by now. God, I just want this to start so it can end and I can head back to my room with a bottle of wine and Skype my sisters.

I feel a hand curl around my wrist. I can't see him, but I know it's him. I know his touch. My body, on instinct, wants to melt into it, but my brain is screaming no. I turn to face him and subtly take a step back, removing my wrist and myself from his grasp. He looks hurt and then frustrated. I look at the entrance. I turn back to him. "Did you have an affair with a teacher's wife?"

His eyes flare and his shoulders tense. "Who told you about that?"

"So you're the type of guy that sleeps with married women?"

His mouth presses together in a hard line, and I can hear the air rush from his lungs. He takes a step closer and lowers that already low voice. "They were already separated because he had slept with his teaching assistant. She picked me because I was in his class. I was a horny, dumb college kid who allowed myself to be her instrument of revenge."

I don't respond. I don't even know why I'm acting like that story is why I'm mad. It's shocking and not what I would have done in college, but it's the past. I can't fault him for that. I can fault him if he's got a girlfriend named Julie at this very moment.

He reaches for my wrist again and pulls me off to the side, near the hallway that leads to the kitchen. He leans down so we're almost face-to-face. "Are you really going to fault me for my past? Are you that type of girl?"

"No. I'm not," I reply and pause, finding the strength to say the rest in a voice that doesn't wobble. "I'm the type of girl that never thought to ask if you were seeing someone when I slept with you."

"What?" he asks, and I can see him struggling to absorb my words.

"Who is Julie?"

Over Eli's shoulder a tall forty-something man walks up to the hostess table in a San Francisco Thunder jersey. The preteen boy beside him is in a Thunder jersey too. I sidestep Eli. "Mr. Jones?"

He turns and smiles. "Yes! I'm so sorry we're late. We live way across town, and traffic was crazy."

"It's fine," I assure him and smile at Charlie, who is staring past me with the brightest smile on his face and wide, starstruck eyes.

He tugs the sleeve of his dad's jersey. "He's here, Dad!"

I turn and see Eli step forward, wearing a bright toothpaste-commercial smile. "Hi there! Charlie, is it?"

Charlie nods. "You're my favorite player. And my dad's too!"

"Well, you guys are my favorite Torontonians!" Eli exclaims.

"Eli, why don't you take Mr. Jones and Charlie to the table. I'll join you in just a second," I tell him, because seeing them in their jerseys reminds me I forgot the gift bag full of Thunder gear I brought for them upstairs in my room.

Eli looks like he wants to argue, but he doesn't. Instead he leads the way to the table. I hurry out of the restaurant and through the bar to the lobby. I'm marching across the marble floor to the elevators when I see Jude. He's wearing the same clothes he was wearing in my room, which is nothing he would ever wear in public. I wonder why…

My eyes catch a glimpse of Levi just behind him. Levi is known for his stern expression, but I've never seen this level of seriousness on his face. It makes my blood grow cold. I change my trajectory so I'm walking straight at them, confusion and fear growing with each step.

They both notice me at the same time. My step falters at what I see next. Jude's blue eyes are filled with tears and his face is awash in anguish. His step falters too.

Oh my God, it's Dad.

24

ELIJAH

I decide to stop at the Starbucks across the street from the hospital and order a bunch of pumpkin spice lattes and a couple mochas, including one for myself with extra whip, and a couple caramel macchiatos and an herbal tea for Zoey, because pregnant women can't do caffeine. Then I get some pastries too.

I yawn so hard as I wait for them that my jaw feels like it's going to lock. Exhausted doesn't even begin to explain how I feel right now. When Dixie didn't come back to the dinner for almost half an hour I was furious. But then Levi appeared and explained to everyone that Dixie had a family emergency and had to leave. Our eyes connected and he looked so devastated—the same expression he wore when he was standing at the foot of my bed after my accident—and all my fury evaporated. I knew something serious had happened, likely to her dad, and my heart started to break for her.

As soon as I'd fulfilled my duties with the fans and Tom, I went straight to Levi's hotel room. He explained Mr. Braddock had suddenly contracted severe bilateral pneumonia, and although the doctors in the hospital were trying hard to treat him, they told Mrs. Braddock to prepare the family for the strong possibility he would not be coming home. Dixie and Jude had gone straight to the airport.

"I'm going to go back and be with her," I announced immediately.

"Elijah, you can't. Even if you don't start, we can't play the game without two goalies. You know that," Levi reminded me and then his expression softened into sympathy as he grabbed my shoulder. "We have a day between the game tomorrow night and the next game in Michigan. How about you fly back home in between them to check on her. We can make up some family excuse so no one knows what you're doing."

"You'd do that for me?" I was in awe. Levi takes his job as captain of this team very seriously, and I never thought he'd lie to the management or coaching staff for anyone, even me.

"You clearly care about her. This isn't some fling. And if it was Tess, I would want to be there for her too."

I reached out and pulled him into a bear hug. "Thank you."

He nodded, and we sat and figured out a story. The next morning over the team breakfast Levi pulled the coach aside and told him we had a family emergency and that one of us needed to head back to California for a day, and he'd like it to be me. The coach was irked but trying not to show it, and Levi seemed to calm him down by reminding him I would only miss the travel day and the one practice in Michigan, and he agreed. It was nothing but a formality to me anyway, because I'd already booked an overnight flight to San Francisco for after the game. I was going whether he let me or not.

Now, although I wasn't regretting that decision, I was growing nervous. Levi had texted Jude right after the game and their dad was hanging on, fighting hard, but it still seemed like the worst might happen. They were a close family, and I didn't want to intrude, but I had to be there for Dixie. Maybe I was selfish. Thinking of the pain she must be going through made me ache like it was my own. Holding her, being there for her, felt like the only way to alleviate that. I hope it will give her strength too. I'm about to find out.

I take my Starbucks haul and walk into the hospital. I know from Levi's text when I got off the plane that Mr. Braddock was holding on and that he was in ICU room 461. I don't want to barge into his room. I haven't even met her mom, and I don't think Jude finding out about us by his dad's potential deathbed is a fantastic idea, so my plan is to go to the nurses' station and ask them to ask Dixie to meet me at the waiting area on that floor.

I don't have to implement it though, because as soon as I get off the elevator, I see her. There's a glassed-in room to the right with a little plaque saying LOUNGE, and she's there sandwiched between her two sisters. Dixie's head rests on Sadie's shoulder, and her eyes are closed. But Sadie's aren't, and she recognizes me even before I come into the room. She smiles at me. "My instincts told me you were a good one. This proves I'm never wrong."

"I don't mean to interrupt. I just thought maybe you guys would want some non-hospital food," I say.

"Starbucks! Oh my God, you're a keeper," Winnie blurts out and jumps up to grab a cup out of the tray. "Pumpkin spice, too. If she doesn't marry you, she's insane."

I laugh at that and feel heat ignite my cheeks. Winnie grabs a second cup as Sadie nudges Dixie and her eyes flutter open. Winnie hands her a latte. Blurry-eyed, she starts to reach for it but then she sees me. Our eyes meet, and she looks like she's seen a ghost. I feel my throat get thick and my chest get tight. Speaking is suddenly hard, but as Sadie stands and takes the coffee tray and bag of treats from me, I tell Dixie, "I wanted to be here in case you needed me."

She stands and throws herself into my arms. I have never held anyone as tight as I am holding her right now. "What can I do?"

She buries her face in my neck, and against it I hear her say, "You did it."

"He's improved slightly," Sadie tells me as she opens the pastry bag and looks inside. "They changed his meds and he's breathing better."

"They won't let more than two of us in at a time, so we take shifts," Winnie explains, reaching into the pastry bag and pulling out a chocolate croissant. "This shift is Jude and Mom. Mom tends to stay through several shifts. She doesn't want to leave him."

I nod and run my hand over the back of Dixie's head, through her tangled hair. She's still in the clothes she was wearing at the restaurant, and I'm betting she hasn't been home yet at all. "When you go in for your shift, give me the keys to your place, and I'll grab you some new clothes."

She nods shakily and gives me a wobbly smile. "I'm sorry. I'm a mess."

"Don't be sorry." I kiss her forehead.

She looks up at me with the most savagely broken expression I've ever seen. She wipes at her eyes, where tears are hovering. "I don't want you to see this side of me."

I cup her face in my hands and dip my head so only she can hear. "Sweet Dixie. I want to see every side of you."

I hear footsteps behind us and turn my head to see Jude walk into the room. He stops abruptly at the sight of me. Then walks slowly around me and sees Dixie in my arms. She notices him and quickly steps out of our embrace. Jude looks like shit. He has bags under his eyes and emanates exhaustion. I can only hope that means he can't find the strength to freak out about this.

"He's awake," Jude says to his sisters. "And actually kind of chatty, so you should all get in there. Nurse said we could crowd the place for fifteen minutes."

Winnie and Sadie jump up and beeline for the door. Dixie pauses and turns to stand in front of Jude. Jude gives her a small smile. "Go see Dad. I'm sure I'll find something to talk about with my goalie."

Dixie hesitates but leaves, grabbing a latte from the abandoned tray on the chair and following after her sisters. Jude and I are standing there in the middle of the room staring at each other. I walk over and pick up the tray of coffee. "Mocha? Pumpkin spice? I brought an herbal tea for Zoey too."

"I sent her home to rest," he replies and reaches for a mocha. "I'll bring my mom the herbal tea, though, when Dixie comes back."

I nod, and as he moves to a chair and sits down, I do too. He sips the mocha. "Thanks for this. And thanks for being here for Dixie. Not sure how you managed that, because Coach hates when we take time away."

"Levi told him I needed to deal with a family thing," I explain and try to lean back and not look so nervous. Talking around the real topic here is stressing me out. "We won last night, so that might make Coach feel better about it."

"You didn't just win. You got a shut-out," Jude remarks. "Your first in the NHL. It's a big deal."

I nod. It is a big deal, especially with the way I've been playing since I got here. "Things are back on track for me, and a big reason why is your sister," I tell him. "Dixie's brutal honesty about my issues helped me face them."

He grins at that. "She's nothing if not brutally honest." He pauses and sips more of his mocha and then sighs. "Which is why it's hard for me to know she's lying about you to everyone and she's going to have to keep doing it."

"I get the feeling you knew about this," I can't help but say, because although I didn't expect him to punch me or anything, I expected a lot more shock and dismay than he's showing.

He shrugs his broad shoulders. "I had a feeling. But I was hoping I was wrong."

Ouch.

"This is serious to me," I tell him, trying to curb whatever doubt he has. "I don't know how it can work, but I've never wanted anything more in my life."

"It can't work," Jude replies quietly and with pure empathy on his face. "Not without carnage. That's why I was hoping I was wrong."

"I can request a trade. If I'm not on the team, she's not violating anything."

Jude nods at that but once again doesn't look impressed. "Because a long-distance relationship is so much better than a secret one? The closest NHL teams are Seattle and San Diego, and their goalies aren't going anywhere. You could end up somewhere on the East Coast, and you'll both be miserable, and she'll end up quitting to move to wherever you are anyway."

I frown. It's not that I hadn't thought of that. I'd just ignored it. Now I have to face it and the other problem with my plan. "I wouldn't want her to leave her family anyway."

Jude stares at the lid on his mocha for almost a minute, and when he looks up something about his expression has changed. He's not guarded, and his forehead isn't creased with dismay like it seemed to be before. His eyes hold something warmer now, acceptance and even approval. He leans forward, elbows on his knees. "She's dealing with a lot right now, and change and chaos are the type of things that scare her the most. More pressure will push her away."

"And I'm working through PTSD and fighting for a real contract in this league," I assure him, meeting his eye so he knows I mean it. "The timing is a bitch."

"Timing is everything," Jude replies, and then he pauses and shrugs. "Until it's nothing."

"What does that even mean?" I'm baffled. This is the guy whose greatest depth of knowledge used to be knowing which condoms felt the least like condoms.

"It means maybe it's not the right time for you two," he explains. "But maybe the fact that being together will fuck everything up means it is the perfect time. Maybe things need to get fucked up. I've never felt Dixie was really one hundred percent happy with the Thunder. She seemed to be trying to prove a point and impress our dad, which she loves to do. But I think there's more she needs from a career."

I wonder if he's right. I feel bad that I kind of hope he is. "Well, she has to come to that revelation on her own, I guess. Just don't tell anyone about this, okay? Me and her."

"Dude, you don't have to tell me not to rat out my sister." Jude laughs. "Just do me a favor and figure out your own shit so that when she gets out of her own way, you'll be ready for her and I won't have to kick your ass or anything."

I smile at that. "I'm working on it."

Jude smiles. "Good. Oh, and fair warning, this whole family tends to overshare and say things they shouldn't, so I hope you can handle it. That summer Levi lived with us there were more than a few times someone said something that you could tell made him want to die of embarrassment."

"I'd rather have a family that's over-the-top than one that's emotionally constipated like mine," I reply, and Jude nods. He knows what Levi and I grew up with and how we both still struggle with our parents' uptight, judgmental personalities.

I stand up and stretch a little bit. "I'm guessing you have a spare key to Dixie's place? I wanted to swing by and get her some fresh clothes so she doesn't have to leave here."

Jude stands up too and pulls his keys out of his pocket. He hands them to me, holding up a silver one. "It's this one."

"Thanks." I take them and put them in my own pocket. "Levi wants you to call him when you can. He's worried. And tell Dixie I'll be back in a flash and to text me if she wants anything specific."

He nods and I head out the door.

25

DIXIE

I need to go back out there and be with Elijah before he leaves to rejoin the team, but I hate leaving my dad. He's got his eyes closed, but I'm not sure if he's resting or sleeping. My mom is in the corner, looking completely drained, but the crease between her eyes is gone. Still, she's aged about five years in the last forty-eight hours. The doctor checked on Dad while Eli was at my place getting me clothes and officially confirmed we were—miraculously, as he called it—out of the woods. Dad would most likely make a full recovery. Well, as full as an ALS patient can make. His breathing ability had been on the decline before this happened. He was on the low end of normal, but at least he will get back to that level, which doesn't require oxygen or machines.

I glance at the clock on the wall and his voice, gravelly but strong, interrupts my thoughts. "If you need to be somewhere, Little D, then go. Your job and your life are important too. I'm on the road to fine, so don't let me mess things up."

I smile at him. "I'm right where I need to be, Dad. But I have a friend who came to check on me, and he's leaving soon, so I'm going to sneak out and say good-bye to him."

I stand. My mom and dad are both intently focused on me now. "Enid, did she say 'he'?"

My mom nods, biting back a smile. "She did, Randy. Her friend is a boy."

"Honey, run home and get my shotgun from the hall closet, will you?" my dad jokes, and my mom snickers.

"I know you don't own a shotgun, Dad." I laugh. "And I know you have a few questions, like maybe a thousand or so, but right now is not the time for them."

I walk toward the door and hear him say. "But I'm bored and I have all the time in the world right now."

I laugh again. "Get better and get out of here. Your reward will be that you can give me the third degree."

I glance out the door and see Eli standing in the hall outside the lounge. My mom also sees him and smiles. "Oh. He's tall. And rugged-looking. Nice smile."

"Wave him in here, Enid!" my dad demands.

"Family only in the ICU. Don't piss off your nurses, Dad." I start out the door. "I'll be back. No wild parties while I'm gone."

He chuckles a little at that, and I hate the way it makes the stuff in his lungs rattle. I march down the hall, take Elijah by the hand and without a word pull him around the corner to a little alcove with pay phones and a water fountain. I wrap my arms around his neck and kiss him hard and deep.

His hands press into my lower back, pulling me closer to his body. I started the kiss, but he's instantly in control of it. The movement of his tongue, the press of his lips, everything exposes his hunger for me and my own fiery need for him explodes. I press my palms to the sides of his gorgeous face, scared he might pull away before I'm satiated...which may be never. I press my torso into his, relishing the hard delineation of the muscles in his abdomen and the growing fullness in his jeans. Finally, with a low moan he breaks the kiss. "If I don't end this now, I'm going to end up in a room next to your dad being treated for blue balls."

A laugh bursts from me, and I cover my mouth until it passes and is replaced by a smile. "It's your fault. You brought me tooth-paste and a toothbrush."

"I should have brought you a condom too," he retorts and winks at me. He runs a hand over the back of my head, stopping to cup my neck, tilting my face toward his. "Are you okay?"

"I will be because he will be," I promise him. "Thank you for coming. I don't know how you did it, but it means everything."

"You mean everything to me," he says in a quiet, firm voice. "I know it's not ideal timing, and I'm working through my own stuff with a sports psychologist."

"You are?"

"Yeah. Some incredibly good-looking, overbearing woman kind of forced me into it," he kids with a cheeky grin. "But I thought you should know, even if the timing doesn't work right now, I will be around when does. Because for maybe the first time in my life I'm serious about something, and it's you."

The desire inside me starts to flicker and reality seeps back in. "Who's Julie?"

He laughs, which is not what I was expecting at all. He pulls his phone out of his pocket and goes through his contacts, pulling up one with that name. "You are Julie."

I stare at the screen and it is my number under that name. "Dixie isn't exactly a common name, and I didn't want to risk someone seeing you call me or accidentally see one of our texts. Like the half-naked ones."

A tidal wave of relief crests inside me. There's no one else. I look up into those perfect green eyes. "Why Julie?"

He shrugs, a little bit of a sheepish expression covering his features. "I had a thing for the character Julie Taylor on *Friday Night Lights* when I was younger."

"Oh my God! I had a thing for Eric Taylor!"

"Her dad?" His face contorts in disgust. "He's like a hundred."

"I've always been into older men," I admit with a shrug, and then I wink at him. "You're the exception, not the rule, boy toy."

He grins and pulls me into him, holding me tight, and I cling to him just as fiercely. He gently pulls away, stopping to kiss my forehead, then claiming me in another kiss just as passionate as the last. I'm the one who breaks it this time, because if I don't, I'll have to find an empty room and fuck him senseless. "I wish I could take you home."

"You need to focus on your dad." He kisses my neck and then my cheek. I shiver with need. "And the fact is, we still have a big problem and no solution. So that's our last kiss for a while."

Right. The rules. Him or my career. The rock and the hard place.

His expression darkens, his smile fading and his mouth slipping into a serious line. "Remember, I'm not going anywhere. If you need me, I'm here."

"Okay."

He hugs me so hard he lifts me off my feet, and everything inside me feels warm and relaxed. He takes my hand and we leave the little alcove and walk to the elevators.

"So, am I listed under a fake name in your phone?" he asks as we wait.

"Yeah."

The elevator arrives, and he steps inside next to an orderly and a doctor holding a chart. "Who?"

"Justin Bieber."

His horrified face as the elevator doors close is priceless.

I walk back into my dad's room, grinning, because I can't wipe it off. He watches me intently as I plop down on a chair next to him. "Enid, honey, forget the shotgun. Any boy who makes my Little D smile like that is okay by me."

That makes my grin grow. "He's a good friend for now. That's all."

"Sweetie, we raised you not to lie," my mom says in a serious tone with a giant smile.

I cover my face with my hands and laugh. "You guys, cut me some slack."

"Okay, for now, but when I get home I'm going to grill you," he warns and coughs again.

My mom stands. "I'm going to get you some fresh water." She takes the small plastic cup with the lid off the tray beside his bed.

"Make it a beer."

My mom chuckles as she heads out of the room. My dad is silent for a few minutes, with his eyes closed. I assume he's drifting off, but then he says, "Dixie, honey, shouldn't you be back at work?'

"I would only be getting back from the road trip this afternoon if I'd stayed there," I explain and inch my chair closer so I can lean on the edge of his bed. "And I need to be here. If they don't like it, they can fire me."

"I don't want you and Jude messing up your careers over me." The guilt in his voice slices through me as if it's a buck knife.

"Don't worry about that. First of all, Jude is their top player. He can do virtually anything he wants," I say. "Players would have to murder someone at center ice to get their hand slapped by the management."

His blue eyes flare at that, because my bitterness is more than apparent. He moves, struggling a bit to pull himself up a little on his pillows. I reach for the remote and tap it, moving the top part of his bed up a bit. He smiles gratefully, but his expression quickly turns back to concern. "The players are the heroes, and you and the rest of the people behind the scenes are the unsung heroes. It's the way it is in any sport. You knew that going in."

"I did. But the team is owned by a woman, the most incredible businesswoman I've ever heard of, so I guess maybe I thought they would be different." I sigh. "I'm just tired and cranky. It happens when your dad scares you to death."

I smile at him, and he smiles back. "You know I'm just as proud of you as I am of Jude, right?"

"I know."

He reaches out and puts his hand over mine on the edge of his bed. "I'm proud of all my kids for following their hearts and doing what they love. It wouldn't matter if Jude was a fourth-line player on a farm team or if you were still an intern. If you're giving it your all and passionate about what you do, that makes me proud."

I nod and drop my other hand on top of his, sandwiching it between mine. His skin feels thin and his hand is cold. "I'm great at what I do." I pause and find myself admitting to him something I haven't even admitted to myself yet. "But I'm not sure I'm passionate about it anymore."

Wow. It feels good to say that. I hadn't realized how much this has been weighing on me until I finally said it out loud.

"Really?" my dad asks, obviously a little bit shocked.

"I went in there thinking I could change the culture," I explain quietly. "And maybe I could, after a couple hundred more years. But now I feel like there's things I'd have to give up that are worth more than the job, you know?"

I tilt my head to look right at him. He doesn't look disappointed at all. He just nods and squeezes my hand under his. His grip is still strong and calms me. "Then move on. I want you to smile about your job the way you smile about that mystery boy."

I laugh. "Is that your way of trying to get me to talk about him again?"

"Maybe." He laughs and it turns into a cough.

"Rest, Daddy," I command as my mom walks back into the room.

He has some of the water she brought him and closes his eyes. He starts to snore lightly, and a few minutes later Jude and Zoey appear at the door. I get up and offer Zoey my seat. She gives me a quick hug before sitting down.

Jude walks over and hugs Mom and whispers. "Everything good?"

"He still seems to be on the mend, thankfully," Mom tells him. "Did you book your flight back to the team?"

"I leave tonight," Jude says and he looks and sounds upset about it.

Mom pats his cheek. "Honey, he wants you to play. He's out of the woods, and if that changes, I will call you immediately."

"I know." He still doesn't seem convinced.

"I'm going to work tomorrow too," I say to make him feel better. "I have a meeting at the ALS Foundation, and then I'll spend the entire day in the office because he wants me to. You know how he hates disrupting our lives."

He nods. I tell them I'm going to head home. Jude says he'll walk me to the elevator. As soon as we're out of the room he says, "So, Casco, huh?"

"Yeah. I mean, not right now, but yeah." I try not to sound as awkward as I feel. My comfort zone around my brother is being annoying and bossy, not serious and vulnerable.

He pushes the button for the elevator and then leans against the wall across from it. His eyes land on mine. "You've got some pretty complicated choices to make."

I nod. "I do."

"Well, I just want you to know that I support you, no matter what."

He's being so damn sweet I can't handle it. The last few days have been way too emotional already. So I give him my best smartass smile. "Good, because when it all goes to hell and I'm jobless and penniless, I am totally moving in with you. I can be a nanny for your little girl."

The elevator doors open, and I jump in and hit the Close button, but I still hear him call out, "It's a *boy*!"

26

ELIJAH

She looks amazing. It's just a plain, short-sleeved navy dress. It's not even tight or clingy. And a pair of low-heeled brown leather boots that hit at her knee. Somehow, though, what might look like librarian wear on someone else looks sexy as fuck on my Dixie. Which is why I don't make eye contact when she walks into the locker room. "Great job, boys! Fifteen-minute media scrum, and then hustle through the shower because the bus to Ms. Bateman's is parked outside ready and waiting."

She marches out. I steal a glance at her perfect ass as it swings out the door. Levi nudges me. "You might want to wipe that drool from the corner of your mouth before someone sees it, little brother."

I glance over at him and smirk guiltily. It's nice to have him in the loop—and Jude too. It's been three days since the hospital talk. I'm trying to get used to this weird holding pattern Dixie and I are in and not to dwell on how much it sucks, because there's nothing I can do to change it. Jasper was called up last week when one of our forwards broke his foot blocking a puck, and they put him in the same hotel as me, on the same floor. I love Jasper and I'm happy to have him here and be playing with him again, and he's a welcome distraction that keeps me from thinking about my romantic limbo.

"You like having a car again?" Levi asks me, because Jasper also drove my car up.

"Yeah. Definitely beats begging you for lifts."

"So you're getting over your commitment issues slowly but surely," Levi quips with a smile. "Next up, you get a permanent place to live."

"As soon as I know I'm getting a real contract, I'll pull the trigger," I promise. I've started looking for places, but Coach hasn't said I'm staying here past this season and management hasn't offered me a new contract, so I'm still not willing to buy anything. It feels like counting my eggs before they're hatched.

He pulls off his jersey and starts to remove his shoulder pads. "Well, with the way Rollins is playing, that should happen any day now."

"It's not about Rollins," I argue quietly, even though Eddie has been pulled in the last two games he started and I've come in and saved the games. "It's about me. They need time to see I'm back and this isn't a fluke. I'm okay with it, and I'll give them that proof."

Levi is looking at me with this weird expression and I can't decide if it's amusement or respect or what, because Levi doesn't do expressions often. He's more of a poker face or resting bitch face kind of guy. "Who are you and what have you done with my emotional, chaotic, temperamental little brother?"

"Get bent," I tell him with a chuckle.

Jasper walks over, already changed into workout shorts and a crisp new Thunder T-shirt and baseball cap, and sits down beside me. He's about to participate in his first post-game NHL presser, and I figure he's coming over because he's nervous but instead he says, "How are you guys able to stare at that fine piece of ass all day and not make a move? I mean, I know we're not supposed to, but she's…damn. She's worth getting your hands smacked for if you get to smack that ass first."

"Dude, enough with the locker room talk," Levi tells him bluntly.

"But…it's a locker room," Jasper replies, baffled.

My shoulders are so tight they start to ache. "She's Jude's sister, Jasper. Tone it down, or else he'll make your time here hell."

Jasper looks stunned. "Really? Holy shit."

He is stunned into silence…for now. Thank Christ.

Forty-five minutes later I'm standing in Ryanne Bateman's insanely opulent mansion in Pacific Heights. I've been here before, after one of the preseason games last year. But I feel like I have a right to be here now. Back then they were testing me out, and I tanked in the game and felt like a poser. Like the little kid sneaking into the adult party. I'd spent my night in the corner drinking Piña Coladas and feeling sorry for myself until Dixie walked over and let me flirt with her relentlessly. God, that feels like a decade ago, not a year.

"Nice game, Elijah." Her soft voice hits my ear as she walks by me toward the bar the catering service has set up in the corner of Ryanne's expansive living room. I watch her go and try not to leer. Then I also walk over and stand beside her, a couple feet away so that it looks casual.

The bartender walks over, and before I can say it, Dixie orders. "Two coconut pineapple Margaritas please."

I lift an eyebrow. She grins. "You'll love it. I promise."

"I'm sure I will," I say casually and pause to make sure no one is close enough to overhear. "I love everything you've brought into my life."

Her smile goes from cheeky to flattered. My body feels like it's magnetic and being pulled to her. The bartender slides our frosted Margarita glasses across the bar, and I move the little yellow paper umbrella to the side and take a sip. It's fucking heaven. "Holy shit, I have a new favorite Margarita."

She smiles proudly, but before we can continue our conversation Jasper is standing beside me. He looks at my frozen cocktail and then at Dixie's and smiles at me. "What? Did you lose a bet and you need to drink girlie drinks all night?"

"No" is the only answer I give.

Jasper just shrugs and leans across the bar. "A beer, please!"

The bartender hands him a pint glass filled with some foamy pale ale. Before he can drink it, though, I see Dixie's eyes attach to something behind me and the casual ease of her expression tighten as her shoulders straighten. And then the focus of her attention speaks. "Well, if it isn't the two newest additions to my dynasty."

I turn and am face-to-face with Ryanne. She's stunning, as usual, in a sleek black wrap dress that hugs her ample breasts and clings to her curvy hips. Her long brown hair is stick straight, and her makeup is sultry and smoky. She's in her forties and has accomplished more and acquired more wealth than most men have, even ones ten and twenty years older. She knows it, and she enjoys it.

I smile and extend my hand. "Ms. Bateman, thanks for opening your home to us again."

"I love showing the team some relaxing fun while I'm in town," she replies, and her thin, perfectly symmetrical pink painted lips part in a smile. "Especially when you boys are on a winning streak."

She turns her attention to Jasper and introduces herself, because he seems to be completely starstruck and unable to speak. He's looking at her like she's his favorite porn star. Since the attention is off me, I use the opportunity to look at Dixie. She's standing quietly, absently touching the sugar on the rim of her glass with the tip of her index finger while her eyes, as wide as saucers, take in Ryanne. I know she's met her before. I was there one time when she did, but she still looks like she's seeing some kind of messiah. It's cute, but I worry, because unlike Dixie, I know the rumors about Ryanne are true.

"So have you found a place to live yet, Elijah?" Ryanne asks casually.

"No, Ms. Bateman. I've found a few possible options but haven't committed to anything yet." I take a gulp of my Margarita because the way she's looking at me makes me uncomfortable. She's like a leopard sizing up her prey.

"Drop the Bateman stuff, please. Call me Ryanne. The whole team does, and you're part of the team," she explains and sips her red wine. "A permanent part, Elijah. The contract offer is being drawn up by the lawyers as we speak."

Is she serious? She looks serious, even with the smile on her lips. She leans a little closer and drops a hand on my forearm. It's a flirtatious move, and the level of uncomfortable it makes me is hard to contain, but I have to. She literally owns me.

I look at Dixie. She hasn't noticed the flirty gesture. She's just staring back at me with pure joy on her face. "You did it!" she mouths silently.

"Coach Schneider didn't want me to say anything yet, but the way you played tonight was so impressive and has me so riled up I just couldn't help but let it slip." Ryanne laughs, airy and carefree. It's a pleasant sound but doesn't make my heart swell like Dixie's maniacal laugh. "So get your own permanent place, Elijah honey. I'd offer you this place, since I'm only here a couple weekends a year, but I have security cameras everywhere, even the bathrooms, and I check them all the time. I would end up watching you twenty-four seven and my companies would tank."

"You have cameras in your bathrooms?" Dixie blurts the question out and immediately looks horrified she did.

Ryanne doesn't seem bothered at all. She just shrugs. "Not pointed at the toilet or anything. Just on the door so if need be my security team knows when someone enters and exits." She pauses and swirls her wine around and then looks up with devious eyes. "But if *he* lived here I'd reposition them to face the shower."

She laughs and doesn't realize that although we're all laughing with her, it's forced. My eyes lock with Dixie's again, and I hope she can see discomfort in my eyes. Over her shoulder I see Levi standing with Tessa by the massive onyx marble fireplace on the other side of the room. I touch Ryanne's hand, which is still clinging to my forearm, and smile. "I'm going to go tell your captain, and my brother, about the contract."

"Of course!" Ryanne smiles and takes her hand off me, thankfully. "He's going to be so proud, I'm sure."

"I don't know about that, but he should be relieved he won't have to face me on another team. He knows he'd lose." I smile again and then turn to make my way through the crowd. I can only hope Dixie follows. I want her near me even if I can't wrap an arm around her like Levi is doing to Tessa right now.

But Ryanne puts a hand on my shoulder again, stopping me from fleeing. "Seriously, stick around after the party and I can give you some real estate advice. I own half this town, not just the hockey team. I know where the best up-and-coming neighborhoods are. I'd love to share my skills with you."

She did it. She propositioned me. The rumors are true.

I turn around to face her. It's so hard not to look past her to Dixie. All I want to do is make sure Dixie isn't freaking out about this. I smile at Ryanne, the biggest, friendliest and most easygoing smile I can muster, but before I can figure out how to turn down sex with the owner of my team, Dixie speaks again.

"Ms. Bateman, I've been meaning to speak to you, if you have a moment."

"Ryanne, Dixie, honey, please." She sips her drink again and smiles. "And since I have loose lips tonight I might as well tell you how incredibly impressed I am with you, Dixie Braddock."

"Thank you. I've worked very hard for the Thunder," Dixie says, but there's something in her voice that says she's not overjoyed with the compliment.

"I have to tell you, even though I shouldn't," Ryanne says, her eyes still on Dixie. "You're my vote for replacing Ann. So you might as well consider it a done deal."

Ryanne finishes her drink and places it on the bar before turning back to me. "Elijah, how would you like a tour of the house?

Although I have to warn you, it's so big we might get lost in one of the bedrooms."

"Ms. Bateman, " Dixie interrupts again, and I can see a quick sharp flicker of annoyance dance across Ryanne's features. The tone of Dixie's voice—firm and cold—sends a shiver down my spine. Even Jasper is riveted to the conversation. "I want to thank you for the years of experience and the truly wonderful team I had a chance to be a part of with the Thunder. However, I'm resigning effective immediately."

"Holy shit." The words escape my mouth in an awed whisper. Dixie looks over at me and smiles.

"I'm sorry…did you just quit?"

"Yep," Dixie says, her voice strong and resolute. "I have a boyfriend who is going to need help finding a place to live. And then after that I think I'm going to find a job where there's not so many rules and goddamn double standards."

The beautiful, elegant owner looks completely and utterly baffled. Dixie puts down her glass and walks right up to me. She kisses me on the lips. Nothing obscene, but she's definitely claiming me, and I have never been so happy in my entire life. "Congratulations on your contract, boyfriend."

"We have bigger things to celebrate," I tell her and take her hand in mine. Lacing our fingers together, I look up at Ryanne. "Excuse us."

I lead us through the house and out the back door into the lush backyard. When I find a private corner I turn to face her. Dixie looks like she just did the ice bucket challenge. She's shocked by her own behavior, and I get it. She just changed her whole life. I cup her face in my hands. "Are you okay?"

"I think so." She looks up at me. "She sleeps with the players. It's fucking true."

"Yeah. I knew that. I tried to tell you a while ago when you were putting her up on a pedestal," I explain. "I'm sorry. I know that's disappointing."

She sighs and puts her hands on my waist. "I'm disappointed in myself for wasting so much time trying to emulate her. But whatever. It's done. And I'm yours if you still want me."

"I'll always want you," I promise her.

She smiles. "Even though I might end up a hobo if I can't get a new job."

I grin. "I can be your sugar daddy if you need one."

She laughs. Suddenly Jude is standing beside us with a very pregnant Zoey. "Did you just kiss him? In front of Ryanne? Like directly in front? Like less than two feet away?"

"Hell yeah, I did," Dixie says confidently. "But don't worry, it was after I quit."

"Oh Mylanta!" Zoey exclaims, which is the weirdest expression ever and it makes me laugh.

"Now if you'll excuse us, I'm going to take my boyfriend home and have some really great sex to celebrate his new contract and my unemployment," Dixie announces and starts to pull me away.

Behind us I hear another "Oh Mylanta!" and Jude's groan. We stop only for a second to tell Levi I'm getting a full-time contract. He's so happy it makes my chest feel tight. We grab a Lyft, make out in the back the entire way, and barely make it into her apartment before undressing. But once we're naked on her bed, everything seems to slow down. I gently lay her down on top of me, and let my fingertips glide through her hair and down her delicate neck. I kiss her gently, as the weight of everything seems to settle around us. "Are you really okay with everything?"

"Yes," she replies firmly. "I mean, I'm panicked and terrified, but I can't keep working there. It's not what I want in my life. And she's a fraud, making people like Nadine stick to rules and then turning a blind eye with Eddie and using her own team like a sexual supermarket. I don't want any part of that."

I try not to smile at the sexual supermarket comment, but I can't help it. She smiles back but it wobbles. "But I need a job. Fast. I can't lose this apartment, and I don't have much savings."

"You could move in with your parents for a while. You'd get to spend a lot more time with your dad."

"I can't." Her expression turns stricken. I suddenly feel bad for even suggesting it. "I see my dad almost every day, but I can't live there. I can't be like Sadie, who is trained to watch people die. I'm not like Winnie, who seems to be able to absorb pain like a sponge. I can only handle helplessly watching him die in fits and starts. I need a job, because it's something I can win at. It gives me purpose and sanity."

"Dixie, you're incredible at what you do. You'll find a job. And if you don't, you can borrow money from me until you do. I promise I won't let this decision backfire on you," I tell her.

She bites her lip, like she's contemplating telling me something. Before I can ask her what she's thinking she confesses. "When I was at the ALS Foundation last week, they mentioned they had an opening in their PR department."

I feel a spark of excitement for her. "That sounds like a match made in heaven."

"It does, doesn't it?" She smiles softly. "I'll apply tomorrow."

She kisses me softly, with tender lips and a gentle tongue. It's different for us, and I like it. Actually I fucking love it. So I match her tender touches with my own. The sex is like that too—soft, and gentle and slow. It's longing as much as sensation. It's promises as much as pleasure. We climax one after the other, and it's the most intense orgasm I've ever had.

We don't say anything afterward. We just lie there tangled up in each other, her back to my chest, my arm across her hip, our legs intertwined, and I lay a kiss on her shoulder. "You should probably know I love you."

When I don't get a response I worry, but as I look down I realize she's asleep. I laugh to myself. This is why I stick to cheesy pickup lines. It's too easy to screw up the stuff that comes from your heart. Luckily, I'll get another chance with her because this isn't a secret hookup anymore. It's real life.

27

DIXIE

The next morning I'm fighting waking up. I want to stay here, naked in my bed wrapped around his perfect naked body, for the entire day. I could technically do it—since I'm unemployed. Ugh.

I feel him shift, but I refuse to open my eyes even as he untangles himself from me. I feel his lips on my forehead and I make a little mewing sound. "Sweet Dixie…I have to get to practice."

"Right now?" I murmur in protest more into the pillow than to him.

"In an hour, which is why I'm waking you up now," he replies in a husky voice. He gently kisses both of my closed eyelids. My eyes flutter open as his fingertips trace a path south, across my ribs and over the curve of my hip and down between my legs. I turn onto my back to give him the access he needs. I arch my back as his fingers move and reach back to grab a condom off the nightstand.

He leans forward, captures my lips in a sweet kiss, and then grins. "You're in a rush to get to the point."

"It's a really great point," I reply with a smile.

His hands move to my hips. "Turn around."

I start to slowly move, but he basically grabs me and flips me onto my stomach. God, I love how controlling he can get. It's the biggest turn-on ever. I bend my knees and get on all fours. I hear him tear the condom wrapper and arch my back in anticipation. One of his hands smacks my ass, not too hard but enough that it leaves a sting that turns into a tingle I feel all the way to my clit. His other hand slips around my hip, down my belly and right to my clit. He starts teasing it—relentlessly. I'm cresting toward an orgasm almost immediately. His chest hair tickles my back as teeth gently sink into my shoulder. Then he moves to my neck, sucking the skin just below my ear.

"I'm going to come soon," I warn him in a pant.

"That's the idea," he whispers back in his gravelly voice.

It's coming, closer and closer and…just before it hits he leaves me teetering on the brink as his fingers disappear and he grabs my hips and pushes into me. It's fast, hard and deep. A pleasure-filled groan escapes his lips and mingles with the moan escaping mine. He keeps a hard but slow pace, and his hand moves back to my clit, but again when I'm close his hand disappears. I groan in frustration—delicious, crazy frustration.

He bends forward again. I feel the scrape of his short beard against my shoulder as he smiles at my irritation. "Relax. I'll get you there. I promise."

But he doesn't. He gets me close again—so blindingly close—and then he stops. "Elijah Casco, I am going to scream."

"Yes, you are," he agrees, and when I try to move my own hand to my clit to finish what he started, repeatedly, he won't let me. He pushes me down onto my forearms, which changes the angle of my hips and his angle inside me. He's deeper and I hear him groan again. Then his fingers are on my clit again and I fight against the pleasure because he's going to take it away anyway. Only this time he doesn't, he lets me fall and it's one hell of a fall. My orgasm is deep, long and intense. His must be the same, judging by the noises he makes as he comes with me.

I collapse onto the bed, and he collapses onto me. As we come back to earth, I hear him laughing. "It's egotistical but I fucking love that you say my name when you come. Or in this case, scream it."

"I screamed? Your name?" I ask because, honestly, I don't have a clue. That orgasm was blackout good.

"Yeah. You know, we should probably videotape us," he suggests, and I squirm and fight until he gets off of me, then I sit up and glare at him.

"No way in hell," I say flatly.

He's grinning, so I know he's just teasing. "But that's clearly the only way you're going to know what you say when you come. And also, how fucking hot you are when you do it."

"No video. I need a job, and employers Google people nowadays," I explain and crawl off the bed. "If that ends up on the internet my life is over."

He laughs as I try to walk confidently to the bathroom but my legs are wobbly. "Your orgasm legs are adorable."

"Shut up and shower with me," I reply as I bite back a smile.

Twenty minutes later we're both getting dressed and I've just finished sending my resume to my contact at the ALS Foundation. He gives my shoulders a supportive squeeze, and as I close my laptop he grows serious. "What are your plans for the day?"

"I was going to swing by my parents' and have lunch with them.

Then I have to go to the arena at some point and collect my personal belongings. I'm dreading that. They'll probably make the security guard escort me and Trish will have a superior little smirk on her face and...ugh."

"Let me grab your stuff," he volunteers. Before I can argue he says, "So you don't have to deal with any drama."

"I created the drama. I should face it," I argue back softly as I pull an oversize gray sweater on over my black-and-white splatter-print leggings. "But I honestly don't want to."

He nods. "Then don't. I'll do it for you."

He wraps an arm around my shoulders and pulls me into his side. "The ALS Foundation will hire you. You're incredible, and it's a great fit for you and them."

"I hope so."

We get to the corner where the trolley stop is, and he cups my face and kisses me good-bye, only it's a hell of a lot more passionate than an average good-bye kiss. "Whoa," I whisper when he finally lets me go.

"We can finally kiss in public," he reminds me. "I am not going to take that for granted by giving you some pansy peck."

I laugh as he winks at me and walks away.

I head to my parents' place, and as I use my key and open the door, I'm greeted by the sound of laughter and yelling. Not angry yelling, just typical boisterous Braddock banter. *God, I hope Eli can handle us,* I worry as I follow the noise through the kitchen into the dining area. Eli's family, from everything he says, is prim and proper, which is definitely not my family.

Everyone is seated around the long oak table. Dad is in his wheelchair at one end. Mom is to his left, Jude is at the other end with Zoey to his right, and Winnie and Sadie are in the middle. There's an empty seat on Jude's left, but there's a plate of eggs and bacon in front of it. He notices me first because the others are listening to Sadie and Winnie talk over each other as they tell a story.

"I told you she'd be here," Jude calls out, pulling everyone's attention. He kicks out the empty chair.

I smile. "Aren't you supposed to be at practice?"

"It's optional. I opted out," Jude explains. He points to the plate in front of the empty chair. "We made a plate for you, freeloader."

"Slacker," I quip, and take the seat next to him, pulling the plate of food closer and reaching for the fork.

"She's an unemployed freeloader now," Sadie reminds everyone.

"That's okay. She can live on love," Winnie pipes up and laughs at her own joke.

"Leave Little D alone," my dad says. "We're very proud of her for following her principles. And her heart. Life is too short not to."

That last sentiment silences the table for a moment. My mom clears her throat, not wanting to let everyone start to get sad thinking about my dad's short life, and looks over at me. "We'd like Eli to come over for dinner. Jude said they don't have a game tonight or tomorrow, so can you ask him to join us one of those nights?"

I nod. I knew this was coming. "Just don't embarrass me, okay?"

"Please. That's our job, honey," my dad replies and winks as he sips his coffee.

"Speaking of jobs…" Jude interrupts. "Do you need anything? Like a reference or cash until you get a new position somewhere? Let me know."

I nod. "I'm okay. I can take care of myself. Besides, soon you'll have your own little girl to take care of, so you better save your money for that."

"It's a boy!" Jude argues back instantly, and Zoey laughs.

"I don't care what it is, as long as you let me babysit a lot," Mom says with an excited smile.

I spend three hours hanging out with my family and then decide to head home and start the job search. As I get off the trolley the phone rings. I have the number saved in my phone as "Kelsey ALS." She must be calling about the social media campaign.

"Dixie! How are you? Do you have a moment to talk?" she says. Her voice is friendly and upbeat, which fills me with hope.

"I'm good, and yes, I'm free to chat. How are you?"

"I'm good, but I'll be great if you take a job with us," she says. "We got your email and we're sending you an offer to be our social media director as we speak."

"Seriously?"

She laughs. "Yes. Normally there might be an in-person interview, but we know you, and the work you've already done for us has been exceptional. We're confident in making the offer."

"Thank you so much, Kelsey!"

We talk for a minute more and she tells me to review the offer and send it back with an electronic signature to make it official. The email comes as soon as we hang up and I look it over. The salary is a little less, but the benefits are better and I get more time off. My start date is a week from today. I squeal and do a little dance on the sidewalk. Then I immediately call Eli and tell him the news.

"I'm on my way to your place right now, and I'm taking you out to celebrate!" he announces.

I can't stop smiling, and when he knocks on the door twenty

minutes later I've already signed the offer and sent it back. He's carrying a box with my stuff in it from the office. He carefully puts it down near the kitchen and then picks me up in a hug and spins me around. "Congrats, Dixie!"

"I knew it would work out. I just didn't know it would be so quickly."

He lets me go and heads back over to the box and grabs a small frame out of it. I had a motivational motto in that frame. It said IN-HALE CONFIDENCE, EXHALE DOUBT. He smiles deviously as he hands it to me. "I replaced it with my new favorite pickup line, so you can put it up here and it'll remind you of me when I'm on road trips."

He's replaced my motto with something he must have printed on a printer. It's white paper with thick, large black print. YOU WANT TO KNOW WHAT THE BEST THING IS IN MY LIFE? IT'S THE FIRST WORD IN THAT SENTENCE.

I look up at him and his goofy grin and I feel deadly serious suddenly. "I don't need reminders. I don't intend to forget you," I admit with nervous butterflies. "Because I love you."

His smile drops and a new, warm, sweet one blooms across his rugged features. He steps into me again, circling my waist with his arms and pulling me into him. "I love you too."

He kisses me again, and when he pulls back he's got a cocky smile on his face. "See? Sometimes flying by the seat of your pants works out, Little Miss Plans and Rules."

"Sometimes." I laugh. This relationship tested me in so many ways and catapulted me out of my comfort zone, but as he kisses me again, I know I'd risk everything all over again if I had to. He's worth it.

Epilogue

ELIJAH

Six months later

Two minutes. Two minutes and we will have done it. We will win the Stanley Cup for the third time in four years. I will win my first Stanley Cup. With my brother. Levi skates and he actually smiles at me. He's trying not to be cocky, but it's two minutes left and we're ahead by two goals. I take my position in my crease and glance at my team on the bench. They're all standing, bouncing and shaking with anticipation.

The ref drops the puck. Jude wins it and gets it back to Duncan. He sails it over to Levi. They skate up the ice away from me for one final assault on the beleaguered Milwaukee Comets goalie. They take three shots between them, but no one scores, and I don't care. All I care about is that clock counting down.

A Comets player gets in and starts down the ice toward me, but Duncan checks him into the boards and gets the puck back. They're too close to my end, so I can't glance at the clock, but I fucking want to more than anything. Jude has the puck now and moves behind the Comets net. He's wasting time. We just need to beat the clock now. I hear the fans' thunderous countdown: "*Three! Two! One!*"

A deafening roar shakes the arena. I never actually hear the final buzzer, but when I look up, the clock's at zero. I toss my stick and throw my gloves off and lift my arms in victory. I throw off my helmet and start skating down the ice toward my team. Every single Thunder player is hopping the boards. Equipment is flying everywhere, and the next thing I know I'm colliding with everyone. We topple over onto the hard ice in a pile of bodies, but I don't feel a thing. I'm euphoric.

Levi's face swims into my vision. He's grinning, tears brimming in his eyes. I grin back as he grabs the back of my head. "We did it! You did it! You fucking did it, Eli!"

I laugh. Jude grabs us both in a hug, roaring in victory. I hug everyone and anyone I see, and then Coach Schneider is in front of me grinning and he hugs me and kisses my cheek and hollers, "Fuck yeah! I knew you could do it, kid!"

"No, you didn't." I laugh, and he laughs too.

"I'm so fucking happy you proved me wrong." He turns and bear hugs Levi next, and I skate a little away from the group, looking up at the section reserved for friends and family, but I can't see her because everyone is jumping and hugging and high-fiving, and it's just a blur of limbs and bobbing heads. God, I really want to see her.

"Handshakes!" Levi bellows because it's his job as the captain to rally us for this act of sportsmanship so the despondent Milwaukee team can get the fuck off the ice and lick their wounds, they can give us the Cup and family can join us on the ice. I can't wait to share this with Dixie and the Braddocks, who have accepted me like family. I push back the slight sting of knowing my own family won't be here. Todd is in Europe for work, and although my parents are well aware of what's going on and I've told them they have tickets if they want them, they won't be here.

Fifteen minutes later, they bring out the Cup and hand it to Levi. I can't believe it's happening to me. Winning this is a lifelong dream, and I earned it. I started every single playoff game. I got us here. Levi takes a lap, kisses the brilliant metal, and then he turns and brings it to me. The camera flashes are blinding. I get that this is a moment. Not many brothers win the Cup together.

I kiss it, lift it over my head and roar. As I take my lap around the ice my eyes find her by the doors they'll be opening to let family onto the ice in a few minutes. Her cheeks are pink with excitement and her eyes are blurry with tears of joy. I grin even larger at the sight and give her a wink. As I skate by to hand the Cup to Jude, I notice Winnie is on one side of her…and my parents are on the other.

I stare at them, blinking to see if this is just some hallucination brought on by mass levels of joy. But no, they're still there. They look more uncomfortable than excited, but they are here. Our eyes meet, first mine and my mom's and then mine and my dad's. My mom waves her trademark little royal wave, a tentative smile on her lips. My dad nods.

I skate toward Levi, who is watching Jude spin around with the Cup above his head. I grab his jersey at the shoulder and tug him closer. "Mom and Dad are here."

"No," he kind of laughs.

"Levi, they're here." I turn him. I can tell the minute he lays eyes on them, because his expression changes to bewilderment and his eyes get a glimmer of hope. "They came?"

"Yeah…shit. They actually came."

My eyes find Dixie's again and she looks sheepish. She did this. That beautiful, uncontrollable, stubborn, nutty little firecracker did this. God, I love her.

DIXIE

I lean closer to Mrs. Casco. "They're going to open the doors now and let us onto the ice."

"The ice? But it's slippery. Won't we all just fall?"

I smile reassuringly. "Just walk slowly and with short steps. It's easier than you think."

"You can hold on to me, Catherine," Mr. Casco tells his wife and bends his elbow like he's escorting her to the debutante ball. It's stuffy but also cute as hell.

They both look unbelievably uncomfortable right now, but the whole night hasn't gone that way. Tessa and I picked them up at the airport forty minutes before the game. Neither of us told Eli or Levi about their visit in case they decided to cancel at the last minute. They didn't, and although it was super awkward for me to meet them like that, without Eli there, it was worth it. They were as uptight and cool as Eli has described them, and at first I fretted that they would get annoyed or even upset watching the game, but they didn't. In fact, they got pretty into it, clapping and gasping and cheering. I think it helped that the rowdy bunch of hooligans that share my DNA were sitting in the row right behind them. My mom seemed to bond with Mrs. Casco, and my dad was all too happy to answer Mr. Casco's questions about the game.

Zoey reaches over and squeezes my hand excitedly as Declan

Randall Braddock squirms in his BabyBjörn at her chest. I reach up and caress his pudgy little cheek and wish for a second that he was more than three months old so he would remember this. But knowing his dad, there will be other Cup celebrations in his life. They open the door and we spill onto the ice with the rest of the families. I make sure the Cascos stay near me. Tessa is right beside me, and my family is right behind me, but they break off with Zoey to rush to Jude, who is standing just left of Levi and Eli. Both Casco brothers are looking at us as we approach like they're seeing ghosts.

I rush to Eli and jump into him. He wraps his arms around me and squeezes me breathless. "You won a fucking Stanley Cup!" I say against his ear, my face smarting from the giant smile I can't wipe off.

"I fucking did!" he replies and laughs as he loosens his hold on me and my feet hit the ice again. His eyes move over my shoulder quickly, and I turn and see Levi hugging his mom. "You did this?"

"It actually wasn't that hard," I reply with a shrug. "I just used my incredible charm."

He laughs and takes my hand and he glides closer to his family. His dad smiles at him. "Congratulations, son. You're very talented. So is Levi."

"We are!" Eli agrees with a smile. "Thank you, Dad. I'm really happy you guys came."

"I'm so glad your lovely girlfriends convinced us," Mrs. Casco says, and Eli squeezes my hand as Levi leans over and kisses Tessa's cheek. "It's scary to watch you out there but...I've never seen you two happier."

"We just won the hardest trophy there is to win in sports,

Mom," Levi tells her with a grin. "Together. This is one of the best days of my life."

"We're proud of you," Mr. Casco says, and I can tell by both of the boys' faces that they haven't heard that a lot, or maybe at all.

Mrs. Casco looks at me. "So, where is your brother?"

I point a few feet away, closer to the middle of the ice. "I should go over there."

She nods. I look up at Eli. He kisses the top of my head and lets go of my hand. I take quick short steps and scurry across the ice to get to my family. Jude is lifting Declan out of the BabyBjörn. My heart just melts, and a wave of happy tears hits the back of my eyes. I fight them off, because he'll tease me mercilessly if he sees me cry. He still razzes me about how I was a weepy mess when I saw Declan for the first time, and he doesn't believe my lie that I was upset he wasn't a girl. I was thrilled he was healthy, and seeing Jude hold him had opened the floodgates, but then Jude handed him to my dad and, in front of everyone right there in the hospital room, put a gorgeous ring on Zoey's finger, and well, it was game over.

He sees me and grins wildly. I shuffle over and hug him. "Congrats."

"You don't sound as excited as you should," he tells me.

I shrug. "You do this all the time now. It's really not a big deal."

He laughs and ruffles my hair.

"Jude, let's get a picture of Little D in the Cup!" my dad says, talking about Declan, because he's inherited my nickname. His words are slurred, like they always are now, but we've all gotten really good at understanding him.

"Let's do it!" Jude agrees and skates off toward the Cup, which is sitting, surrounded by people, at center ice. We all follow, Sadie pushing Dad in his wheelchair.

Ten minutes later, after tons of family pictures with Little D in the bowl of the Cup and the family around him, Jude picks Declan up and hands him to Dad, and Eli skates over. He hugs my mom and lets my sisters maul him, and then he's skating toward me. I only have time to lift my arms and then he's grabbing me around the waist, lifting me up and spinning me. I wrap my arms around his neck, and he kisses me long and hard. When we break the kiss I laugh. "Put me down! I'm getting dizzy."

He gently lowers me to the ice but keeps his arms around my waist and rests his forehead against mine. "What you did…getting my parents here. There are no words."

I smile and cup the side of his face. Well, the side of his thick scruffy beard. "I'd do anything for you."

He grabs my waist and tugs me closer and I squeak because I almost lose my balance. "I love you, sweet Dixie."

I suddenly feel like crying again. He sees the tears in my eyes and laughs. "I'm sorry if that upsets you, but I do. You'll have to learn to live with it. For a very long time."

I nod. "I can handle that. In fact, there's nothing I would rather handle, because I love you too."

Don't miss Jude and Zoey's story.

Score is available now!

Please turn the page for a preview.

1

JUDE

I lock my car and make my way across the hospital parking lot. It's a gorgeous day—the sun is shining in the cloudless sky, and the temperature is a perfect seventy-eight degrees. I'd be bitching about having to spend it indoors if it weren't for such a good cause. Today I'm doing a meet-and-greet at the children's hospital with a few of my teammates and the Stanley Cup, the second in a row for the San Francisco Thunder. The only thing that beats lifting that Cup above my head on the ice after our win is sharing it with kids.

Not everyone is back from summer break yet, so it's a small but excited group. I normally wouldn't be back in San Francisco yet either, but this hasn't been a normal summer for me. Nothing has been "normal" for me in a long while. It's not that things are bad; they're just…different. And I have been realizing I am not the best with dealing with changes on my own.

The last big change I'd faced in my life was being traded to San Francisco from the Milwaukee Comets, but I didn't do that alone. They traded my teammate, my best friend since I was seventeen,

Levi Casco, as well. And then there was my dad getting sick, but I had my family to go through that with me.

As I reach the sidewalk where the team is gathered, I see my youngest sister and Thunder publicity dynamo, Dixie, pacing a hole in the concrete a few feet from a bunch of guys from the team. I make my way toward her, stopping to hug and high-five a couple of the guys on my way by. Dixie's got her face buried in her phone, which is typical when she's working. She doesn't look up, but somehow she knows I'm coming. As soon as I'm standing beside her, she says, "Are you sober? Are you hung over? Oh, and no hitting on the moms or nurses."

"Nice to see you too, sis," I reply and roll my eyes.

The word "sis" finally gets her blue eyes off her phone screen. They land on me with an expression that could wilt flowers. "Do not use that word in public, Jude."

"Sorry." I roll my eyes again, and she frowns. "And FYI, I'm sober, and I will keep my dick out of the staff and mothers. Thanks for thinking you have to tell me that, though."

"Of course I have to tell you that," Dixie replies matter-of-factly. "Unfortunately, I know your dick and your brain are mortal enemies. Anything your brain says, like 'don't bang people at team events,' your dick purposely defies."

"You are a total weirdo," I tell her for what's probably the millionth time since she was born into the family. "And you need to stop saying 'dick' in front of me."

She stops pacing, just out of earshot of the team. She shoves her phone in the pocket of her off-white summer blazer and tilts her head up to hold my eye. "If it makes you feel any better, this is Dixie Wynn, publicist for the San Francisco Thunder, talking, because it's my job to keep the dick of our best player in its pants at public events. It's not your sister Dixie Braddock talking. That said, both of us—Dixie Wynn and Dixie Braddock—are still disgusted your Little Jude ended up on the internet."

"There's no proof it's my not-so-little Jude. And you don't think it's weird that your job is to keep my dick in my pants?" I can't help but ask because, damn, she could have gotten a job anywhere else. My two other sisters, Winnie and Sadie, are living and working in our hometown of Toronto.

"Oh, it's weird," she agrees and gives me a humorless smile. "But you know what's really weird? You're the only player on the entire team who needs to be reminded to keep his dick in his pants at team events. Not even creepy Eddie Rollins needs the reminder."

Ouch. I must look as wounded by that as I feel, because her expression softens for a second before her eyes dart around to make sure no one is watching. She's ridiculously anal about keeping the fact that we're related a secret from the rest of the team. A lot of the management is aware, but no one from the team except Levi knows. It's kind of weird that no one has guessed. Especially since we have almost identical blue eyes and high cheekbones. We're both blond too, but my hair is more of a sandy color than hers is.

"We're scheduled to be inside in five minutes," Dixie tells me, and I simply nod as her eyes scan the players gathered on the sidewalk. "Where's Levi? He's never late. In fact, he's usually the first one here. Can you call him for me?"

"No." She frowns at my quick and assertive response.

"He called you a lot this summer," she counters.

"Yeah, because he thought my dick was on the internet, and management made him," I reply. Her frown deepens, as does that little crease between her eyebrows she gets when she's annoyed. The truth is Levi had called me a few times this summer, and some of the calls came before the dick pic scandal. I just ignored them because I was still pissed at him for dating my ex-girlfriend behind my back.

In an effort to avoid Dixie's judgmental stare, I look away, and my eyes land on Levi. I knew he'd never be late. He's the same old calm, reliable, emotionless Levi. Only I can't help but notice as he gets closer, he doesn't look like that Levi anymore. His posture is loose, his hair longer than I've ever seen it, careless stubble covers his jaw, and his smile is light, jovial. Everything about him seems to be the opposite of the cool, emotionally detached, almost moody guy who was my best friend until two months ago. Now he looks like someone I don't know, and that stings, like a sunburn inside my chest.

He glances up, our eyes connect and he gives me a Levi smile I recognize—tight, small and quick. I smile back, but it isn't completely authentic. This is what we are now. This is what we've become. Best friends with a deep crack running through the foundation of our friendship. One I don't think can or will ever go away. And it's eating at my soul to admit that. But I don't know how to get around the fact that he started sleeping with my ex-girlfriend without telling me.

"Hey!" Levi reaches out and grabs me in a hug. I hug him back, but it's awkward and brief. "How was your vacation time?"

I shrug and keep my smile light. "Fine. Not long enough."

We are due back for training camp in two weeks, after only ten short weeks off. Levi nods. "Yeah. It's gonna be a long season, but it was worth it."

He rolls his shoulder, probably without even thinking about it. He was injured last year in the playoffs, and I'm sure the shoulder is still not one hundred percent. "When did you get back to San Fran?"

I shrug again. "Two weeks ago. I went back to Toronto for a while, but after the picture thing happened, I came back here. Needed some alone time."

His brown eyes grow dark, and he nods tersely at that. I'd sworn to him it was a misunderstanding, the picture wasn't me, and in true Levi fashion he didn't believe me but backed me up anyway. Between his support and the fact that the dick pic taken by the puck bunny didn't have my face in it, the team management decided not to cut me loose. Thankfully.

"How's your dad doing?" Levi asks, his face filled with sympathy. It's the only unfiltered expression he gives me now. I know he truly is gutted about what I'm going through with my father, who was recently diagnosed with ALS, and I do appreciate his concern. My family is also like a family to Levi. He became an honorary Braddock the summer after high school, when he lived with us.

But the fact he's been like a brother to me is why the shit he pulled with my ex hurt me so much.

"He fell this summer. Had to spend a couple days in the hospital with a fractured wrist and some broken ribs, but you know him, he's bouncing back," I explain quietly. I'm still having a hard time dealing with the fact my big bear of a dad may only have a year or so left.

I pull myself together as Duncan Darby walks over, his phone to his ear. "Okay, babe. Yeah. I'll call you when I'm done. Love you."

He drops his phone from his ear and pulls me into a bear hug.

I hug him back easily. Duncan is a giant, hilarious man-child. He's a defensive beast on the ice and as sweet and loyal as a puppy off. "Braddock! You *Playgirl* centerfold, you!"

I roll my eyes. "Wasn't my dick."

He nods emphatically. "Right. I forgot."

I ignore the completely un-ignorable exaggerated wink he gives me. Levi clears his throat. "Was that Carla on the phone?"

I watch Duncan nod. He started dating Carla Soto almost a year ago. She's best friends with Tessa Haynes, my ex and Levi's girlfriend. Yeah, we're one big happy family. Not.

"Yeah. She wants me to swing by work when I'm done."

"I was going to swing by and see Tessa too," Levi tells him. "I was going to surprise her with lunch. Carpool?"

They're like suburban husbands now. The realization makes me feel very lonely. Luckily, I don't have to stand here awkwardly and listen to them talk any longer, because Dixie is walking toward us. She stops in front of us and claps her hands to get the group's attention. "Okay, everyone! We're going to go into the lounge on the main floor, and the kids will filter in a few at a time to get pictures with you guys and the Cup."

Everyone nods. "The PR staff will be giving out Stanley Cup cookies and little stuffed mascots. Any questions?" Dixie asks.

No one has any questions, so she leads everyone inside. A couple minutes later we're in the long, antiseptic-smelling room, and the kids are starting to come in. It's brutal to see so many kids pale, frail and in some cases attached to tubes and IVs, but there's no place I'd rather be. I always take the time to shake their parents' hands and chat with them a little bit. Not because I'm trying to flirt with the hot moms, but because I can only imagine how hard this is on them. I'm feeling helpless and furious about my dad's health; I assume those feelings are even deeper when it's your child.

As the event winds down and the last of the kids finish with the photos and make their way to the cookies and toys, I see Dixie huddled in the corner with one of the nurses. She glances at me but doesn't really acknowledge me. That crease between her eyebrows seems deeper than normal, so I walk over to find out what's going on.

"He's just devastated," the nurse says to Dixie as I approach.

"Who?" I ask. Dixie hasn't realized I've joined them, and she jumps a little when I speak.

"A little boy," the nurse tells me as she smiles a big, flirtatious smile and smooths her bright pink scrubs. "Christopher. He's a huge Thunder fan, but his white blood cells got low last night. He's in isolation until we can pump them up again, so he couldn't come today. I'm Kina, by the way."

I smile at her and shake her hand. She bats her eyelashes at me with a smile that tells me I could violate Dixie's little rule with her.

"He's one of the reasons we organized the event," Dixie explains, and her brow pinches so tight I'm tempted to press my thumb between her eyes and flatten out the crease. I decide against it, because she'd probably slap me. "His mom wrote us with a few of the other moms and asked us to visit."

I feel for this kid. I hate the idea that he's going to miss us. Dixie's expression perks up a little. "Could we have Levi hold the Cup up outside the window to his room?"

"Why Levi?" The question flies from my mouth with a hard edge that has both Dixie and Kina startled. "I mean, I could do it."

"Well, you are his favorite player," the nurse explains with that flirtatious smile, adding, "And mine."

I ignore her last comment, because Dixie told me to, and nod. "Well, I'd love to see him. Can't I go in the room if I'm sanitized or whatever?"

"You'd have to wear full scrubs and a mask and everything," she explains. "It's a bit of a pain."

"You know what's a bigger pain?" I ask and smile. "Being a sick kid and missing your chance to see the Cup and meet your favorite player."

The nurse smiles; this time it's more excited than flirty, thankfully, because I've never been great at ignoring a flirty woman. Dixie, on the other hand, is staring at me with a stunned and confused look rather than a happy one. I shrug at her. "What? It's not a big deal."

She doesn't respond, so I ignore her and ask Kina to take me to his room. Twenty minutes later, wrapped in a bunch of scrubs and booties and with a giant mask on my face, I'm in Christopher's room. He's pale and skinny, but his smile is hearty and full of life. I give him a jersey with the whole team's signatures and I have Levi hold up the Cup outside his window and all the other guys wave at him. He's only nine, which guts me, but I don't let him see it. I joke with him and take pictures. We talk hockey and how when he's better his mom is going to let him play on a team. I tell him I'll get him tickets to a Thunder game when he's well and take him around our arena. He's thrilled. Then I let his mom almost strangle me with a grateful hug before I leave.

I strip out of all the special clothes and find Dixie waiting for me by the elevators with the rest of the team. "That was amazing of you."

"It was nothing."

"Jude!" I turn as Kina jogs down the hall toward me. "Thank you so much. You're amazing."

She shakes my hand and then hands me a folded piece of paper. "My number. Call me if you're wondering how Christopher is doing or, you know, you want to hang out."

She flashes that flirtatious grin again before heading back to the nurses' station. Dixie glares at me and shrugs. Duncan, Levi and the guys are chuckling as we all crowd into the elevator. "Only Jude turns a good deed into a lay," Duncan quips, and it instantly pisses me off.

"I didn't do it because of that," I say, my tone flat and even.

"You do everything for that," Eddie Rollins, our backup goalie, chimes in, and the elevator erupts in laughter.

"Fuck you guys," I mutter and storm off the elevator as soon as the doors open.

I'm already opening my car door when I hear Dixie call my name. I want to ignore her and just drive away, but knowing her, she'll hunt me down, so I stop and wait for whatever it is she wants to say.

She is almost breathless when she reaches me, and I realize she must have been chasing me. She stops half a foot away and smooths her blond bob. "Thank you for doing that. You went above and beyond."

"It was nothing," I reply casually, but I'm happy she was impressed enough to say something. "He's a kid. He deserves a little above and beyond."

"Yeah, he does. So thank you for being an awesome human." She lowers her voice before adding, "And I'm proud of you, as a sister."

"Yeah, well, you could have defended me in front of those assholes," I reply and sigh.

She glances over her shoulder toward the guys who are jumping into their own cars. "They were just teasing you. And besides, it's not like it's a wild accusation."

"I wasn't nice to the kid because I wanted to bang the nurse." I can't believe I have to defend myself on this. "I don't bang every girl I meet, even when I can. And trust me, I could have gotten in those scrubs with or without being nice to the kid."

Dixie rolls her eyes, but she's smiling. "If you don't bang every girl you meet, then why are you currently staying at a hotel and not your apartment?"

"What?" Fuck. How did she find that out?

"I was coming out of the coach's office after a meeting last week, and I heard Duncan tell Eddie you'd moved into a hotel because too many of your prior hookups were showing up at your place unannounced trying to get another ride on the…how did he word it? Braddock-mobile."

She shivers—actually it's more like a convulsion—as she says that. I clench my jaw in anger. Fucking Duncan Darby and his big mouth. She's staring up at me with a smug smile on her face, and I know the only answer is to lie. "Darby is talking out of his ass. I checked into a hotel because I wanted a staycation."

"A staycation? Did you just honestly feed me that bullshit excuse with a straight face?" Dixie questions. She is the most annoying sister on the planet. She really is.

"Yeah."

"So why is it that for the first time since you moved here you aren't letting Sadie, Winnie and me stay with you for our annual girls' weekend?"

I wish my dad had indulged me when she was born and I requested we trade her for a puppy. "I thought I'd treat you all to a five-star hotel. It's not like I'm making all of you cram into that shoebox you call an apartment. But if you all want to stay with me instead, by all means, go ahead."

"Thanks. We will. See you tomorrow night." She turns and marches off toward her car.

Goddamn it, I think as I watch her walk away.

I pull the nurse's number out of my pocket and tear it into pieces.

The unexpected guests that were showing up at my apartment weren't just annoying; to be honest, it was embarrassing and a wake-up call. I was way too liberal with where I put my dick. I wanted to say it was because of everything that happened with Levi and Tessa, but even I couldn't sell myself on that lie.

Dixie's red Fiat buzzes by me, and as my sister catches my eye through the windshield, I stick my hand out my window and let the torn-up phone number trickle out of my hand and to the pavement. I don't even think twice about it.

Read on for a peek at *One More Shot*, Book 1 in the Hometown Players series.

Drafted by the NHL at eighteen, Jordan Garrison was headed for fame, and there was only one person he wanted to share it with—Jessie Caplan. He was crazy in love with her, and had finally told her so. They shared an amazing night…and then everything fell apart. Now, Jessie can't tell whether she loves him or hates him. But Jordan has learned enough to know a connection like theirs is rare. He was lucky to find her once. No way will he lose Jessie ever again.

1

JORDAN

Despite my better judgment, my eyes flutter open. I'm not at home. I think I knew that before I opened my eyes, but I'm not sure exactly where I am. I'm…on a bed. A big bed. Probably a king. But not *my* king. I would have nicer sheets.

I squint against the light, not that there is much of it, but it's still more than I would like to have hit my pupils after what feels like only fifteen minutes' sleep. There's a desk in the corner and a flat screen on the wall and dark blue and white striped curtains. There is also a naked woman lying facedown beside me.

I shift onto my side, ignoring the mild throbbing in my foot and, as the sheets turn and twist around me, I realize that I'm naked too. I look down at her. All I can see is pale skin—like never-been-on-a-beach pale—and dyed blond hair. I'm thinking it's enough to take care of my morning wood.

I run a hand down her bare back, over her ass and down the back of her thigh. She stretches and makes a little moaning sound as my hand makes it to the back of her knee.

"Round three?" she giggles into the pillow.

Three? I guess I was a busy boy last night. A drunk, busy boy. She rolls toward me.

"Such big blue eyes…" She leans closer and kisses me, her hands wandering under the sheets. "Such big everything."

The night is slowly coming back to me. We won a home game. I sat and watched from the team box high above the ice, ridiculously frustrated. Afterward, I joined my teammates at a bar to celebrate. I wanted to drink away my frustration at not being able to play thanks to my stupid ankle.

Hours later, my teammate Alexandre invited a bunch of people back to his place. That's when I had decided to screw my frustration away with one of the girls who tagged along because obviously drinking alone wasn't going to improve my mood. It never does but I've yet to stop trying. Fucking random girls has never helped my problems either, but I keep doing it. I've never been one to learn from my mistakes, at least not quickly.

Her name was…Jenny? Julie? Jackie? It began with a fucking J, I know that because I avoid girls whose names begin with J. Normally that's a deal breaker for me, especially when I'm drunk. But desperate times called for desperate measures, and I was so over being injured and unable to play hockey—the only thing I've ever done for a living—that I was desperate for a distraction. This J girl was it.

"You're a freaking animal," she coos, her hand moving from my ass to my hard-on. "I had no idea hockey players had so much stamina."

I just grunt, gently turn her toward the mattress and move myself over her back. I nudge her legs open, kneel between them and then pull her backward by her hips so she's on all fours.

I grab a condom off the bedside table where there is a pile of them in a bowl. I realize I'm still at Alexandre's apartment because he's the only one ballsy enough to leave condoms around his house in candy dishes.

I tear the condom wrapper with my teeth and start to put it on when my cell phone starts ringing. My head begins to pound in rhythm with the shrill ring. Great. I stop what I'm doing and extract it from the back pocket of my jeans, which for some unknown reason are draped over the lamp beside the bed.

I see my parents' number on the call display and roll my eyes as my dick deflates.

"I have to take this," I tell Julie-Jenny-Jackie.

She groans in dismay and I ignore her.

"Hi, Mom. It's a little early to call," I say into the phone as I yawn.

"Jordan, it's one in the afternoon," she lets me know tersely.

I blink. Shit. "Sorry, it was a late night."

"Should you be having late nights when you're still injured?" she asks pointedly.

I try not to be annoyed and remind myself she's just doing her job. Moms are supposed to ride their sons' asses.

"We won and went out to celebrate," I defend myself. "It's fine. I'm fine. The ankle is getting better every day."

"Okay, then…" I can still hear the judgment in her voice, but we both ignore it.

"When do you leave for New York?" I ask, changing the subject. My parents were supposed to be going to Brooklyn this weekend to visit my older brother, Devin, his wife, Ashleigh, and their two-year-old son, Conner.

The girl beside me gets out of bed and gathers her clothes. "I have to go. Work," she whispers, and disappears into the bathroom.

"Well, we were supposed to go tomorrow but we had to push back our flight to Monday. Honey…" She pauses and there's something in her tone that makes my stomach clench uncomfortably. "Lily Caplan died."

I feel a wave of relief to hear that my parents aren't sick, but as the news settles in it instantly feels like a bomb has exploded in my chest. My heart skips a beat and my mouth goes dry. "Mrs. Caplan?"

The name conjures up images in my head of three beautiful, spirited but sad teenage girls, not the silver-haired shrew of a woman it belongs to.

"Yes. I guess it happened a couple days ago. I just found out this morning," she says, and her tone is soothing. I know she knows this news makes me feel off-balance—like a hormonal, impetuous teenager, because that's what I was the last time the Caplans were in my life. She also knows that because of my turbulent past with one Caplan in particular, this news hits me harder than the rest of my family. "It was sudden but not completely unexpected. She had those heart problems."

"I know…" I swallow and ignore the dyed blonde with the J name as she leans in and kisses my cheek before heading for the bedroom door.

"Call me," she whispers a little too loudly. I nod quickly at the blonde and she frowns as she leaves the room.

"Are they back?" I bark out the question gruffly because I don't want to be asking it. I don't want to care. I don't want to know…only I do want to know. Badly.

"Rose arrived last night. Callie got here this morning," my mother volunteers easily. "Jessie is supposed to be arriving this afternoon."

She's back. She said she would never go home again. Everyone swore she was gone forever. But Jessie is back. The vault in the recesses of my brain, the one where I crammed all the memories of her, suddenly bursts open, and my breath catches in my throat and I cough.

"The funeral is Saturday. We're going, of course, but I thought it would be nice if you could come as well," my mom goes on. "You boys were all so close to them, and Devin and Luc can't make it because they're playing. But since you're not playing right now..."

"Isn't Cole going to go?" I ask quickly, almost nervously. I fucking hate that I feel this out of sorts all of a sudden.

"Yes, but Cole wasn't best friends with her," she says simply. My mom has never been one to get too involved in our romantic lives. She doesn't want to be that kind of overbearing woman. But clearly she feels strongly about this. "You should be here, Jordan."

"I'll see what I can do," I mutter. "Thanks for telling me, Mom."

"Do you want me to say anything to...them? From you specifically?" she asks quietly in a voice full of unspoken words.

"No." My mother sighs her discontent so I clear my throat, roll my eyes and add, "Fine. Tell them I'm thinking of them and everything."

"I will. I love you, Jordy," she says in a voice that clearly says she approves of my message.

"Love you too," I say, and hang up.

As I throw on my underwear, slide my injured foot into my air-cast and dig around the room for the rest of my clothes, Alexandre appears in the doorway. He's in nothing but Seattle Winterhawks track pants and he's holding two coffee mugs. His dark blue eyes are twinkling and his dark brown hair is askew.

"You sure know how to make a girl scream," he says with his heavy French Canadian accent and a wry smile. He hands me one of the mugs. "I'm surprised you didn't set off car alarms last night."

I smile, but it's short-lived, and take a sip of the coffee before putting it down to pull my shirt over my head. "I have to go to the rink. I need to talk to Coach."

"Why? Did she rebreak your ankle or break some new part of your body?" He laughs.

I make a face at his crappy joke and shake my head. "A friend of the family died."

"Je suis désolé, mon ami," he offers condolences in his native French.

"Yeah," I reply because I don't have time to explain to Alex that after the way Lily Caplan treated her grandkids, she wasn't exactly my favorite person.

I grab the mug again and take a few more sips as I walk out into Alex's main living area, which has floor-to-ceiling, south-facing windows and reclaimed barn board floors. A sultry-looking brunette in nothing but Alex's plaid dress shirt from last night stands behind the kitchen island cooking eggs on the stovetop.

"Hey." I give her an awkward wave.

"Jackie says to tell you to stop by Hooters any time and she'll get you free wings," the brunette tells me.

"Tell Jackie thanks," I say, and try not to roll my eyes. Even after all these years as an NHL player, I'm still always shocked when the same girls who throw themselves at you the first night they meet you just because you're a professional athlete expect a shot at girl-friend status. Of course, in their defense, I'm not turning them down.

"Why do you need to talk to Coach?" Alex wants to know.

"I need to go back home," I explain, and try to tame my wild bedhead with my hands. "For the funeral. Just a couple of days."

Alex shrugs and then gives me a hug. "Okay. Take care, eh?"

I nod and smile. "Thanks for the guest room."

"Sure." Alex smirks. "But next time remind me to buy earplugs for my neighbors."

Outside I'm greeted with a crisp, sunny fall afternoon. It's not raining, which in Seattle is always a plus. When I was traded to the Seattle Winterhawks last season, I wasn't all that thrilled about living so far from home. At least when I played in Quebec City, it was only an eight-hour drive from my hometown in Maine. But Seattle is fun, my team has been great and the fans here are a small but passionate bunch. I'm happy now professionally. At least I was until I broke my left ankle. Hockey is the only thing I've ever wanted to do with my life. It's the only thing I've ever been *great* at and the one thing I have never screwed up. This is the first injury in my professional career. It's a big one, and I couldn't be handling it worse if I tried.

As I drive to the rink I call my brother Devin.

"Hey, Jordan," he says easily, answering on the second ring. "What's up?"

"Lily Caplan died."

"I know." Devin sounds stunned for a minute. "Mom told Ashleigh."

"She wants me to go home for the funeral," I respond as I

pull my SUV off the I-5 and down the familiar downtown Seattle streets to the hockey arena.

"Makes sense," he says.

"How does it make sense?" I demand. I was calling him for support—so he could help me brainstorm excuses for not showing up. "Mrs. Caplan hated me. She hated all of us. She thought we were—and I quote—'derelict hockey punks.'"

"She's dead," Devin reminds me snarkily as I slow at a stop sign and lean my head against the leather headrest. "This isn't about her. It's about supporting your best friend."

"Ex–best friend," I retort. "We haven't talked in years."

"And whose fault is that?" Devin mutters almost under his breath—almost inaudibly—but I hear it and it pisses me off.

"She left town, remember? Why does everyone blame that on me?"

I wave my players' pass at the security guard at the gate to player parking. He's obviously a little surprised to see me on a day off, but he raises the gate without question. "I should be concentrating on getting my leg healed. My family should be supporting that."

"Oh, I'm sorry," Devin counters, and the sarcasm rings loud and clear through the Bluetooth. "Is your leg going to stop healing just because it's in Maine instead of Seattle?"

"Go fuck yourself."

"Love you too, bro." He laughs, enjoying this way too much if you ask me. But when the laughter dies he grows serious. "Look, Jordy. I would be there if I could and so would Luc. The Caplan girls are family. We've all given you and Jessie enough time to figure out how to be grown-ups, yet you can't seem to do it. So I'm telling you be a grown-up and go and support her."

"Fine. I'll go if the coach lets me."

"He'll let you."

"Shut up."

"Shutting up," Devin promises, and then the line goes dead. I sigh loudly, get out of the car and slam the door. Hopefully Devin is wrong and Coach Sweetzer has some reason he needs me here. Because as painful and frustrating as it was to be here dealing with my injury and not being able to play hockey, seeing Jessie Caplan again would be worse—*much* worse.

ABOUT THE AUTHOR

Victoria Denault loves long walks on the beach, cinnamon dolce lattes and writing angst-filled romance. She lives in L.A. but grew up in Montreal, which is why she is fluent in English, French and hockey. You can visit her online at www.victoriadenault.com or facebook.com/authorvictoriadenault.